Life and Death in Venice

I0639750

A novel by
Victor Lana

"Pale Death, with impartial step, knocks at the poor man's cottage and the palaces of kings."

— Horace, *Odes* Book 1:4

For Susan, Lauren, and Victor

TABLE OF CONTENTS

CHAPTER ONE – Writer's Block

I am a writer. I love writing, and that is why I hate it. Now, I am living in Venice, Italy. I hate Venice, and that is why I love it. There is something for a writer here that is palpable as the murky waters of the canals. At night there is a shroud around every lamppost and a specter on every bridge over the canals as life passes by in the gondolas below. Working to alert the Grim Reaper, they wait patiently to collect those whose time will eventually come.

I walk to the Rialto Bridge every morning despite the crowds assembling there in good weather and wander through the vast open market, but I never buy anything because it is too overwhelming to deal with the hordes of tourist zombies taking selfies as they buy neck ties, fruit, veggies, souvenirs, and smelly fish. The absurdity of it all would be soul crushing if it were not so wickedly intriguing.

Today, I buy an apple from an old vendor named Tinno who talks about his life. "It is all over for me now. My wife died last year. This stand and these fruits and vegetables are all I have left."

"What about your kids?"

"They have left me now. My boy lives in your country."

"Where does he live?"

"Las Vegas. He performs in shows for the tourists."

"It gets very hot there," I say as I wipe my sweaty neck with my handkerchief. "A lot like here right now."

Tinno, his face leather-dark from standing in the sun every day, moves under the shade of the crooked canopy over his stand. "I try to stay out of the sun as much as I can, but I'm lucky I have Italian skin."

"You should wear sunscreen," I say. "I put it on every day before I go out."

"Ahh," he says with a wave of his old, gnarled hand, "Don't need it. I told you I have Italian skin."

I rub the apple on my shirt and shove it into a pocket in my cargo shorts. "I'll save this for later. *Arrivederci,* my friend."

"Goodbye," Tinno says in a hoarse whisper.

At this point I go down the old alleyways, over bridges, and down narrow lanes where one can barely pass another person walking in the opposite direction without moving to one side. There is one street – *Calle Varisco* – that is the narrowest of them all, where I must squeeze by someone and exchange sweat.

I have walked all over this city, and yet I still do not know it. I can get around without a map or my phone, but this is not my city, at least not yet.

When I walk through Piazza San Marco, I casually glance at the basilica and carry on, much as I used to do with the Empire State Building back home. I did not take it for granted because I knew it so well, just as I do with things here now. The basilica – like the skyscraper – will be there again tomorrow. I will always have time to admire it when I choose to do so.

I stare out over the waters of San Marco Basin glittering in the sunlight, the tied-up gondolas bouncing in the waves. Others are filled with tourists baking in the heat, and the gondoliers in blue or red striped shirts are pushing them out for another tour of the canals. These men are the best tour guides because they know the city and cheerfully prove themselves to be cordial despite the heat and the tourists' annoying questions and requests.

This city is known to be one for romance – as can be visually confirmed by some gondolas with red heart seats – but, like Paris, it is a mausoleum for those not in love or someone like me who has lost their lover. Why did I come here then? Because Beth and I had planned to come here, and

I was determined to conquer the angst I was feeling and write a novel just as I promised myself to do 20 years ago.

I do not even know what my novel will be about. When I ruminated about the idea before Beth and I broke up, I thought it would be a grand story about castles and kings, but then I read something about Hemingway saying that you should write about what you know, so then I thought I would write about growing up near JFK in the Queens section of New York City, but now that I am here, I wonder about the wisdom of doing this. James Joyce wrote all about Dublin while he was not in Dublin, so I guess it can be done.

To get connected to my Venetian muse, I even joined a writers' group comprised of some people who are expatriates like myself; however, there is the Serge, the leader of the group, who is Venetian, Pietro – a Florentine who loves Venice almost as much as himself – and then there is Mireille, a beautiful young French woman whose prose is ugly, but because of her glowing face, no one tells her the truth. I have thought about attempting some helpful criticism, but does it really matter in the bigger picture? Perhaps it does, but I am too tired to be brave and speak the truth. I always told the truth and, because I did, I threw away my relationship, and now I am here alone. Trust me, honesty is not the best policy, at least in love.

As I navigate the streets and lanes and cross bridges over canals, I am wearing my standard Venice attire – Mets cap, sunglasses, plain polo shirt, cargo shorts, and sneakers. I try to keep in mind that there are people who live and work here who are not tourists. They cook in the restaurants, clean rooms in hotels, maintain the streets, and present their goods in lovely shops. I sometimes feel sorry for them having to compete for pedestrian space, especially in the Rialto Bridge-San Marco zone, where the visitors seem to overwhelm even the most kindhearted natives.

I do my part as a former tourist – I once came here 20 years ago and always wanted to return – who is now living here respectfully. I appreciate the good nature of the people who suffer the tourist trade with a genial smile, a gleam in their eyes, and patience that is indeed a virtue. Probably, deep down, besides their good nature, the Venetians know the deal – despite their annoying tendencies, tourists are the lifeblood of this island city that is wondrous because of all it has to offer – architecture, history, art, music, great wine, and the legendary cuisine.

*

I start walking home as the sun starts to crash against the buildings and slide into a place beyond the lagoon waters for the night. I cross the Rialto Bridge again, still packed with tourists taking selfies and group photos and blocking the steps for people like me who want to just go home. I walk away from the bridge, still smelling fish from the stalls where hopeful seagulls line up to get some discarded scraps every day.

I go down a long lane in the *sestiere* of San Polo –
one of the city's six districts. It is the city's smallest and
more elevated neighborhood that never floods. I stop in my
local *supermercato* to grab a few things. The owner Marco is
an older gruff fellow with a gray mustache who is always
reading a newspaper when I come into the store. We rarely
exchange words, but he grunts *"Buonasera"* as I leave with
my groceries.

After unlocking the front door of my building, I must
navigate the 62 steep steps up to my third floor flat. I bought
the place after seeing nice pictures of the rooms online;
however, there was no mention of the steps; it did highlight
"on the third floor with a nice view of San Marco's
Campanile or bell tower." All good things come with some
costs, sometimes exhausting ones.

My flat has one bedroom and a living space of
combined kitchen and living room. There is a fireplace that is
covered with a metal door that does not open. The windows

do face southeast with the promised view of the bell tower, and sometimes a nice breeze can drift through them in the evening. I had an air conditioning unit installed because my first week in the heat was unbearable. It cost a staggering amount, but it was worth it.

I shut the windows, turn on the AC, and put my things away. I run the cold water for a minute or so and then stick my head under the faucet for a drink just like I used to do back home in my mother's kitchen. She would always slap my ass and say, "Bobby, use a glass!" I miss that type of love from someone who cared about me.

Feeling sweaty and gross, I decide to take a shower. I go into the bathroom, peel off my clothes that are sticking to my body and take off my gold wedding ring – I only take it off when I shower because it once slid off my soapy finger and almost went down the drain. Yes, I still wear the damn thing because, even though we are divorced, I feel married to Beth in my soul. Perhaps I am trying to trick myself, but it gives me some satisfaction to wear it for some strange reason.

After drying off and putting on a Mets T-shirt and shorts, I sit down at my dining table where I eat my meals and do my work – alas, always alone – and open my laptop and click on the story I have been working on for the group. Since I cannot get the novel going, I figure that writing a story that can become a novel is something; at least this is one way to go. It is a story about my boxing days back in New York City and the fight I had with Adamu, a hulking half Italian, half Ethiopian boxer. I am trying to capture it the way that it happened, but there seems to be no way to tell it successfully because so much is going on in the story that my readers will be overwhelmed. I must find a way to simplify it because fiction does not need to include everything that happened in real life, at least that is what the sagacious Serge tells me.

Since I am getting nowhere, I check my email. My brother Vinny has sent me a message. We have not spoken since Mom died – that is almost seven months ago now – and he never emails or even sends me a text. His last text was sent when I left for Italy a few months ago, and he wrote the words *"Bon voyage."* That was all, and that fact portrays my brother perfectly, using French when I was leaving for Italy.

He is coming to town for business and wants to get together. I am shocked that he wants to have any contact. I am four years younger than he is, and when we were growing up, I followed him everywhere. I worshipped him because he was a great athlete, handsome, and super intelligent. One day when he was 16, I followed him to the bleachers by the paved city ballfield where he met this blonde girl. They were going behind the bleachers and holding hands. When he saw me, he screamed, "Get lost, Bobby." That was the beginning of the end for us.

I respond to his email. "Sounds great. Looking forward to it." Short and not so sweet, but at least I did respond. I wonder how his wife Melissa and his kids are doing. Sara (now 17) and Vince (now 15) both used to call me "Uncle Bob," and I loved them, but even they were taken away from me. As the cliché goes, "That's the story of my life."

After dinner – leftovers from a place over in San Marco – I sit and watch Italian TV. I have picked up enough of the language to understand the news, and I watch soccer, which I believe is a universal language. That is the wonderful thing about sports.

The truth is I do not care so much about TV anymore. Since I have come here, I realize that there are many things I can do without that I used to think were indispensable back home. While the Internet is a must, I do not have all the apps on my phone and TV anymore. I have kept Netflix, but the rest are gone. To keep up with things back home and in the world, I have CNN and *USA Today* apps on my phone, which are especially helpful to keep tabs on news and sports.

I drink another can of Moretti and knock back a shot of Smirnoff Red. I can never get drunk enough here. I change channels and *Die Hard* is on. It is fun seeing Bruce Willis as John McLane kicking ass and speaking Italian. Although I try hard to stay awake, I fall asleep sometime before Hans Gruber gets tossed off the building by McLane. I will have to try to watch it again tomorrow.

CHAPTER TWO – Comfort, But Not Joy

Once a week I visit her flat in the Cannaregio section of the city, walking over the Scalzi Bridge across the Grand Canal to get there. It is very noisy and busy on this side – very close to the train station – and it is seedy and nothing like my street in San Polo. It seems as close to gritty urban as anything that I knew back home.

Just like in my building, I must climb numerous steps to get to Elena's flat. I tap three times on the door, and she throws it open. "You're late!"

"Sorry," I whisper as I put my money on the counter.

Elena is petite and wears only a short shirt that barely covers her full breasts. She has bleached blonde hair and eyebrows and dark brown eyes that almost appear black at times. Elena is pretty, but sometimes a scowl flashes on her face like a hologram.

I take off my shorts and hug her. She kisses my cheek and pulls the lower part of her body away from my penis, shaking a finger at me as if I were a naughty schoolboy.

She leads me over to her sofa bed – she will not let customers in her bedroom – and I take off my shirt. I notice the pink condoms lined up in a row on her lamp table. Elena takes one and pulls off her short shirt ready for action. She is all business for the most part.

Afterwards, I lie on my back and look at her full naked breasts as she smokes a harsh Italian cigarette sitting cross-legged. I see a big bruise on her underarm for the first time. "Hey, that's quite a welt."

She blows some smoke out of her mouth. "Nino!"

Nino is her pimp. I see him in the bar always looking for fresh blood. He is a short man but built like a fire hydrant with beady eyes that seem to be always rapidly scanning everything all at once. Perhaps he puts the scowl on Elena's face. "Hey, why does he do that?"

She finishes her cigarette, falls onto her pillow, and puts her arm over my chest. "He's showing me who's the boss," she says with smokey breath.

"Oh, I see," I say. "He is a creep."

"What is this *creep*?" she asks.

"Not a good guy."

She giggles. "Yeah, you can say that."

"Why do you stay with him?"

Elena sighs. "He says that he loves me."

"I'm sure he tells that to all his girls," I say with a touch of anger in my voice.

"Yes, probably," she moans.

I touch her arm and rub the spot that he damaged. "He shouldn't be hurting you like this. My father raised me to respect women."

Elena puts her arms around me and kisses my cheek. "I know you would be good to a woman. I can tell."

As she stops hugging me, I stare at her dark eyes and say, "Do you realize that this is the only affection I ever get."

"What do you mean?" she asks.

"You're the only person I have physical contact with."

She nods her head. "Oh, I see."

"Yeah, so I look forward to coming here because…"

Elena snuggles against me and touches my cheek. "How is this for you? Do you like it?"

I close my eyes and whisper. "Yeah, I do."

"Did you never have a wife or lover?" she asks, sounding younger than what I believe is her age, almost like a teenager. She touches my hand. "This looks like a wedding ring."

"Yeah, there was someone once, my ex-wife," I say. *I see Beth standing in our yard holding our cat Trixie. She was a real blonde with hair that fell on her shoulders.*

"What happened to her?"

"I blew it," I whisper, like not saying it louder would change anything.

"My other clients have wives or girlfriends, and they cheat on them," she says caressing my face. "You're the only good man I see."

I saw tears in Beth's eyes as she was packing her bags. I watched as she walked out the door with Trixie under her arm and got into a taxi. "Uh, I don't know about that, Elena."

She hugs me tighter. "You are a good man. I know too many others and can tell they are all bad."

"I guess you would know," I say.

After hugging me for a while, she jumps up and walks over to the kitchen area. "Would you like a beer?"

"Uh, yeah," I say as I pull on my underwear.

This little semblance of domesticity is intriguing, but I know not to let myself get any ideas. She hands me a bottle of Moretti, and as I sit on a kitchen chair she asks, "Where are you from in the States?"

"New York," I whisper.

"The city?"

"Yes, I grew up in Queens near JFK Airport," I say. "My father worked there and wanted to live close to it."

Elena sits on another chair. Stark naked, she looks lovely sipping the beer. "Was he a pilot?"

I laugh. "No, he was a mechanic. He worked on the planes for American Airlines," I say.

"Interesting," she says with a smile.

"Where are you from, Elena?"

The slight scowl returns to her pretty face. "I was born in Milan and grew up there."

"I love the Duomo there," I say.

"Yes, so does everyone else," she says with a frown. "It was a big, gritty city with lots of tourists coming to see that stupid Duomo. When my parents finally got divorced, my mother brought me to live with her family in the southeast of the city. They were very poor but also hardworking people. My life changed forever then."

I lean forward on the chair. "So, how did you end up here?"

Elena leans back in her chair, sips the beer, and some of it drips down on her beautiful breasts. "My mother had to work long hours in her brother's factory. She ended up getting sick and unable to work anymore. My uncle said I would finish high school and then start working in her place. It was a terrible job that I would never do.

"The day after I graduated, my mother died. Her last words to me were 'Run away.' She didn't want that life for me. So, I had a little money saved and Carla, a friend who had moved to Venice, invited me to come stay with her in what she described as 'a wonderful place,' so I bought a train ticket and came here seeking a better life."

"And then what happened?"

"Carla worked for Nino, and he got me drunk the first night and raped me. I was a virgin – a very innocent girl." Tears start rolling down her cheeks. "And *that* is how I got here."

I put down the beer bottle and stare at her. "I'm sorry."

Elena looks at me as she wipes away her tears. "Why are you sorry?"

I think quickly and say, "Because I am a customer. I wish I had met you in a different way."

Elena shakes her head. "It doesn't matter now. I've been doing this so long I don't care anymore."

I have been seeing her every week for the last two months after meeting her in a bar. I did not know it then, but Nino was standing in the corner at that time watching us. I only found out who he was when Elena explained why she wanted money when I went to her apartment the first time. In some ways I wish I had left when she said I had to pay. I get up, put on my clothes, and head for the door.

Elena puts on a pink bathrobe, follows me to the door, and hugs me from behind. "I'm going to see you again next week, yes?"

I turn to her and touch her soft cheek with my fingertips. "Yeah, I guess. I need my weekly dose of affection."

She stands on her tiptoes and, for the first time, she kisses me on my lips. "I'll see you next Tuesday, Bobby."

I nod my head. "Yeah, see you."

As I am going out the door, a girl around Elena's age is going into the flat next door. She is not as pretty as Elena but is physically fit and has dyed bright red hair.

"Hey, Carla," Elena says.

Carla glances at me. "Is he the one?"

I look back at Elena. "What does that mean?"

"Nothing," Elena shrugs her shoulders as I stare at her, and then she smiles. "Okay, you're my favorite client."

I smile, touch her cheek, and skip down the winding steps. As I go outside, I see Nino coming up the street. He looks me up and down and says, "You're a good customer!"

I feel awkward and nod. "*Grazie!*" I keep walking and turn around and watch Nino going smugly up the steps. I suppose he has come to collect his money and have his way with Elena and probably Carla too. I know I cannot change any of this, but as I continue walking, I think about how good it would feel to beat him to a pulp.

CHAPTER THREE – The Seahorse

On my side of the Rialto near Campo Erberia, there are bars that remind me of home. They are less raucous than ones in New York, but they have a mix of local regulars, expats, and tourists. There is music and laughter, and in my solitary life it gives me a place to go to do some socializing.

I have been coming to one of these tavernas because of a beautiful bartender. She is Indian/English and hails from London, but she lives and works here now. I like to stay at the bar because in most places there is a cover charge when you sit at a table. Besides, standing at the bar here gives me a chance to talk with the lovely Paula.

She comes over to me with a short glass filled with ice and a bottle of Smirnoff Red. Paula winks at me as she pours the vodka over the ice. "Haven't seen you in a while," she says. Paula has big hazel eyes and a beautiful smile that causes them to twinkle. On this night wisps of her brown hair dangle onto the sides of her cheeks, and she wears a Chicago Bulls T-shirt that leaves nothing to my imagination. Her super short shorts complete the package, making my heart flutter.

"I've been busy," I say as I sip my drink.

"With a lady friend?" she says with that dazzling smile.

"No, with work." For the first time because of the way her T-shirt is cut, I notice a seahorse tattoo above her upper right breast. "Hey, that's cool." I point to it and say, "I haven't seen that before."

Paula stares at me and says, "It's relatively new. I'm in therapy and recently came to terms with who I am."

I sip my drink and ask, "Who are you then?"

Paula leans her lovely elbows on the bar and puts her face closer to mine. "I was a seahorse in another life. I used to swim in the ocean and play with my kind, but I would also rise to the surface and see that different world. My mother warned me to stay away from the world of sun and sky and people. She said it was dangerous, but that made me even more intrigued.

"One day I swam to an island and saw people sitting on a beach. They were basking in the sun, and the children were laughing and playing. I figured they were just like us only above water."

I stare at her. "So, has the therapy helped?"

"Yes, t 'was a little painful at first, but I came to realize why I have always felt like 'other' in my life." She looks down at the service area and sees a waiter needing drinks for a table. "See you later."

I nurse my drink and notice Nino standing over a table with three young girls sitting around it. He is dressed in tight jeans and a dark polo shirt with a big gold cross hanging around his neck. I have seen him doing his recruiting routine before, but he has never been successful at least when I have been here. The girls are trying to ignore him, and he eventually throws his hands up into the air and walks away.

I remembered all the bars I used to go to back home when I was younger. As I got older, we went to the clubs to try to meet girls. It never felt wrong to me, but it did not feel right either.

Always wanting to be a writer, I tried to get a job in that field. I eventually found a position at a small local weekly in Queens. I would write articles about leaking fire hydrants, lost dogs, the grandmother who won the lottery, and the teens wanted for robbing a convenience store. It did not pay very well, but I had achieved my goal – to be paid for my writing.

My father would come home from work and find me tapping away at my keyboard. He moved his big cigar to the corner of his mouth and said, "So, is this article gonna win you a Pulitzer?" He would then laugh sarcastically and walk away. I wanted to show him that he was wrong, but I knew

there was truth in what he thought too.

After confronting the truth about my writing about

boring topics, my uncle – my father's brother – offered me a

job in his insurance company in Manhattan. I really did not

want to do the 9-5 thing like so many other people, but I

wanted to get my own apartment, and this was the only way I

could do that.

I got a place on Forest Avenue in Ridgewood, just a

few blocks from the M train that would take me right into

lower Manhattan to a stop a couple of blocks from my

building on Chambers Street. I figured I would do my writing

at night and on weekends, but the job sucked so much energy

out of me that all I could do when I got home is eat and have

a few beers while watching the Mets' game.

My world would change when Beth came to work in

the office. When I saw her, she glowed from head to toe like

an effervescent being. We would chat a bit at first, and then I got up the courage to ask her to go out to lunch. That was the beginning for Beth and me.

"Hello!" Paula says loudly, breaking me out of my spell.

Suddenly, I am back in the bar with music pulsing and looking at Paula's beautiful face. "I guess I zoned out there," I say.

"Yeah, you were in another dimension I think," she says with a smile.

I stare at the seahorse tattoo and ask, "So, why a seahorse again?"

She leans her elbows on the bar and says, "I was a seahorse in another life."

I remember now. "Oh, yeah, right. I don't know much about seahorses."

Paula stands up straight and pours more vodka into my glass. "What if I told you that seahorses were monogamous?"

I sip my drink. "Then, I'd have to believe you."

"My seahorse mother and father were together for life," she says.

I think about Beth. "Hmm, I wish I had that kind of experience."

Paula's eyebrows move up on her forehead momentarily. She lifts a tray of clean glasses onto the bar and starts putting the glasses into the rack above our heads. "Another thing that is kind of cool is the males carry the babies and give birth."

I find this surprising. "Wow, that is an unexpected twist."

Paula nods and continues placing the glasses in the rack. "Seahorses are not only monogamous, but they die for love."

"What?" I ask.

"It is true!" Paula says and laughs because I am shaking my head. "If their mate dies, the other seahorse will die soon after. They can't face life without their lover. This is the most important thing to know about seahorses."

I raise my glass. "A toast to seahorses – they are much better people than we are."

"I'll say they are," Paula says. "That is why I got the tattoo – a reminder of what I used to be."

I wonder about Paula because she is beautiful. Could she still hold true to her origins as a human? "So, do you feel this way now too?"

She brushes the strands of errant hair from her face and then her expression softens. "I have had my share of disappointments; alas, I did feel a pressing need to remain monogamous, but I can't say that my previous partners shared those feelings."

I finish my drink and hold the glass up for a refill. "Another, please."

She takes the glass, drops some new ice into it, and pours the vodka. When she hands it back to me, I briefly brush her fingertips – another fleeting case of physical contact. "I have to say, I have had my own experience with the challenge of exclusivity," as I hold up my hand and show her the wedding band.

"I've noticed that before," Paula says as she bends her head sideways to study me. "I take it that you were the one who transgressed."

I sip my drink and nod my head. Putting my index finger up in the air, I say, "Yes, it is true but only one frigging time."

Paula crosses her arms. "Like the number of times has any significance?"

I lean both elbows on the bar and hold my head in my hands. "It was at the office Christmas party. She was a new girl who started in November. Julie was young and pretty and flirty."

Paula leans both hands on the bar and stares into my face. "Like that has anything to do with fidelity?"

I shake my head and sip my drink. "Yeah, you're right. I was just vulnerable because my wife was away on a business trip, and I was lonely. She would have been at the party otherwise, and it would have never happened."

Paula crosses her arms again and skews her eyebrows. "You mean to tell me that your wife worked in that same office?" I nod my head and sip my drink. "Oh, Bobby, you're making this former seahorse very angry."

"I'm an idiot, okay?"

"That's a start," she says.

"Of course, I tried to leave the party discreetly after Julie had left, but other workers put two and two together. Anyway, we went back to her place and…"

Paula puts up her hand and says, "Stop! I don't need to hear the rest. You're guilty and now you're alone."

I look up and imagine Paula wearing a judge's wig and a black robe holding a big gavel in her hand. "Yes, yes, I am guilty, and the punishment has been meted out."

"Is that why you're here, Bobby?"

I look up at her, and Paula is her smiling self again. "Yes, I had to get away. Beth still works there, so I quit my job, sold the house, and moved here to write a novel I was supposed to write 20 years ago."

"Well, maybe something good can come from this then," she says.

"I wanted solitude and a place where I felt I could be creative, but Venice has too many detours, too many long narrow alleys where I can wander."

"Well, you're always welcome here when you want to stop your wandering," Paula says. "It's getting busy, but I'll be back."

"Ciao," I say and finish my drink. There is no reason to wait for her to come back; I have already told her enough about my ugly self.

I go down the steps and out into the hot Venetian summer night. People are walking on both sides of the Grand

Canal; illuminated gondolas are floating by with passengers aboard, and there is music playing in the distance. This is too much activity for me; I want and need to go home.

Wandering in and out of narrow streets, there are too many detours. One street leads to another; one narrow lane leads to a dead end. This is the glorious confusion of navigating Venice. Manhattan's streets go east and west, and the avenues go north and south. There is a simplicity back home that makes it easy to navigate, but Venice is a labyrinth that makes a Rubik's Cube seem easy.

Finally, I make my way back to my building, stagger up the steps, and burst into my flat. I put on the AC, grab a cold beer from the fridge, and go sit by the window and stare at San Marco's illuminated Campanile in the distance. I take a sip of beer and think that when I die, I want to come back as a seahorse.

CHAPTER FOUR – The Boxing Story

Having convinced myself that I had to write something for the writing group next week, I stock up on food, beer, and booze. I realize that I must focus on writing the story that I never wanted but need to write. I must deal with my past because it is inexorably catching up with me.

I eat a good breakfast of scrambled eggs, toast, and three cups of black coffee. I turn on the AC, sit at my table, and stare at the blank Word Doc staring back at me with a blinking cursor. Now it begins…

When I was a kid, my father gave me a pair of boxing gloves for my birthday. He grew up in the streets of Brooklyn, and a fight was always just around the corner. He wanted to teach me how to box, but I was kind of a baby at ten, so those gloves hung on the wall in my room for over a year gathering dust.

One day at school, this big bully in my Spanish class

named Lem Kawalski started bothering me. He made fun of

my hair, my clothes, and my sneakers. Lem seemed to always

be around and saying something about me. One day he would

not let me go down a hallway to class. "Watcha gonna do

about it, Bobby?"

My math teacher Mr. Jacoby looked out of his

classroom door and yelled, "Kawalski, leave Valenti alone."

"Later," Lem said threateningly.

I never saw him the rest of that day, but that night I

told my father about what happened. He was a big man –

saying he was overweight would be an understatement – and

he put his large hand on my shoulder. "Do you think those

boxing gloves hanging in your room should stop gathering

dust now?"

We went into the basement, and I slipped on the

gloves. He showed me how to set my feet and to punch with

power. I was hitting him in the palms of his hands – left-right and right left – and I realized I could throw a punch for the first time. We practiced all weekend, and he went out and bought me a weight set. I was finally motivated to get stronger and to know how to protect myself.

Monday came and Lem was bothering me again. I just smiled at him and kept walking. In the cafeteria he came over to my table. My friend Probie – his name was Jack Probst, but Probie was my nickname for him – said, "Oh, crap, here comes Kawalski."

I calmly sipped my milk and ate my crummy pizza that was served cold. Kawalski stood over me and said, "What if I shove that pizza up your ass?"

I stood up and stared at him like I never stared at anyone before. I felt like I could see past his skin and bones and look at his beating heart that I wanted to tear out of his chest. "Try it," I said.

Everyone in the cafeteria was watching, and then one of the teachers who was on duty came over and said, "Break it up, boys."

Kawalski looked at me like he was scared, turned around, and walked away. I sat back down and Probie whispered, "You looked like you were going to kill him."

I sipped my milk and said, "Yeah, I wanted to."

After that my father sent me to a local gym after school where a guy named Cookie ran the place. Cookie was a Puerto Rican man who was short but stocky. My father and Cookie went to high school together. He had asked him to help me to learn how to fight.

"You have to have patience, Bawbee" (that is how he said my name). He showed me how to box, got me hitting the heavy and speed bags, and started me on a regime that involved running every morning and lifting weights.

I graduated high school and started going to Queensboro Community College, but I still made time for the gym. At this point, I had become bigger and stronger from the weightlifting, so that Cookie allowed me to get in the ring and spar with the guys who were prepping for real fights.

Most of the guys knew me from my hanging out at the gym, and I got along well with them. There was one big guy – an Ethiopian/Italian named Adamu – who kept giving me dirty looks and making threatening gestures like banging his gloves together as he stared at me.

"Why doesn't he like me, Cookie?" I asked one Saturday morning after punching the heavy bag.

Cookie let go of the bag and came around to stand next to me. He looked up at me and said, "He doesn't know you."

"Well, I don't feel that way about anyone," I said.

"Look, he's had a hard life. His Italian father left him and his mother a few years ago and moved back to Italy. Maybe he didn't get to go to college like you are doing. Who knows?"

I looked at Adamu as he got in the ring and started sparring with an Irish guy, whom we all called Murph, a big redhaired kid from Woodside. I watched Adamu's moves, and he looked sharp. Murph was down for the count in less than three minutes.

*

About a week later, I had just finished my workout routine with Cookie and was heading for the showers when I heard Murph calling my name. "Hey, Bobby!"

I turned around and asked, "What's up, Murph?"

"They need a sparring partner for Adamu."

"What's wrong with you?" I asked.

He held up a bandaged right hand. "I hurt it last week sparring with him."

I started thinking this is executive decision time. The easy thing would be to turn it down and hit the showers, but I could hear my father saying, "Don't always take the easy way out."

"Okay," I said, "let's do this."

I walked back into the main gym and saw Adamu standing in the ring. His light brown skin was covered with sweat, and he already had on a headguard, and I could see the blue mouthguard between his teeth.

As Murph helped me put on my gloves, Cookie came running over to me and put his hand on my shoulder. "You can do this, Bawbee."

Cookie adjusted the elastic straps on my gloves and headguard. He slipped a mouthguard into my mouth, and I mumbled, "Have the doctor on speed dial, Cook."

Cookie shook his head. "Just do everything I've taught you."

Once in the ring, Adamu and I tapped our gloves and started dancing around. He had a longer reach than I did, and he took advantage of it and popped me in the head. This was not sparring; he had hit me hard. Cookie was in my corner and moving his arms like he was playing a virtual boxing game.

I planted my feet and, as he swung at me, I avoided his glove and came up and caught him in the center of his chest. He lost his footing and staggered backwards. I moved in with a flurry of heavy punches to his head. Adamu went down hard and the ring shook, the ropes swaying like they were hit with a brisk wind.

Cookie came running over to me and lifted my arm over my head. "I knew you could do it, Bawbee!"

I hit the showers after that, went to my locker, and started getting dressed. Murph came up to me and said, "You really did great, Bobby."

I shook my head. "I just got lucky."

"No, you really looked good," Murph said enthusiastically.

I passed the office and Cookie motioned for me to come in. "There was a guy in the gym today who saw you. He left me his card."

I took the card and looked at it – the name was familiar to me. "Doesn't he manage fighters?"

"Yes, he would like to take you on," Cookie said.

I put the card in my pocket. "I'll think about it, Cook."

"Hey, he works with some big pro boxers. You must have impressed him, Bawbee," Cookie said.

"Yeah, okay, thanks. Goodnight, Cook."

When I went outside, I found Adamu standing by the side entrance with his big arms crossed over his chest. I nodded to him. "Hey, Bobby."

"Yeah?"

"I know I hit you hard on that first punch, so what you did was okay," Adamu said.

"Thanks, man," I said as I started walking away.

"In a fight, I'd want you on my side," Adamu said.

I put my thumb up and said, "You got it!"

After finishing the story, I sit back in my chair and feel exhausted. Hemingway was right; writing is hard work. I go the fridge, grab a cold Moretti, and sit by the TV and watch some news show, and a lovely blonde woman is doing the weather report. They always seem to get pretty girls to do the weather report back home too.

I am happy that I wrote that story; I will go over it and tweak it before going to my writing group next week. Writing it proves something to me – *I can write something*. It gives me hope that I will eventually write the novel I have always wanted to write.

The novel I want to write is about home – my neighborhood in New York City. I can still see every street and the stores and houses and trees. I can smell the odor of good food drifting over those houses like culinary angels spreading their wings, the scent of many cultures intermingling. I can visualize my old public school with the yellow buses in the parking lot next to it, and I can feel the cold air on my face when the wind whipped across JFK from Jamaica Bay and swooshed along the streets of my neighborhood. And, most importantly, I can remember my friends and me playing in the streets and having the times of our lives. I guess that will all be in the book that I want to write.

CHAPTER FIVE – The Writers' Group

The writers' group that was formed by leader Serge and convenes in the ballroom of his palatial home has just finished meeting. For the first time since I joined the group, we have gone from a generally supportive and safe space to an adversarial one. The beautiful Mireille is crying because my friend Pietro has just told her that her poem is garbage – "Come on, it's just rubbish," he said, after old Anna said the poem was nice.

I watch as she is running out of the room while sobbing. I glance at Pietro and ask, "Calling her poem garbage? What about giving her a chance?"

"I don't know – I guess I am tired of lying," he says with a wicked smile. Pietro speaks perfect English. I am talking like a presenter on the BBC English.

I lean back in the chair and sigh. "I had hopes that she would get better with practice."

"Sadly, writing is not playing the piano," Pietro says as he takes out and looks at his phone. "Oh, Brian has just gotten us tickets for *Turandot* at La Fenice." Brian is his partner whom he talks about incessantly.

I nod and say, "Puccini, right?" I do not tell him, but I saw an ad for the opera in the street.

"Yes, you are quite correct," Pietro smiles and says, "You always surprise me, Robert." He insists on calling me that. "You're proof that there's hope for you Americans yet."

Pietro stands up as I do. I am looking down like I used to do with Cookie back home because Pietro is five foot nothing. He has a graying mustache to match the hair on his head. His nose is slightly pointy, and in some moments with his whiskers he reminds me of a possum. "Why thank you, Pete." I call him that because he insists on calling me Robert.

Pietro gets Anna's attention. She is an older woman – a white-haired grandmother of seven – who has joined the group to write stories about her late husband and the rest of her family. The ones that I have heard have been achingly beautiful. "Anna, why don't you check on our girl?"

Anna struggles to stand up but with quiet dignity. She leans on her cane and says, "There was no reason to hurt that girl's feelings."

"Well, am I supposed to keep on lying?" Pietro asks with his hands out at his sides.

Anna shakes her head and starts walking toward the bathroom saying, "*Pazzo! Pazzo!*"

Pietro glances at me. "Poor old woman! She would be much better off playing with those grandchildren than being here telling stories."

I shake my head. "Now you have problems with her writing too?"

"Now, Robert, I am very fond of Anna," Pietro says turning to me. "I just sense that you're getting rather aggressive. I don't want to see any of the pugilistic behavior here. Save the fighting for your stories."

"Sorry, Pete," I say. "I've put those fighting days behind me now."

"I must say I am surprised by your story of fighting that beast. I find it odd that you have that in your past," Pietro says with a raised eyebrow. "I saw you as something of a romantic – American writer in Venice and all – not some New York brute. I guess my illusions are shattered."

Before I have a chance to respond to Pietro's comments, Serge walks over to us, an unlit pipe clenched in his teeth. He is in his late thirties like I am. Touches of gray tint his sideburns, and he has piercing blue eyes. When he was a kid, his mother's nickname for him was Sinatra, named after the Old Blue Eyes American singer Frank, whom she loved to listen to while she sat in the parlor having a brandy.

"I believe it was rather cruel to make that comment to Mireille," Serge says as he adjusts his pipe. "The Three Germans think so as well." We all glance over at the three large men taking food from Serge's sumptuous buffet.

"Oh, my, we don't want to offend those ogres now." Pietro glances at me and says, "Since I can't get anyone else to be honest, the burden has fallen upon me."

"Well, I for one do not appreciate your honesty, Pietro," Serge says with a frown. "If it happens again, I will have to ask you to leave the group."

"But I am a founding member of this group," Pietro says with flared nostrils.

"I don't care if you were Dante," Serge says, "I am not accepting this kind of behavior. Do you understand?"

Pietro takes his worn binder filled with stories, stuffs it under his arm, and walks out of the room mumbling to himself. Serge looks at me, and I smile. "I almost laughed there for a moment."

"Pietro is not used to people confronting him," Serge says.

"Well, it is *your* group," I say.

Serge looks around the room with its high ceiling with Renaissance paintings on it and magnificent chandeliers hanging from it. "This ballroom is where my parents held elegant affairs long ago for people from society. I remember them vaguely because I was sent off to school in England when I was a young boy."

"Must have been hard to leave this place," I say.

We walk toward the ornate windows and look out at the Grand Canal. "My family has lived here since this place was built in the late 1400s. By the time my siblings and I came along, the heft of family history and legacy seemed more of a burden than a gift."

I look out the window and see the gondolas and water taxis going by on another beautiful but hot summer evening. "I cannot even imagine that kind of situation."

"My sisters married well; one is living in Spain and the other in the U.K. My younger brother works in the family business; I let him run it now. This frees me up for more creative pursuits."

"Well, I appreciate this setting for our workshop," I say.

Other members of the group say goodbye and leave the room. Serge glances down the red carpeted hallway heading toward the bathroom. "I do not know what I am going to say to Mireille."

I shake my head. "I don't know what to say except to apologize."

Serge nods his head. "Yes, this is something I must do." He glances out the window. "I've been approached by people who want to turn this place into a hotel."

"I can imagine they would want this location," I say.

"They've done it with other grand homes along the canal, but I will hang onto it for my own purposes," Serge says defiantly.

Anna and Mireille come down the hallway slowly. Mireille's lovely face seems puffy from crying, and the ends of her shoulder length dark brown hair are damp from tears. Anna is holding her hand and patting it. Anna looks at us and says, "She is better now."

Serge puts a hand on her shoulder and says, "Mireille, I am so sorry for what Pietro said. You know he doesn't speak for all of us."

Mireille nods her head and glances at me. I say, "Yes, he doesn't speak for the rest of us."

Anna looks at Serge and me. "She is saying that she doesn't think she can come to the group anymore."

"I…I don't know if I can come back, Serge," Mireille whispers.

Serge shakes his head. "Please, you are welcome here. I want to hear what you are writing. So do Bobby, Anna, the Three Germans, and all the rest of us."

I nod my head. "Oh, yes, I want to hear what you're writing."

Anna touches Mireille's arm. "Please come back, *mia amica*."

Mireille looks at all of us and smiles. "I...I will come back."

Serge smiles broadly. "Excellent! I will see you all next week!"

Anna, Mireille, and I leave the magnificent building. Anna looks up the street toward where the vaporetto stop is located. "I am going home now. Why don't you two get some coffee." That Anna is a sly one – quite the matchmaker.

I look at Mireille and ask, "Would you like that?"

Mireille nods her head. "Yes, that would be nice."

*

We wander silently away from the Grand Canal and find a café located on a small canal with a narrow bridge going over it. As a few pedestrians walk over the bridge and gondolas go under it, we have found a somewhat peaceful corner of Venice. There is even a slight breeze coming over the water.

We get a table under the shade of an umbrella and both order *caffè americano* and bottles of still water, and Mireille sits there stirring her coffee and looking out over the canal. Her face has an elegant fragility to it, with green eyes that reflect the light and water like they are shards of crystal. I wonder about how hurt she must have been by Pietro's rude comments and if she has ever been hurt this way before.

"I am sorry you had to experience that," I say and take a sip of coffee. She looks up at me silently. "You know, you really shouldn't take anything Pietro says seriously."

"I'm not sure that I should discount it," Mireille says with just a hint of a French accent.

"You shouldn't let him ruin the experience for you," I say.

"You know in Paris we have a big river which is very grand," she says and sips her coffee. "But there is something elegant about these canals, something admirable too."

"Well, I love Paris too," I say. "I took classes there when I was younger."

"Oh, I suppose writing classes," she says, smiling for the first time.

"Yes, it was something I had saved up for working during high school and college. I fell in love with that city."

Mireille sips her coffee and then takes her water bottle and pours some water over the ice in the glass with a straw in it. "Paris is an easy city to love, but I find this place also romantic."

I look out over the canal and see two old people holding hands in a gondola. "Look at them – still in love after all these years."

"Yes," Mireille whispers, "I wonder what their story is."

I get an idea and lean forward and say, "This is your challenge!"

"My challenge?" She asks with a hand over her heart.

"Yes! You will write a story for next week about those two old people."

"I don't…think I can," she says.

I reach over and squeeze her hand. "You can do it – I believe in you!"

She shakes her head. "I…I don't know where to begin."

I lean back and sip my coffee. "You will begin here. Start with the two old people in the gondola. You can then flashback and see how they got here – how they met, fell in love, and lived their lives."

She puts one hand on her cheek. "It is such an enormous task, Bobby."

"Yes but think about it. You have mentioned that finding subjects that you seem to care about is difficult. Now, you have one given to you. I am certain it will be wonderful."

Mireille nods her head and says, "Okay, I will do it! I am not sure how, but I will." She looks at her watch. "Oh, I have to get back to work. This is my late night this week."

She gathers her things, and I say, "Good luck, Mireille. I am looking forward to your story."

"Thank you, Bobby."

As she walks away, I yell, "I believe in you."

She stops walking and smiles. "I know you do. *Au revoir!*" The way she said "au revoir" has a tint of hope in it.

I watch her gracefully walk away. I could easily find myself falling in love with Mireille, but I like her and would not want to do that to her. I sip my coffee and look at the gondolas in the canal going by as they have done for centuries. Somehow, I find that oddly comforting.

CHAPTER SIX – Probie

Jack Probst texted me and said he was going to be in Milan on business, and he wanted to know if we could get together. Now, I have known Jack since kindergarten, so he is my closest and dearest friend; however, I suppose he is not too up on geography because it is not like Venice is around the corner from Milan.

To get to Venice's Santa Lucia Station, I must take a vaporetto (water bus) to get to its location on the other side of the Grand Canal from San Polo. I could walk all the way by going over the Scalzi Bridge, but I want to make my train on time. People are getting on the watercraft with big suitcases. I find a seat toward the back and sit next to an old man who has a cat on his lap. I do not know what kind of cat it is, but it stares at me with sinister green eyes when I sit down. It must sense that I am a dog kind of person.

Once I arrive at the stop for the train station, it is a long walk until I am inside the area to get to the platform. I show the ticket on my phone to security, and soon I am inside a nice, air-conditioned car and on my way to Milan. I close my eyes and think about my old friend Jack.

Jack was walking about a block away from school when Lem Kawalski grabbed him. He ripped the backpack from Jack's shoulders and shoved him up against the wall. I was on my way to school and saw this from across the street.

"Okay, Probie, you're gonna get it for always laughing at me in Spanish class," Lem said with spit spraying out of his mouth.

"I didn't do anything," Jack screamed as he put his hands up in the air to express his innocence.

A NYC bus came rumbling down the street, so that I lost sight of them for a second, and then it was gone, and I saw Lem punching Jack. I raced across the street, threw down my own backpack, and grabbed Lem by the shoulder.

As he turned around, a big smile brightened his pimpled face. "Oh, great, I get two for the price of one!"

As Lem took a wide swing at me, I ducked under his arm and came in with a punch to his chest just like my father had shown me. This backed him up a bit, but Lem charged me, and I popped him once in the chin with a left jab and then used a right hook to flatten him. Jack was breathing heavily and whispered, "I didn't know you could fight."

"Well," I said shrugging my shoulders, "that's a surprise for you today!"

We both picked up our backpacks and started walking toward school. Jack looked back at Lem sprawled out on the sidewalk and asked, "What about him?"

I laughed. "I guess his mother will have to write him an absence note."

When I wake up, I find that the train has almost reached Milan. I look out the window and smile as I think back to those times. After that day, Lem avoided me and stayed away from Jack. That was my first real fight, and the last one until I went to Cookie's gym.

I take a taxi to Jack's hotel that is very close to the illuminated Duomo that we pass in the dusk. It amazes me how the taxi drivers here can plow down a narrow street and not hit the clueless tourists walking inches from harm's way. Once I pay the driver, I go into the lavishly decorated lobby, go up to the desk, and ask a lovely young lady to let Jack Probst know that I have arrived.

She looks at the computer screen and says, "Mr. Probst has left a message and asks that you join him inside the cocktail bar." She helpfully points to the direction I must go, and soon I am inside a slightly darkened room where a guy is playing the piano, and couples are sitting at tables.

"Hey, Bobby," Jack calls to me from the bar. He is short but not as short as Cookie or Pietro. Because of his height, it is easy to see that he has put on a little weight in almost a year since I last saw him. His naturally blond hair is starting to thin and turn white, but his face is smooth without any signs of age.

I walk over to him and shake his hand. "It is good to see you, Probie."

"Same here," Jack says. He turns to the bartender and says, "Please make a Tanqueray martini, very dry, straight up with olives."

"Very good, Mr. Probst," the bartender says.

I sit on the stool next to him and smile. "You haven't forgotten my go-to drink order."

"Of course not," Jack says with a grin. "How have you been since the…"

I take a few pretzels from the snack bowl and slip one into my mouth. As I crunch one, I say, "Since the debacle of my stupidity that resulted in Beth leaving me you mean?"

"I didn't mean it that way," Jack whispers.

The bartender brings my drink, and I take a sip. "That gentleman really knows how to make a good martini," I say.

"So, how are you, Bobby?"

"I am getting by, Jack," I say. "I came here to get away from everything. My parents are gone, and frankly New York just reminded me of Beth no matter where I went."

"Well, you took her everywhere," Jack says and then sips his martini.

"Yeah, all our old haunts," I say. "There was no place I could go without thinking about her."

"But did you have to go so far away?" Jack asks. "It's been a long time, and I really miss you, buddy."

I put my hand on his shoulder. "I miss you too, Probie. That's why I took a two-and half-hour train ride to see you."

"Well, thank you, I appreciate you making the effort," Jack says with a big smile.

"Are you still working for Walsh and Benneck?" I ask. Jack nods his head and sips his martini. "So, what's this business you're up to here in town?"

"I am meeting with a client tomorrow that is looking to bring their business to good old NYC," Jack says with a big smile. "They are an up-and-coming fashion company and want us to handle all their legal issues. If I land this account, I will be set for life."

I raise my glass and say, "Then a toast is in order – to my friend Probie – may you have success in this venture!"

We clink glasses and sip our drinks. "So, I have reservations for us to have a fine dinner. I have taken the opportunity to place our orders since they know we are coming."

"Should I know what it is or can you surprise me?"

"Veal Milanese with a delicate risotto. I'm told to always opt to keep the bone in the meat because they overcook the boneless elephant ear."

"Elephant ear?"

"Yes, the *cotoletta* is sort of shaped like an elephant's ear," Jack says. "We will order a nice pinot noir that goes very well with it."

"So, you have been there before," I ask.

"Oh, no, this is my first day here," Jack says. "The concierge has told my everything, and he claims it is the best place in town to get the city's signature meal."

I think about it for a second and say, "What the hell, let's go for it."

*

After the dinner, which was truly amazing, Jack and I end up in a club in the shadow of the Duomo. It has a rooftop bar where we can sit and look at the city. Jack and I have switched to Smirnoff Red on the rocks – a drink we always had when we went out back home. The music is pounding over speakers and young people are dancing under the stars.

"So, Probes, how is it going with Mandy?" I ask because he has not spoken about his wife all night.

Jack stares at the illuminated Duomo and the city around it and shakes his head. "She took the kids and went back to her parents," he says with no emotion in his voice. "I decided not to stop her this time."

Mandy and Jack have been having troubles since their wedding day when I served as his best man. They got married 13 years ago, and I tried to tell Jack that they were too young – Beth and I got married 10 years later, but I was probably still too young even then. The difference is that Jack and Mandy have three kids – Sally, Jackson, and Madison – and Jack loves them more than anything.

"I'm so sorry, Probie," I say.

"Remember when Sally first said 'Da-da' and I was over the moon?" he asks with his voice breaking.

I put my hand on his shoulder. "Yeah, I remember, pal."

Jack stands up and walks over to the railing. "I worked hard to make money. I know it was long hours and business trips. I didn't inherit money like you."

"Ouch!" I say, "I wish my parents were still alive and that money was still in their house and accounts."

"I know, Bobby; I'm sorry I said that," Jack says as he sips his drink. "I'm just frustrated with my situation."

I join him standing at the railing. "You did your best, man."

"Yeah, but my best wasn't good enough – not for Mandy. She wanted more and more each year."

"Do you get up to Brewster often to see the kids?"

"I have them every other weekend," Jack says robotically. "Because of the distance, I just get a motel room and take them to playland or a movie. She really screwed me by moving back up there."

I look out over the beautiful city and say, "You've got your dignity, man. That's how you move on from this."

"I really tried," Jack says. "I went to Jackson's games, and all the soccer matches for Maddy, and Sally's recitals. I did everything I could. It just wasn't good enough."

"Listen, you secure this deal tomorrow, and then you have the rest of your life to live it your way from now on," I say, speaking from experience.

"Thanks, man, thanks for being here," Jack says. "Are you going to stay over tonight?"

"Yeah, I'm kind of out of it," I say as I finish my drink. "I'll take the train tomorrow."

We look out over the illuminated cityscape with the Duomo's sparkling gem in the middle of it all, and there is nothing left to say. I will be there for Jack whenever and wherever he needs me, and it does not matter if he cannot do the same for me. I am okay with that.

CHAPTER SEVEN – Murano

Mireille and I take a vaporetto for a 15-minute ride to the island of Murano. This is a place known for glassmaking since the thirteenth century. We have come here to see the town and visit Museo del Vetro, where we can learn about the history of the island and see how they make glass using the old traditional methods.

We walk along a canal toward the lovely Church of Santa Maria and San Donato, which has a bell tower made of distinctive dark red and brown bricks. Inside, there is respite from the heat of the day, and we walk across the multicolored mosaic floor before sitting in a pew. We have been quiet since getting off the boat, and I noticed Mireille blessing herself and whispering a prayer.

She glances at me and asks, "Are you at all religious?"

"I was – *I am* – Catholic. I just haven't been practicing the past few years due to circumstances beyond my control."

She turns to look at the altar. "See the statues of the saints on the altar?"

I look and nod my head. "They are very lovely."

"Do you see the bones hanging behind the altar?" I nodded. "They are from a dragon slain by San Donato. You can see that they are unique and not like any creature we know now."

"Wow!" I say, wondering if she really believes this story is true or not.

She turns to me and whispers, "I used to come here during my lunch break just to visit this church. I have never been to the museum or the factory."

"Are you very religious, Mireille?"

She turns and stares at the altar. "I went to Catholic school, and I thought about becoming a nun for a while, but my mother tried to talk me out of it."

"Why did you leave France?"

She closes her eyes. "Because I prayed hard one night for God to help me make a choice about being a nun. The next day my mother told me that her brother had a job for me in his hotel in Venice. I figured God answered my prayers."

We leave the church and head toward the museum. It is hot now approaching noon. As we look in the shop windows at the various glass items for sale, the bells in the church starts ringing. Mireille puts her hands over her ears and laughs. I find the sound of the bells delightful, like chimes from the past.

In the Museo del Vetro, we get a complete history of glassmaking from the Golden Age Venetian beads – the fourteenth century to the seventeenth century – and everything up until the present day. There are so many jars, birds, butterflies, statues, glasses, bowls, and even characters from popular culture. All these items chronicle the history of glassmaking. I turn to Mireille and say, "These pieces from the past are like new in a way that seems impossible."

"They were artisans, Bobby. I think in some ways that they strived to make their work eternal."

I nod my head. "Yeah, I guess so."

After the museum, we head over to a less busy factory – the popular one right near the vaporetto stop has a long line to get in – to see demonstrations on the art of making glass. An older man stands at a table with many different colorful glass pieces on it. "Hello, I am Rodrigo. It is wise that you came here instead of that commercial place by the water."

I look around and am happy that there are no tourists with cameras – Mireille and I are alone in the place. "Hello," I say.

"I am a master glassmaker. It takes 10 – 15 years to qualify to be a master." He motions toward two young men behind him who stand near a huge furnace with two open doors revealing the flames. These are my sons who are my assistants, and one day they will be masters. Right now, we are making a pitcher and glasses to go with it."

I look at Mireille and her crystalline eyes are bright as she listens to Rodrigo intently. He continues, "They are now putting the blowpipe with glass into the flames. At 1,000 degrees Centigrade, the glass glows orange. Then it is ready to start shaping it."

The men bring the hot glass over to where they have tools and a marver – a metal table that they roll the molten glass over to start to shape it. Rodrigo points to a bin that has shards of blue glass in it. "They will roll the now shaped glass over the blue pieces to create a design and give it color, and then they have to go back to the furnace to continue the process."

We watch as the men do their work so gracefully, blowing into the pipe, molding the glass, and returning to the furnace again and again. It is like a carefully choreographed ballet of man, tools, pipe, glass, and heat that results in an amazingly beautiful set of glasses and a pitcher.

Mireille says, "May I purchase that set, Rodrigo." She looks at me and says, "I want to send it to my mother."

"Oh, I am sorry, but the glass takes about 24 hours to cool down, but if you wish to go down this hallway," Rodrigo says pointing to a doorway, "there is a small shop where my wife and daughter will take care of you."

We go down the hallway and walk into a little shop like the ones we passed when we left the church. There are two customers, and a young girl is helping them. An older woman is behind the counter and smiles at us. "Please, look around," she says softly.

Mireille scans the shelves quickly, and she looks at me and says, "Let's go."

When we are outside, she takes a deep breath, and I ask, "What's wrong?"

"I only wanted that set of blue glasses and pitcher; they have nothing like that in the store," Mireille says.

"Okay, I understand," I say.

"It is also because I saw it being made," she says anxiously. "I could tell my mother that story. It is something that would make her happy."

"I get it," I say, but I am not quite sure if I do.

"Let's get lunch, Bobby," she says.

We walk for a few minutes and come across a nice café right on a canal. We sit in the shade of the umbrella and glance at the menus. I say, "I'm getting a cheeseburger."

"Very American," she says with a little smirk.

"Truthfully, I haven't had one in all the time that I have lived here," I say.

The waitress comes over to us and Mireille orders a salad and still water. I order the burger and a beer. She leans forward on the table and says, "I'm sorry if I seemed strange in that store."

"What's really going on?" I ask because I am curious.

She sits back and takes a deep breath. "Seeing that woman and her daughter working in the store together did something to me."

"Why?" I ask as her eyes sort of glass over.

"I was thinking that I have been away from my mother almost four years now. I realized how much I envied that mother and daughter."

"You haven't seen your mother in almost four years?" I ask.

Mireille looks at the canal. The water is still and has no boats or gondolas on it now. It is so much quieter here than in the heart of Venice. "It is complicated, Bobby," she whispers.

I sit back as the waitress comes with our drinks. I look at Mireille's face, and she seems to be on the verge of crying. "We don't have to talk about it if this upsets you," I say and take a sip of beer.

"My father left us when I was a teenager," she says, trying to not cry. "It was very difficult for my mother, but she worked hard to keep my sister and me in school. I can never repay what she did for me."

"So, why is it complicated now?"

"My father came home shortly before I got the job and moved here," Mireille says, taking her napkin and dabbing her eyes. "He and I do not get along; otherwise, I would go home to visit."

"Why doesn't your mother come here?"

"He...he won't let her," Mireille says.

"What happened to your sister?"

"Colette is two years younger than I am," she says. "But she got out of the house as soon as he came home. The last time I heard from her she was in Amsterdam, but that was almost two years ago."

Our food comes and Mireille pokes at her salad with her fork. I take a bite of the cheeseburger and nod my head,

"This is really good!" I look up and see Mireille staring at the canal again. I wish I can find a way to help her.

She watches me eating, and I can see she is noticing my wedding ring. She asks, "Are you married, Bobby?"

I swallow my food and dab my mouth with a napkin. "I was married for almost three years, but we broke up late last year."

Mireille sips her water. "Why do you still wear the ring?"

I look at it and say, "It is a reminder – sort of way to keep reality in perspective. I guess it lets me remember my mistakes as to not repeat them."

*

When we get off the vaporetto back in San Polo, Mireille looks up at me. "I know I am not good company."

"No, I had a nice time," I say. "I'm just sorry that you got upset about your mother."

"I am okay now," she says. "We were so close, and now not to see her for four years is very difficult for me."

"Well, I have a brother that I don't see anymore, so I kind of understand," I say.

She leans toward me and kisses my cheek. "Thank you for being so kind to me."

"Oh, it is just being there for a friend."

She starts walking away but turns around. "Will you be at the writers' group on Friday?"

I nod my head. "Yes, I'm looking forward to your story."

"My story?"

"Yeah, you know, about the old people in the gondola," I say.

"Oh, yes, I've been working on it." She turns and floats away gracefully, disappearing around a corner.

I think, "Damn it, Mireille; you're making it hard not to fall in love with you!"

CHAPTER EIGHT – Comfort Visit Surprise

Elena shrieks and rolls off my body, breathing heavily. I turn, put my elbow on the pillow, and lean my head on my upturned hand. "Hey, is everything okay?"

"Yeah, more than okay," she says, catching her breath.

"What's going on?"

"Bobby, I just had an *orgasmo incredibile!*"

"Really?" I ask.

"Uh, yes, very fine," Elena says, still catching her breath. "That has never happened to me before." She sits up and turns to me cross-legged, her lovely naked breasts partially covered by the ends of her hair. We are both sweaty from the our lengthy and happily satisfying session for Elena.

I lie back on the pillow and look at her. "Oh, wow!"

"Well, truthfully, I have only had sex with Nino and customers. Nino raped me when I was a virgin, so I really am not into it with him, and with the customers I usually get robotic with them and wait until they're done. You know, *finito*, and that's all!"

"I get it," I say, "it's just a job."

Elena puts a hand on my arm. "But not with you. Since you told me about how you only have affection with me, I feel a little different about you now. I feel like you like me not just as, *you know what*, but who I really am."

I put my hand on top of her hand on my arm. "I like you for who you are. You're just a special person to me."

"Well, *l'orgasmo* is amazing for me," she says with a big smile. "I've always heard about it, but to have one is *just amazing*!"

I sit up and touch her cheek. "I don't know what to say to you."

"Well, did it feel so wonderful for you?"

"Yes, it has always been good with you," I say.

"I just wonder if this means something more."

"We like each other, and that's okay," I say as I get up. "Hey, I'm really sweaty; can I take a shower?"

Elena takes me by the hand and leads me into the bathroom. She runs the water as I take off my wedding ring and put it on the shelf over the toilet. We walk into the flowing water together, and she starts soaping my body, and I return the favor. I get erect again, and we start to make love. She kisses me deeply, and I press her against the wet tile.

When we are finished, she turns off the water, and we stand there looking at one another dripping on the tiled floor. She whispers, "That's the first time I've ever had sex without a condom."

"Really?" I ask, and she nods her head. "What about when Nino raped you?"

"Oh, he put on a condom; *the creep* – see now I'm using that word – always wants to make sure he doesn't get anyone pregnant."

"He's such a calculating bastard," I say.

We dry one another off, and then I go out into the living room and grab my underwear from the floor and slip it on. As I stand there staring at her, I realize that Elena really is quite beautiful, and her face is glowing. "Today was the best sex I ever had," she screams.

"I wouldn't repeat that," I say, "I think Nino wouldn't like it."

"What do I care what he likes?" Elena screams and throws her hands up over head. "Nino, *quel bastardo!*"

I start getting dressed. "Look, Elena, you always say he is dangerous and that you're afraid of him."

She runs up to me with fiery eyes. "When he sleeps, I think about getting a knife from the kitchen and…"

I put my hands on her upper arms. "Elena, you're not a killer."

"Maybe not, but I would use the knife to cut off his cock!"

"Elena, you would still go to jail," I say.

"Maybe we can just run away together," she says.

I take a deep breath. "You're just a kid. I am too old for you." She is starting to make me feel nervous now.

"No, Nino is too old for me. He is over 40. You are not old at all. You are perfect for me."

"How old are you?"

She looks away from me and whispers, "Going to be 21 next month."

"Well, I'm going to be 38. People would see us together and think that I'm a dirty old man."

Elena turns to me and touches my hair. "You have wonderful thick hair and not even turning gray yet."

I am buttoning my shirt. "Look, if you want some money, I can give it to you to get out of here."

"But where will I go, Bobby? Back to Milan to work in my uncle's factory? To work myself into getting sick from the chemicals and dying like my mother?" She asks glumly.

"Well, you could get on a train and go as far away as possible." I say, sorry to see the sadness etched in her face.

Elena takes her robe from the back of a chair and puts it on. She leans against the wall and shakes her head. "It doesn't matter where I go. Nino has told me, if I run away, he will find me. I guess I should forget about this because even if I went with you, he would find us. I wouldn't want him to hurt you."

"I can take care of myself," I say.

"Just go, Bobby," she says. "I have another customer coming soon."

I kiss her on the cheek. "I won't come next week if you don't want me to come."

Elena closes her eyes. "No, just be here at your usual time."

*

I wander the streets for a long time, and I end up near the Rialto and detect that fish smell from the market despite them watering the ground around the stalls earlier in the day.

I go up on the bridge, and it is not that crowded despite the sun going down. Tourists like sunset pictures, and there is something awesome about looking at the sunset from the bridge, but there are not many of them here for some reason this evening.

A haggard old man leans on the bridge wall next to me, stares at the sunset, and whispers, "The sun never sets in Venice; it just lingers out of sight." He glances at me and walks away. I have no idea what he is talking about.

I keep thinking about poor Elena. I wish I was not the only guy who ever gave her an orgasm. Now she is thinking all these crazy things. I hope she does not say anything to that nutcase Nino, and I also hope she will not do anything stupid with a knife.

After the sun goes down or perhaps lingers somewhere like that old man said, I come off the bridge on my side of it and walk aimlessly until I go into the taverna to see Paula. I lean on the bar and watch her as she talks with the waiters while filling their orders; she makes bartending look like it is easy, which I know it is not. I look around the room and listen to the music – Frankie Goes to Hollywood's "Relax" always reminds of my younger days.

Paula comes over to me with a big smile. "Haven't seen you in a while."

"I was just here last week," I say.

"Yeah, but you're usually here almost every night," she says.

"I'm writing a book," I say.

"Am I in it?"

"Yeah, you're the beautiful female bartender with a seahorse tattoo!"

"Funny!" she says with a smile. "What are you drinking?"

"Tanqueray on the rocks," I say.

She pours my drink and looks me up and down. "What's going on? You seem out of it tonight."

"I am," I say. "I want to help a friend, but there is no way I can."

"Why is that?" Paula asks with a raised eyebrow.

"Because there is no way out," I say.

"No, Bobby, there is always a way out; you just have to find the right door!" she says with a smirk. It is getting busy at the service bar, so Paula winks at me and says, "See you later."

I turn my back to the bar, lean one elbow on it, and sip my drink. The place is getting crowded, and I see mostly couples sitting at the tables. I wonder why I come here sometimes. It would be so much easier to get drunk in my flat, but I do not like drinking alone all the time, then I might as well be dead.

Paula comes back after a few minutes, wiping her hands on a bar towel and then moving all the dirty glasses on the bar into the trays to be cleaned. She has so much energy that it amazes me. I turn around to look at her. "Seems like the regulars are coming in now," I say.

"Aren't you a regular?" Paula asks.

I nod my head. "Yeah, I guess I am now."

"You ready for another?"

I suck down what is left in my glass and hand it to her. "I'm ready, Paula."

She dumps out the old ice, replaces it with some fresh cubes, and generously pours more gin into my glass. Paula hands it to me and leans her elbows on the top of the bar. "How come you never take any garnish in your drink?"

I look at the glass and say, "I don't want anything getting between me and the gin."

"You're a funny bloke," Paula says. "Hey, why aren't you wearing your wedding band tonight?"

I look at my left hand and then see myself taking off the ring and putting it on Elena's shelf before we showered. I guess I will get it back on my next visit. "I...I took a shower and forgot to put it back on."

"Do you always remove your ring when you take a shower?"

"Yeah, because I almost lost it down a drain," I say, sipping the drink. "Ah, nectar of the British gods."

"How come I never see you trying to talk to any of the girls that come in here?" Paula asks.

"I've been burned before, so I'm not looking for any complications," I say with a grin.

Paula nods her head. "I see. I was just wondering because you're the only guy that never flirts with me."

"Oh," I say, "well, you and I are friendly, so I wouldn't want to ruin that. Besides, you pour a great drink.

Wouldn't want to mess that up either." I am telling lies – *I really like her*, but I am afraid to be rejected by her.

Paula laughs. "You have your reasons then. But you may have also noticed that I don't flirt with any guys."

I sip my drink and realize that is true. "Yeah, now that you mention it, that's true. Is that one of your rules?"

"No, it is because I am in love and live with my partner," Paula says.

"Was he a seahorse in another life too?" I ask.

"It is *she*, and no, she was not," Paula smiles.

"Ah, I see," I say as I sip my drink. *Damn it*, I think. I do have a crush on her, but now I do not stand a chance. "Monogamy is a beautiful thing if both partners stay true."

"What are you saying?"

"I'm talking about myself, Paula," I say. "The reason I am here and not back in NYC is because I cheated on my beautiful wife. Remember?"

"I must say I was surprised when you first told me that story," she says. "I was a little sad because I thought you were one of the good ones."

I stare at myself in the mirror behind the bar. "I was until I wasn't." No one knows the truth of those words more than I do, and I must live with this every day for the rest of my life.

Now, the hope I had that I could have something with Paula is kind of dead. I am not sure what is happening with Mirielle, and Elena's situation is too complicated. Once again, I am out of options in the game of love. Maybe I should just give up and stop playing it because I aways lose in the end.

CHAPTER NINE – The Gondola Story

Serge's writers' group meets for the first time since Pietro's comments about Mireille's poem abruptly ended the session. As usual, Serge has a nice spread for this event that he purposely holds at teatime – 4:00 pm sharp – since he once lived in London and adopted the practice but has also added some Italian delicacies. His British majordomo Whitman checks to make certain that everything is just perfect before exiting the room.

Pietro comes in with his battered binder under his arm. He glances at me and nods. "Robert."

"Hey, Pete," I say as I prepare to place a small cucumber sandwich with no crust into my mouth.

Anna waddles in with her cane, her white hair flowing on her shoulders instead of up in a bun. The rest of the members come in and gravitate to the serving table, where the Three Germans are taking hefty portions on their plates. I see Serge at the doorway, and he motions for me to come over to him.

"Bobby, where is Mireille?" Serge asks.

I look at my watch and say, "I expect her to be here. She texted me last night and said her story is ready."

Serge peeks into the room and spots Pietro shoving food into his mouth. "I heard from other members during the week. They feel Pietro should be forced to apologize to Mireille. If he refuses, they want him expelled from the group."

I think about it and say, "He will never apologize."

"Then I will handle things after the meeting," Serge says. "This is nothing to be done in front of the group."

Mireille comes running down the hallway, looking spiffy in a gray business suit and black pumps. Her beautiful face is flushed from apparently running from the vaporetto stop to Serge's home. She pulls papers out of her laptop bag and says, "I have my story, Serge," she says as she is catching her breath. "I would like to go first."

Serge looks at me and nods. "That is the least I can do for you."

We walk into the room, and Serge closes the doors behind us. He walks up to the podium while Mireille and I take our seats. Pietro glances at me and asks, "What did he want?"

"You'll see," I say with a grin.

"Good afternoon, everyone," Serge says. "This is our first meeting in August, so at the end of the readings, I will go over July's monthly minutes and take any questions." Serge mentally keeps tabs on everything that goes on during our meetings, and then he composes the minutes afterwards. He claims to have a photographic memory. Judging from his meticulous minutes, I believe that he does.

"Mireille has requested to go first today," Serge says, with Pietro responding by tapping his fingers on the top of his binder. "So, Mireille, please come up to read."

Mireille walks gracefully to the podium as Serge sits down in the seat adjacent to it. "Hello, everyone. Last week, Bobby presented me with a writing challenge, so this story is the result of that. It is called 'Two Lovers in a Gondola.'"

George and Harriet Wilson, from Connecticut in the United States, sat in a gondola in Venice, Italy, for the first time in their lives. Both were 90 years old and on their first trip to Europe. They sat holding hands and kissing with the enthusiasm of young lovers on a red heart shaped seat. As the gondolier pushed them along the canal under Rialto Bridge, they closed their eyes and hugged one another.

Harriet remembered meeting George at her cousin Millie's high school graduation party in the backyard of Millie's Brooklyn home. He looked dashing in his Army uniform. He poured some lemonade into a glass for her, and they sat down in the shade of an oak tree to eat their hotdogs and talk.

"How long have you been in the Army?" Harriet asked.

"A little over a year," George replied.

"How do you know Millie?"

"Her boyfriend Johnny is my brother," George said.

Harriet smiled. "Oh, he is a nice feller."

"Are you still in high school?" George asked.

Harriet sipped her lemonade, "I graduated last year. I just turned 19 last month and work in Woolworth's."

"Oh, that's swell," George said and bit into a hotdog and chewed quickly. "Next week I am shipping out for Korea."

Harriet put her hand to her cheek. "Korea! Oh, I am sorry to hear that you have to leave."

"Well, I'd like to take you to a movie tomorrow if you would like to go," George said. "And maybe we can see each other a few more times before I go away."

Harriet put her paper plate on the table. "I would like that, George."

Les Baxter's "Because of You" was playing on the radio, and George stood up and said, "May I have this dance?"

Harriet got up, and they started dancing a waltz. The little kids in the yard started laughing, and the adults were clapping. This would be their song played for the first dance at their wedding.

They came out of from under the bridge and opened their eyes. Harriet realized that everything that happened to them started with hotdogs and lemonade and a dance in her cousin's backyard.

"We've had a good life, George," Harriet whispered to him.

"The best life," George said. "I couldn't ask for anything more. You gave me three beautiful children."

"Who gave us eight grandchildren," Harriet said with a smile.

"And we finally made it to Venice," George said.

"You promised me that we would come here years ago, but there was always something that came up," Harriet said.

"But we finally made it," George said.

"Thank you, George."

The gondolier was moved by the elderly couple. He saw them hugging each other as he went under another bridge, and they remained in a loving embrace for the rest of the ride. When they got to the end the trip, he stepped forward to help them get out of the gondola.

George and Harriet's eyes were closed, and there were smiles on their faces, but they had both passed away. The gondolier wiped tears from his face with a cloth and, although he was sad, he felt that the couple went to their final

rest happy and fulfilled.

Mireille looks up from her paper, smiles, and says, "The end!"

There is a period of brief silence – an uncomfortable kind usually reserved for wakes – and then Pietro stands up, starts clapping, and says, "*Brava*, Mireille! *Brava!*"

We all look at one another as Serge stands up and starts clapping. We all stand and applaud as well. Mireille looks around at everyone as tears fall from her eyes. Then, as she did last time when Pietro had made fun of her, Mireille takes her papers and laptop case and runs down the red carpeted hallway toward the bathroom.

The applause ends, and Pietro looks at me and says, "There is just no pleasing that girl."

Anna takes her cane and starts waddling slowly down the long hallway to check on Mireille. Serge adjusts his tie and walks back towards the podium. "Please be seated, everyone."

"I think she was just overwhelmed," I whisper to Pietro.

"Now, who would like to go next," Serge says in an exquisitely deadpan way.

*

As the group starts to leave the room, Serge walks up to me. "What happened with Mireille?"

I look at my phone. "I texted her, but she has not responded as of yet."

Serge puts his unlit pipe in his mouth and holds his chin pensively, reminding me of an Italian Sherlock Holmes trying to solve the case. "Seems rather odd that she was rattled by such a supportive reaction."

"Well, it may have taken her by surprise," I say. "After all, nothing she has read here in the past has gotten much of a reaction at all, except last week when Pietro was so negative."

Serge looks around the room. "Speaking of him, where the hell did, he go so fast? He usually lingers to take more food."

"If I hear from her, I will let you know," I say.

"Very good, Bobby," he says. "And maybe you can find out what happened to Anna too."

I suddenly feel like I am Dr. Watson to Serge's Holmes, and I say, "I will let you know."

Outside of Serge's palatial home, I stand and watch the gondolas and a vaporetti on the Grand Canal, and I feel the intense heat. It will be good to get on a vaporetto and be out on the water for the ride home.

I walk for several minutes, and I see Anna sitting in the middle of a bench and holding her cane with both hands. She is watching pigeons that are lined up on the railing with the canal water flowing behind them.

"May I sit down?" I ask.

Anna scoots over to make room for me. "Mireille went back to work."

"Ah, so how was she doing?"

Anna turns to me and says, "Pietro was so cruel to her last week. She wasn't sure if he was sincere or mocking her."

I nod my head. "I can see why she feels that way, but I think we all showed her our approval."

"Perhaps it was too much for her," Anna says.

"Perhaps you are right," I say, and I turn to see the pigeons fly off over the canal.

*

That evening as I drink a glass of wine after dinner, Mireille finally responds to my text. She writes, "Sorry I left so abruptly."

"Are you okay?" I write back.

"Can you talk?" she asks.

"Yes!" I type quickly.

She rings my phone, and I answer it. "Bobby, I just couldn't handle the reaction."

"I'm sorry," I say. "I think the reaction was sincere."

Mireille whispers, "I...I don't doubt that."

"What can I say. Serge was concerned about you."

"Please let everyone know that I apologize," Mireille says.

"I certainly will," I say.

"Bobby, I can never go back there," Mireille says.

"Oh, Mireille, I hope you don't mean that!"

"I'm sorry, Bobby. I am done with the writing."

"Maybe you will feel differently after some time passes," I say. "Just take some time to think things over."

"Okay, maybe," Mireille says as she starts to cry. "I have to go now."

"Mireille?"

"Goodbye, Bobby," she whispers and hangs up.

I pour myself another glass of wine and go to the window and look out at San Marco's illuminated bell tower. I am not certain, but that "Goodbye" seems very final. I sip some wine and wonder if I will ever see Mireille again.

CHAPTER TEN – My Brother's Keeper

My brother Vinny texts me after he goes through customs at Marco Polo Airport. There is a driver waiting for him who takes his single suitcase – I know because he always travels with one small suitcase that can be a carry on – and then the driver opens the door of the limousine for him. He texts, "I'm in the limo now."

I grin as I read this; he is always trying to impress me. I write back, "A limo cannot get you to the hotel. You will need to take a water taxi."

"I'm not coming over to Venice," he writes.

"What are you talking about?"

"I'm staying at the Venezia-Marghera Hotel Mercure," he responds.

"You are not coming over to see *the real Venice*?"

"My hotel is 15 minutes from the airport. My meetings are being held in the conference room there."

I realize that my brother is the only person I know who would come to Venice and not want to see the actual city. That explains Vinny's personality much better than I can.

"So, you want to get together tonight?" he asks.

"Yes, that will be fine."

When I first came to Venice, I stayed in that same hotel for a week while I was settling the details for buying my flat. It is nice enough – there is even a view of the real Venice from the hotel room.

Now, I can take the train to Mestre and get the number 6 bus that will take me to the hotel very quickly. I just thought "going out to dinner" meant eating in one of the many fine places in my neighborhood or across the Rialto in San Marco, but my brother puts convenience over ambiance every time.

I take a shower and shave – for the most part I have only been shaving once a week since I am here. Guessing that Vinny will want to eat in the hotel restaurant, I put on a pair of black slacks, a gray polo shirt, and slip a blazer on my arms. I stare at myself in the mirror and realize this is the first time I have not worn cargo shorts and sneakers since being here.

*

Walking from the bus stop to the hotel, I am reminded about how sedate it is here on this side of the Ponte della Liberta – Liberty Bridge – that connects the islands of Venice to the mainland. There is a light volume of traffic and pedestrians. When I was staying here, I had yet to experience the tourist frenzy that occurs in Venice proper, especially around Piazza San Marco.

I go to reception and ask them to let Vinny know that I am here. A few minutes later, he is coming out of the elevator dressed in white shorts and a blue Hawaiian shirt with white tropical flowers on it. When we were kids, we used to watch reruns of *Magnum P.I.* Vinny seems to be recreating the look of the star Tom Selleck.

"Hey, Bobby, this isn't a formal event," Vinny says as he rushes over to me and shakes my hand. Vinny is a couple of inches taller than my six feet, and he has maintained his muscular physique. I have been working out in my flat, but it is not the same as hitting the gym a few times a week.

I wonder what his plan is and ask, "So, where are we going?"

"I have it handled; let's just take a taxi," Vinny says. We go outside, get in a taxi, and he hands a piece of paper to the driver. He glances at me and says, "The concierge gave me a suggestion."

"How have you been, Vinny?" I ask. "You look great."

"Business is really good, Melissa and the kids are great, and we're living the good life," Vinny says.

The taxi pulls up in front of a rather ordinary looking restaurant, but it seems very busy with a steady stream of people going inside and a crowd of people sitting at the outside tables. Vinny says that we have a table reserved inside, and when we walk through the front door, there is traditional Italian music playing, a crowded bar area, and tables filled with diners.

We sit at our reserved table in a corner near the back of the place, and we are directly in the welcome blast of a ductless AC unit above our heads. An old man comes over to the table who looks like Lou Costello from the *Abbott and Costello* TV series – he could be the long dead comedian's twin brother – and he says, "*Buonasera, signori.*"

He hands us the menus, and Vinny looks at me. "Are you still drinking those straight up martinis?"

I smile. "You might have gotten a good one in the hotel bar, but out here there is less than 50% chance they will make it right." I look up at Lou's twin and say, "Just give us gin over ice. *Due drink, per favore.*"

The twin nods his head and walks away. Vinny turns to me and says, "I don't think I like a country where you can't get a proper martini!"

"When I'm in the mood for one, I make it at home," I say. "But there is one place where the bartender makes them right."

"Then I'd go there all the time."

"I do," I say.

"You're looking well rested," Vinny says. "What are you doing with yourself every day?"

No one else would notice it, but there is a touch of envy in my brother's voice. While he makes a ton of money, Vinny works hard for it. I am sure that he wonders what life would be like without such long work days, so I decide to rub it in. "Well, I get up when I please depending on if I've been out the night before."

"Still burning the candle at both ends," Vinny says with a grin.

The waiter brings the drinks, a bottle of still water, and two tall glasses with ice. "Would you like to order your food yet?"

Vinny picks up the menu and asks, "What is a good Venetian dish, Bobby?"

Without missing a beat I say, "Cuttlefish."

Vinny looks up at the waiter. "And what do you think about that?"

Lou's twin nods his head. "It is a classic local dish. The chef makes it in a special black sauce, and it comes with orzo and spinach."

"I'll take that then please," Vinny says handing him the menu.

I glance at the menu and say, "I'll take country chicken with polenta and peas. Please also bring us a bottle of Soave."

The waiter takes the menu from me saying, "Very good, signor."

"If it's so good, why didn't you get the cuttlefish?" Vinny asks and then sips his drink.

"I've had it many times since I've been here," I say. "In fact, I just had it two days ago, so I wanted to try something new."

Vinny lifts his glass for a toast. "To the Valenti brothers – may success continue to come our way."

I clink my glass against his and sip my drink. "I am happy for your good fortune, Vinny. I just don't know why we haven't been in touch since I left for Italy and then you contact me out of the blue."

"It's not every day that I come to Venice." Vinny sits back and fiddles with his glass. "After mom died, it got pretty frosty between us there."

"Well, mom realized that you were making a lot of money, and I was struggling to make ends meet," I say.

He takes the bottle of still water and pours some over the ice in our glasses. "She left me the beach house! *The frigging beach house!* And you got everything else."

"I think that was very fair, since that was always your favorite place," I say. "Besides, after you got married and moved to Westchester, I was left to take care of mom. She was lucky to see the kids at Christmas if you decided to make a trip over the bridge."

"It just hurt, Bobby, that's all," Vinny says and sips his drink. "She knew I was very busy. I thought she'd understand."

"Look, I had nothing to do with how she set up her will," I say. "I was surprised as you when we went to the lawyer.

"Okay, Bobby," Vinny says. "It's over now."

"Well, six months is a long time," I say, "and I didn't even get an occasional text here and there."

"Okay, well I'm here now," Vinny says. "We can change things going forward after this dinner."

Lou's twin brings the wine and bucket of ice. With a very deadpan face, he struggles with the corkscrew to open the bottle, and then pours a little wine in my glass. I taste it, nod my head, and ask him to not pour the wine now because we are still working on our drinks. He says, "As you wish, signor," and shoves the bottle into the ice.

"Look, Vinny, we are both in different places in our lives. You have everything – a great job, beautiful wife, wonderful kids – I am the one who should be envying you."

"Envy? Who said anything about *envy*?"

"I didn't mean it that way," I say.

The waiter brings our food, and Vinny says, "Let's just eat!"

*

When we get back to the hotel, it is getting late. Vinny looks at his watch and says, "I have to get up early tomorrow for my meeting, but I have time for a nightcap."

I really want to get on that bus and go home. "I'm okay. You don't have to for my sake."

"When am I going to see you again, Bobby?" I just stare at him because I do not have an answer for that. He shrugs his shoulders. "Your guess is as good as mine then!"

We go into the hotel bar; it is rather crowded, and contemporary music is playing in the background. Vinny orders bourbon on the rocks; I get Smirnoff on the rocks.

"Look, I'd like us to have a relationship," I say.

"Yeah, then why did you come all the way over here?"

"Because after breaking up with Beth, I just had to get out of New York," I whisper.

"The kids ask for you all the time," Vinny says.

"I thought that when I left that they'd forget about me."

"They ask about you all the time, especially Sally." He looks at me and puts a hand on my arm. "Next thing you know, she'll be off to college."

"Man, time goes by too fast," I say.

"Way too fast!"

We finish our drinks, head out of the bar, and walk toward the elevators. Vinny shakes my hand and says, "Let's stay in touch."

"Okay, we will," I say.

I walk out of the hotel into the cool dark night. It is eerily quiet as I take the brief walk to the stop for the number 6 bus. No one else is at the stop waiting with me. The bus comes, and I get on board; there are only a few other passengers. I cannot wait to get home – my flat and my neighborhood really feel like home now.

Glancing back at the tall, austere hotel illuminated against the dark sky, I think about Vinny. He is trapped in a gilded cage of his own making. I feel sorry for him in a way, but he engineered this situation, and now he has reached a pinnacle from which there is only going to be a balancing act or a hard fall.

I turn away from the window, put my head back against the seat, and close my eyes. I have an aching heart after seeing him, and I believe I know why – I am never going to see or hear from him ever again.

CHAPTER ELEVEN – Someone We Know?

Paula is very busy on this night, and I am standing at the end of the bar nursing a Smirnoff Red martini with Italian olives – she makes an excellent one worthy of my praise, and the zesty olives add a nice unique touch.

After today's writers' group – the first one sans Mireille – I am feeling a bit down, and Pietro agreed to meet me here, but he has still not shown up. It is not easy to have a deep discussion with the rest of the group there, and Serge seemed particularly upset that Mireille did not attend, so there was no opportunity to talk with him.

Paula wipes her hands on a bar towel and leans her elbows on the bar. "So, how do you like my martini?"

I lift and admire it. "It is a work of art – the *Mona Lisa* of martinis! It is truly something to look at and should be in a museum."

"Well, I appreciate this comment coming from a martini aficionado like yourself," Paula says with a big smile.

I take a sip and sigh. "Nectar of the gods."

She slaps my arm. "You are too funny."

"Very busy tonight," I note as I place my glass down carefully as not to spill a precious drop.

"Fridays are always this way," she says. She scrutinizes my face and asks, "How is life?"

I stare at her and feel like a deer in her headlights. "Now, isn't that the unanswerable *Who Wants to Be a Millionaire* question! Do I get to phone a friend?"

She squeezes my arm. "No seriously, Bobby – are you okay? You don't look so good tonight."

"I'm just a little upset," I say. "This girl I've been seeing has sort of cut me off, and I really like her."

A waiter yells, "*Ehi*, Paula," from the service bar.

She glances back at me. "I'll be back."

I whisper, "That's what they all say."

As if on cue, Pietro enters the bar and looks like a lost possum in my old backyard. He is looking around and sniffing the air, and then he sees me at the bar. I wave to him as he navigates his way through crowded tables until he is standing next to me.

"Hey, Pete!" I say with a smile.

"Hello, Robert." Pietro says as he looks around and spies an empty table. "Are we going to be civilized and sit down? Or are we going to stand here like two ruffians?"

"Well, I'm going to get another drink and one for you if you are so inclined," I say.

He looks around the room and then at me. "I don't usually frequent these kinds of establishments. I wonder if they would even have a decent glass of wine."

I signal Paula, and she comes over to us, and I say, "Pietro, this is the lovely Paula. Paula, this is the always lovely Pietro."

"It is a pleasure," Pietro says.

"Same here," Paula says. "What are you drinking?"

Pietro shrugs his shoulders. "I am wondering if I can get a nice glass of Lugana."

"You've got it," Paula says with a broad smile "And what about you, Bobby?"

"I'll take another exquisite martini," I say.

Pietro points to the vacant table. "Please have it sent over there."

"Of course," Paula says with a wink.

Pietro and I go over to the table and sit down. "Now, there is a little dignity sitting here."

I sip my martini. "It's fine by me. Thanks for coming here."

"Well, I know you are still mourning the loss of Mireille," he says with a snicker.

I take offense at this remark. "Hey, I care about her the way you care about Brian. Do you understand?"

"Oh, I am sorry," Pietro says. "I did't realize the depth of your affection for her."

"Listen, Pete, all of this started when you ridiculed her poem. That set everything in motion."

"I thought you were the kind of guy who would believe honesty is the best policy," Pietro says with a dastardly smirk.

I sip my martini. "Not when it hurts someone – especially someone who is innocent."

A waiter comes over to our table with our drinks. Pietro takes his wine glass and sniffs it with that possum nose, the whiskers wiggling as he inhales. He takes a sip and nods his head. "This establishment does carry this fine wine."

"Pete, you have taken no responsibility for hurting Mireille," I say. "You should have apologized for what you said about her poem."

"Instead, I chose to build her up and rave about her story which, between you and me, I found rather maudlin."

I finish my first martini, and eat the olives that have been soaking up the vodka all this time. "I found it to be good – and for her – a great accomplishment."

"To each his own I suppose."

I lean forward and say, "Serge is very angry with you. Some members are asking for you to be removed from the group."

"That would be an injustice," Pietro says. "Serge and I are founding members. The whole group was my idea in the first place. He just provides the venue and thinks that puts him in charge."

"Well, it kind of does put him in charge since he can decide who comes and goes in his own home."

He points his possum nose toward my left shoulder. I turn around and see a Black man at a back table where he is sitting in the shadows, but he seems to be staring at us. Pietro asks, "Someone we know?"

I try to focus on my martini and savor its luscious mixture of vodka, a dash of vermouth, and the Italian olives. "I don't think so."

Pietro sits back in the chair. "That very, very, very large Black man is walking over to us."

I turn around and, as the man comes into the light, I see that it is my old friend Adamu. He says, "I thought it was you, Bobby."

I stand up and shake his hand. "It is good to see you."

Pietro wipes his head in relief. "Oh, I thought there was going to be fisticuffs."

"Adamu, this is Pietro; Pietro, this is my friend Adamu from New York."

Adamu shakes Pietro's small hand with his enormous one. "Nice to meet you," Pietro says.

"Yes, same here," Adamu says.

"Adamu is the fellow in the boxing story I read for the group," I say.

Pietro shakes his head. "How am I supposed to remember these things?"

I turn to Adamu and say, "Please join us," motioning to an empty chair at our table.

I notice that Adamu is holding a Moretti bottle as he sits down. "What are you doing in Venice, Bobby?"

"I live here now," I say. "What about you?"

"My father moved back here years ago," Adamu says. "I visit him every summer."

I have not seen Adamu in almost ten years. The last time he was running a gym on the East Side. "Are you still working at the gym?" I ask.

"Yeah, but I own it now," he says with a big smile.

Pietro has been watching us as we are talking. He stands up slowly and says, "Obviously, you two gentlemen have a lot to discuss. I am going over to finish my wine and talk with that nice seahorse lady."

"Okay," I say, "thanks for meeting me, Pete." Pietro dashes over to the bar and starts talking to Paula. She glances at me and smiles.

"So, Adamu, where does your father live?"

"He lives in the old family apartment over in Dorsoduro," Adamu says. "My half-brother and his mother are there too. We all get along."

"And your mom is still in Brooklyn?" I ask.

"No, I bought her a house in New Hyde Park," he says. "I have been lucky and wanted to take care of her now that I'm doing so well."

"Good for you," I say, and then I think of my parents and brother.

"What is wrong?" he asks, probably noticing my solemn expression.

"My parents are gone, and I have basically no relationship with my brother," I say. I sip my martini. "You are very lucky to have family."

"Yeah, I know I am. When I come here, I feel Italian," Adamu says. "I can even speak a little. Dad can speak English, but he speaks Italian with his wife and son, but they know how to speak English too."

"Can you believe that I'm half Italian, but I can only speak a few words?" I chuckle.

"You must be picking up something here," he says.

"Slowly, but you know how it is," I say. "Too many people speak English around here."

"It's because of the tourists – there are too many Americans here. I'm walking in the street, and I hear so many Americans talking."

"Yeah, especially over in San Marco," I say. I sip my drink and notice Nino trying to get another young blonde girl to go home with him. This time it seems like she is ready to comply. "Hey, Adamu, I have to stop something."

"Need any help?" he asks.

"No, I've got this," I say as I get up and maneuver may way in between tables until I am standing over Nino and the girl.

Nino looks up at me and snarls, "What do you want?"

"Hey," I say looking at the girl, "is he bothering you?"

She is very young and very pretty – probably 18 if even that. "I am just waiting for my girlfriends," she says, her English accent noted. She seems scared.

"Why don't you get up and go call your friend," I say.

"Hey, *amico*, what are you doing?" Nino says as he stands up and clenches a fist.

The girl jumps up, grabs her phone from the table, and runs to the exit. I stare at him and say, "Don't come in here and pull that crap anymore."

"Yeah, and who is going to stop me?"

By now, Adamu is standing next to me. I lean on the table and say, "Don't come back here again."

Nino is angry, but as he looks at Adamu, he unclenches his fists. "You're lucky you're a good customer, or I would mess you up." He turns around and storms out of the taverna.

"Who is that dude?"

I turn to him and say, "Nobody – truly a nobody."

We go back to the table, get another round of drinks, and continue to talk about the old days. I am happy to be here in Venice, but inside I will always be a New Yorker. Seeing Adamu just reminds me about that fact.

CHAPTER TWELVE – Burano

The beautiful Mireille and I are on a vaporetto heading for the island of Burano. Unlike when we went to Murano when she wore business attire because she was on a break from work, it is a Sunday and she is wearing white shorts, matching sneakers, and a blue blouse with short fluffy sleeves. A stylish blue and white hat with a wide brim completes her relaxed look. We are sitting quietly in the crowded boat, with Mireille looking out the window.

The night before I came home from the taverna a little drunk. Going up 62 steps in that condition was not a pleasant experience. Once I was in my flat, I grabbed a beer from the fridge, turned on the TV, and decided to watch Kubrick's Full Metal Jacket because it was in English with Italian subtitles.

I was just getting into the flick when my phone rang. I looked at the screen and saw a picture of Mireille on it. I had been hoping she would return my calls, but after two weeks I

had given up. I wondered if this was going to be an emotional

call or a more pleasant one.

I answered the phone. "Hi, Mireille."

"Hi, Bobby," she said and then there was silence for

a few seconds.

"Is everything okay?"

"Yes, everything is...okay," she whispered.

"You know that I've tried to call a number of times

the past two weeks, but I was kind of worried that you didn't

answer the phone," I said and then took a swig of beer.

"Bobby, I have been going through some difficult

things," Mireille said.

"Oh, I'm sorry to hear that," I said.

"My little sister is getting married," she said.

"Oh, I guess you're very happy for her."

"I...I am, but it is just a little overwhelming,"

Mireille said and started to cry uncontrollably.

I listened to her for a while and then said, "I know something like this could very emotional."

She blew her nose and caught her breath. "This is just something I was not expecting."

"I understand," I said, thinking about when Vinny got married, and not only did he not ask me to be his best man, but I was not even a groomsman.

"This is not why I called," Mireille said sniffling. "I am going to Burano tomorrow, and I was wondering if you would like to go with me."

I had heard of Burano being a nice place to visit, but I was putting off the 45-minute boat ride until another day. I guessed that day had come because I wanted to see her again. "Of course, I would be happy to go."

Mireille glances at me and smiles. I am happy to see her in an emotionally calm demeanor. She reaches over and takes my hand. Feeling the soft and warm glow of her fingers, I wonder if there is any hope for us.

As we come into Burano, I am amazed by the picturesque old houses painted in vibrant colors on either side of a narrow canal flowing with ripples from the lagoon where our boat bobs in the water. We get off the boat and walk toward the town. Mireille says, "I would like to go to the museum."

Another museum? I guess that she thinks I like this sort of thing, and I do in a way. "What kind of museum?" I ask.

"It is the Museo del Merletto. It used to be a palace, and it is all about lace and the making of it," she says with a big smile. "I guess you don't know that this island is known for its lacemaking."

"Oh, okay," I say. "I was just told that it had colorful houses and was a lovely place to visit."

As we go down the main street, I notice all the shops selling lace and lace products. Many of the designs are quite bold and complex. She stops to look in one store, and I check out my phone for a few seconds. Pietro is going to let me know about his conversation with Serge, and I am waiting for Adamu to get back to me about meeting up at the gym that he goes to here for a workout.

Mireille comes out of the shop with a small shopping bag. "I got something for my sister – an engagement present."

"How nice," I say.

In the museum of lacemaking there is familiar historical breakdown – like the glass museum on Murano – by centuries. We begin the tour with an explanation of how there was a transition to needle lace from biblia stitches, and that the exquisite works are examples "aristocratic female sensitivity" of the sixteenth century lace makers.

"Unlike the male glass blowers," Mireille says as she turns to me with a smile, "this art is exclusively female."

We go through the centuries – each room more impressive than the last – and end in the last room that is dedicated to the Burano Lace School that was in this palace from 1872-1970. It was opened thanks to the patronage of Margherita of Savoy. There are many lovely examples of deeply intricate works of lace art – some with vibrant colors and others equally beautiful in all white and off-white pieces.

As we leave the museum, Mireille's face is glowing. "I have always wanted to come here. Thank you for coming with me."

"I am really impressed by the artistry," I say. "This is an amazing form of art that I knew very a little about before today."

She rubs my arm. "I had a feeling that you would appreciate the craft and skill. You are a writer – an artist and kindred spirit." Mireille is suddenly staring at something over my shoulder with wide eyes.

I turn around and ask, "What is it?"

"That shop offers a lacemaking class," she says joyfully. "Let's find out about it."

We cross the square and enter a small shop with the ubiquitous lace items displayed on its walls and shelves. An ancient woman with sullen eyes wearing a black dress looks up at us from behind the counter. Mireille asks, "Is there a lacemaking class today?"

The old woman comes from behind the counter, takes Mireille by the hand, and leads her to a back room where a young woman sits in a corner making lace. She has a pretty face and bright brown eyes. She smiles at us and says, "I am Annetta. Are you here to learn how to make lace?"

Mireille enthusiastically nods her head. "Yes, I would like to try."

After a few minutes, Mireille is seated next to Annetta who gives her a needle and a thimble. Mireille sees that Annetta has the thimble on the middle finger of her sewing hand, so she places the gold tinted object on her middle finger. "What would you like to make?"

"Something with a butterfly for my mother," Mireille says with a big smile. "My mother loves butterflies."

"Okay, we will make her a doily with a butterfly on it," Annetta says. She takes a fresh piece of lace fabric from a pile and initiates the design rather quickly. Once it is started, she hands the thick fabric over to Mireille with a long needle. She shows her how to put the needle through the fabric, and Mireille follows the pattern and listens carefully to Annetta's directions.

About 45 minutes later, Mireille has a lovely white doily with an off-white butterfly at its center to give to her mother. "Oh, my, I cannot believe I could do this."

"Oh, you would be very good at lacemaking if you practiced," Annetta says.

As we leave the shop, Mireille is ecstatic about her experience. "I've been looking for a creative outlet; perhaps lacemaking is something I can do."

"You seemed like a natural in there," I say.

"I just needed to find an outlet for my creativity," Mireille says. "Maybe I have found something I can do well."

"Yeah, I suppose you're right," I say. "Do you want to get something to eat now?"

"Yes, that would be nice in this lovely place," she says with a big smile.

We stop in a little café with the backdrop of colorful houses and a narrow canal behind us. Mireille orders chicken salad, and I get a hotdog because I have not had one since going to a Mets game a few years ago.

"Hamburgers and hotdogs – you're so American!" Mireille laughs.

"So, you made the doily for your mother. What did you get your sister in that other shop?"

"A beautiful table cloth for their new home – Colette loves lace as much as I do. Every time that they eat or sit at that table, she will think about me," Mireille says with a wide smile, as if all her concerns are gone.

"Will they live in Amsterdam?"

The waiter brings the food and a big bottle of still water, and Mireille stares at me. "I have no idea. Mother did say Colette was at home again, that I missed the party celebrating the engagement as well."

"Will you go home for the wedding?" I ask and then take a sip of water.

"I guess I have to ask Mother more questions," Mireille says. She looks down at my hand and asks, "Where is your ring?"

I raise my hand and look at it, and I obviously cannot tell her the truth. "I took it off when I got into the shower, and I guess I forgot to put it on."

Mireille nods her head. "I just thought maybe you decided not to wear it anymore."

Nino probably took that ring and pawned it, so I guess I will never see it again. I stare at her through my sunglasses and smile. "You know, that's a possibility."

"I guess you will have to think about it."

The hotdog is delicious – even better than a "dirty dog" on the streets of Manhattan – and so are the fries that come with it. I squeeze some ketchup onto my fries. "This is like being home again."

Mireille chews her salad and sips her water. "Do you miss it?"

"Home?" I think about it for a moment. "No, not really. Sometimes I think I do, but then I remember all the reasons why I left, and know I'm happier here."

"Good for you," she says and eats another bite of salad. "You know, I am the same – I used to think I missed Paris, but I like Venice much better. It will be hard to go back for the wedding."

While I am appreciating every bite of my hotdog, I notice Mireille texting someone quickly. I sip my water, and she looks up at me. "What?" I ask.

"I guess you think me rude for texting," she says.

"No, not at all," I say.

We finish our meal and stroll through the town with colorful houses on both sides of the street and go over quaint bridges above the tranquil canals – it is such a welcome respite from the frenzy of Venice that I still secretly enjoy because it is not even half as bad as New York. We turn up the block to go back to get the vaporetto, and Mireille stops abruptly.

"What is it?" I ask.

She is staring at a shop window. I glance at colorful racks outside the shop that have beautiful examples of lace items hanging above the cobblestone sidewalk. Mireille walks toward the shop, and I realize that she is not looking at the towels, shirts, and head scarves displayed outside, but at a beautiful dress inside the window.

"It is breathtaking," she says, putting her hand to her chest.

The lace is all white and off white, and the intricate pattern of the design involves interlocking white roses across the entire dress. A matching headpiece is on the mannequin's head. I do not know what to say, but I manage to utter, "It's very beautiful!"

She starts to cry again, turns to me, and buries her head on my shoulder. I pat the back of her head, and gradually the tears subside. She takes a tissue from her purse, blows her nose, and then wipes away the tears on her lovely face with another tissue. "I'm okay now."

"What happened?" I ask.

"I was texting my mother because I wanted to know where the wedding would be, and she told me Colette wants it to be in Martinique."

"So, that's why you're crying?" I ask.

She nods her head. "Partially. Because I don't know if I can even get the time off to go. But it is also something else."

"What is it?"

"I *want* that dress in the window for myself," she says. "I want to be married in that dress someday!"

"Well, perhaps someday you will," I say.

She looks up at me, and there is that moment I have only experienced once before, when there are no words – knowing the girl wants to kiss me as much as I want to kiss her. I lean down and our lips meet softy at first, but then we kiss deeply as we stand there as people walk by, and it feels like the world has gone away. I do not know how long it lasts, but somehow or other we make it back to the vaporetto stop on time.

As we head back to the city, I sit with my arm around Mireille, and she puts her head on my shoulder. Again, no words are needed. After two weeks of not hearing from her, I feel like we are back to some sort of stability between us. Now, as we sit together on the boat, there is a feeling of serenity. The loud buzz of the boat's motor, the low murmur of conversations all around us, and the gentle spray of lagoon water splashing the boat windows do not matter. It seems like we are on a cloud all our own.

CHAPTER THIRTEEN – Coming Out

On the following Friday evening after the writing group's activities are over, Pietro, Serge, and I go out for drinks and dinner. We find a nice little place on a canal and adjacent to a bridge over it. The street is busy with pedestrians and a steady stream of people are crossing over the bridge. A parade of overloaded gondolas continues to pass along the canal.

We are lucky to get a table because Serge knows the owner of the place – a robust man with rosy nose and cheeks and trimmed white beard – making him appear to be Santa Claus undercover in Venice. He moves a menu sign and a little serving cart to squeeze us into the last vacant table.

After the food is eaten, we are on our third bottle of Soave, and things are very festive and loud between us. The waiter brings us complimentary glasses of grappa – a drink that is reminiscent of tequila but stronger and once wiped me out when I first came to Venice – and Serge waves gratefully to our secret Santa.

After taking a generous gulp of grappa, Serge slaps Pietro's arm and says, "We almost threw you out of the group a few weeks ago."

Pietro takes umbrage to this comment. He sips his wine and says, "*Throw me out?* A group that I created and that you became a member of only because you offered the venue to us? This is simply an outrage!"

Serge looks at me and asks, "Can you believe the set of balls on this guy?"

I nod my head and laugh. "Seems to me that is one of his more interesting traits," I say and sip the potent grappa cautiously.

Pietro lifts his binder that is overflowing with papers. "I work very hard to bring a well-crafted story to the group each week. I feel very unappreciated."

I tap his arm and say, "I appreciate you, Pete!"

He leans back in the chair and glares at Serge. "And I thought of you as a friend – *Sergio Matteo Rossi*! What a fool I am." He lifts the grappa and takes a swig, making a contorted face afterwards. "This is…good!"

The drinks are hitting me now – since I started with a gin and tonic cocktail before the meal – so I sit back and say, "I think we should all be friends here, guys. Why don't we act like friends?" That is drunken me talking here.

Serge nods his head and sips his wine. "Yes, we are all friends." He leans forward and grabs Pietro's arm. "I'm sorry, my friend. No one is throwing you out of anything. It was a poor attempt at teasing you."

"I hope so, Serge," Pietro says with a frown. "I have put a good deal of effort into making that group successful over the years. As far as I can tell, I am the only one who brings something to share every week. When was the last time Anna brought anything?"

"I suppose over a month now," Serge says, "but she is very supportive of everyone and gives good feedback on the peer reviews."

Pietro dismisses Serge's comment with a wave of his hand. "The group is not engaged like it used to be years ago." He turns to me and points. "Even Robert doesn't bring something to read every week."

I shrug my shoulders and sip my grappa. "Sometimes I just have a lousy week and can't generate anything."

"That is understandable," Serge says while Pietro makes faces and rolls his eyes.

I turn to Serge in hopes of changing the subject. "Serge, who was that lovely woman that we saw you with before the meeting?"

"That is the Contessa Christina," Serge says. "We sort of have a thing going on."

"A thing? Oh, I hope she is not married and having you as a lover on the side *thing*," Pietro says.

Serge shakes his head. "No, she is very available, but she is also very young – 27 to my 39 years."

"Perhaps she likes mature men," I say.

"Perhaps," Serge says seriously. "It is more that we have a – connection!"

"So, it is physical attraction?" Pietro asks. "Or do you love her for her mind or perhaps her title?"

"I care deeply for her," Serge says. "The problem is her family."

"Have you met them yet?" I ask.

Serge nods his head and finishes his grappa. "Of course, I have lived and played in the same aristocratic and social circles that her parents inhabit for years, as did my parents and our grandparents before us."

"So, if you're in love, what is the problem?" Pietro asks, seemingly being sincere in his concern for Serge.

"The problem is – my dear Christina is afraid of what will happen when we reveal our relationship to her parents,"

Serge says with a solemn expression. "She feels that despite all our shared experiences, that I will be rejected by them as too old."

I lean forward and say, "You won't know if you don't try."

Serge nods his head. "This is true, but I fear the worst. I'm not sure what we are going to do at this point."

"Look at my situation," I say. "Mireille has gone quiet again after our lovely day in Burano. I am not sure what is happening."

"You have tried to contact her?" Pietro asks.

"Yes, I've called and texted her – no response."

"You've been ghosted!" Pietro says with a smirk.

"Pietro!" Serge says, and Pietro sits back and sips his wine like a seemingly innocent choir boy with a crooked halo over his head.

"Serge, do you know Mireille's last name? Where she works or lives?" I ask.

Serge shakes his head. "I only know her as you know her – *Mireille*."

"Who knows if that is her real name?" Pietro asks.

"I guess I am in bad way," I say. "I really don't know what else I can do."

"Well, you are better off than I am," Pietro blurts out. "My parents don't know that I am gay, and they think Brian is a girl!"

Serge and I both stare at Pietro in disbelief. "Really?" Serge asks. "How have you managed this for so long?"

"Well, Brian is British, so when I go home to see my parents, I tell them that *Brianna* goes back to London to see her parents." Pietro hangs his head and stares at his wine glass.

"Gee, Pete, you always seem so confident and secure in your relationship," I say.

"I am – I mean I was, but things have changed now."

"What do you mean?" Serge asks.

Pietro sits back and taps his fingers on the table. "Brian has been getting restless. We will be together three years in September – that is the longest relationship I've ever had – and he would like us to take the next step."

"Marriage?" Serge asks with raised eyebrows. "You know you cannot get married here."

"Well, we know that we cannot get married, but civil unions are an option, which give us the same rights, benefits, and legal protections as married couples."

"So, what's the problem?" I ask.

"Brian wants this…this Symbolic Ceremony, which in essence, will be as elaborate or even more elaborate than a wedding."

"What is wrong with that?" Serge asks as he pours some more wine into his glass, and then Pietro's and mine.

"What's wrong is that I have not come out to my parents and friends and family back home," Pietro says. "And I have no desire to do so."

"And Brian is upset with that?" I ask.

"Yes, he came out to his parents and family years ago," Pietro says. "He just doesn't understand how I feel."

"Look, I get it," I say, "but you love Brian and want to be with him, right?"

Pietro takes a deep breath and exhales loudly. "I am not – and I am never – coming out to my parents."

"But why, my friend?" Serge asks. "You love him, right?"

Pietro sips some more wine. "I…I do love him, but I cannot destroy my parents. My sister Esterina is a nun, my Uncle Carmine is a priest, and my parents are so involved with their church back home. If I would do this, they would not be able to handle it."

"You'd be surprised what people can handle," I say. "I am Catholic, and I had to tell my parents I was marrying a Jewish girl. I thought that they would freak out, but they handled it rather well in the end."

"So, how did you first approach telling them?" Pietro asks.

"I got a little drunk, I went to my local church, and I prayed," I say. "A few days later, I had a dream about telling my parents, and they took it so well and seemed happy."

"And did the dream come true?" Serge asks.

I laugh. "Actually, no. When I told them my father screamed and my mother cried, but after some time they calmed down. My mother stared at me and said, 'But we thought Beth was Irish?' Of course, I kind of lied and told my parents she was Irish – Beth has blonde hair and green eyes – it was not much a stretch to hint that she was Irish to them to keep the peace at least at first."

Pietro holds both sides of his head with clenched fists and screams, "But I can't tell my parents that I am gay!"

Everyone in the restaurant stops talking for a moment, and the only sounds are a few clinks of utensils against plates. Then, as if nothing happened, everyone starts talking again and laughing.

Serge looks at me and raises an eyebrow. "What can we do to help you?" he asks.

Pietro sits back against his chair and drinks some wine. "You know, just talking to you both has helped me. I haven't been able to tell anyone at work because they don't know either because the museum is so conservative. At least the group was a safe space where I could share my stories and not feel that I would be judged about who I am."

"I understand," I say. "I was unable to write about my divorce, and I really should try it because I think it will help."

Serge nods his head. "I would like to hear that story."

Pietro looks at us both and says, "Thanks for listening."

"So, what will you do, my friend?" Serge asks.

Pietro gets a far-off look in his eyes and whispers, "I have no idea."

On my way home, I lean on the railing of one of the bridges over an illuminated canal. Mireille has not contacted me since our trip to Burano. I have called and texted her, but she has not responded. I do not even know where she lives or works; otherwise, I would go to see her. Since she does not come to the group anymore, I have no way to find her. I do not even know her last name.

Serge has no contact information for her. I even asked Anna, but she only knows her from the group. I try to Google "Mireille" and get names of French actresses and models, but not my Mireille. Searching "Mireille in Venice" comes up with similar results as well. It feels as if she does not even exist. I wonder why she is ghosting me like this.

I see a young couple in a gondola, illuminated by the lantern as the gondolier pushes them slowly until they glide under the bridge. I feel a presence above me, and I look up and see a dark figure in the top window of a three-story building. I squint to focus my drunken eyes, and it appears to be the Grim Reaper, his scythe glistening in the streetlight. I shut my eyes and, when I look again, just a dark curtain is swaying in the breeze. I exhale and figure that I better stay away from that grappa.

As I start walking home, I think about Death stalking me, or was he there for the young couple? No, I think, it is just my imagination. It is not their time or mine. They are so young and have their whole lives ahead of them, and I have so much I have yet to do, but perhaps Death has other plans.

CHAPTER FOURTEEN – Emergency

On a hot mid-August Tuesday, I leave San Polo by crossing over the Grand Canal using the Scalzi Bridge near the train station. It is time for my weekly appointment with Elena. I skipped it last week because of that Sunday in Burano with Mireille, but since she is ghosting me, I feel I must take care of my own needs.

The streets near the station are bustling with people pulling wheeled luggage either coming into Venice or preparing to leave. I make my way toward Elena's place, pass a leafy park where there are no kids on the playground because of the heat, and head down the block to Elena's building. The front door is always ajar, no doubt for the nefarious activities Nino has going on here. Elena has hinted that he is a drug dealer besides being a pimp, so I can only imagine what goes on in this building.

I go up the stairs, knock on Elena's door, but there is no answer. Usually, she throws open the door and is scantily clad. I find her exciting and I like her, and the last time I was here she had an orgasm for the first time in her life. I want to see if I can perform well enough for that to happen again.

After knocking on her door a few more times, I guess that she is not there, turn around, and start to head for the stairs. The door to the apartment next-door opens, and I see Carla standing there – her red hair all messy, and she is wearing a yellow bathrobe.

"You're Bobby, yes?" she asks.

I turn to her and nod my head. "Yeah, I was just here to see Elena."

"Elena is not here," Carla says.

"Yeah, I can see that," I say.

"I…I…" Carla says and starts to cry.

"What wrong?" I ask, annoyed with Carla to begin with because she invited Elena to come here and got her mixed up with Nino.

Carla looks down at her bare feet and then up at me. She says, "I can't tell you." Carla starts crying harder.

I shake my head. "Whatever you say; I have to go."

"Bobby, I wasn't supposed to tell you, but Elena is not here because she is in hospital," Carla says, and tears continue to roll down her cheeks.

I start to get angry and ask, "Who told you not to tell me? That bastard Nino?"

"No," she says as she wipes away tears, "Elena didn't want me to tell you. He beat her up last week – I don't know why. I called for an ambulance because she was really hurt."

"How bad?" I ask, now very worried about Elena.

Carla's expression contorts as she whispers, "Very, very bad!"

"Which hospital? Where is it?"

"It's…it's not far," she sniffles and wipes her nose on the sleeve of her robe. She takes her phone out of her pocket, taps it twice, and shows me the hospital and address.

I take a picture of it and then put the name into the map on my phone. I see that it is not too far away. "What is Elena's last name." Carla hesitates, so I grab her by the arms. "What's her last name? How am I supposed to see her if I don't know that?"

Carla wipes the tears from her face with a tissue as stares at me and whispers, "Gallo."

I turn around, run down the stairs, and burst out of the front door. I am not thinking clearly at all; I am just worried about Elena. I race through the streets without paying attention to the people I am passing or how many bridges I go over, and I finally get to the hospital out of breath. I lean against the wall and try to get myself straightened out. I know I cannot run in there like a maniac and think I can have a chance of seeing her. After catching my breath and composing myself, I go through the front door.

Surprisingly, it is easy to get in. I show them my passport to get a visitor's pass. I am told that Elena is in intensive care, and I am heading toward the elevator wearing a mask that they gave me. I feel my heart pounding in my chest – I start to realize that I care for Elena more than I have realized before.

Once I am inside the ICU, a nurse comes up to me and asks, "Who are you here to see?"

"Elena Gallo," I say.

The nurse's eyes widen over her mask and she says, "Please wait here."

I look around the room, and there are several people in beds covered with bandages, hooked up to wires and tubes, and machines are beeping all around me. The nurse comes back and asks, "Will you please come with me?"

I follow her down the hallway, and she leads me into a room where a beautiful woman in a white lab coat stands up and extends her hand. "I am Dr. Isabella Iannelli. Are you here to see Elena Gallo?"

She is beautiful like a model with blue eyes, blonde hair, and a svelte body under that white coat. I swallow and say, "Yes, I am."

Isabella leans toward me and reads my I.D. tag and says, "Robert Valenti – an American?"

I nod my head. "Yes, I am."

"Please sit down," she says. She turns to the nurse. "You can go now, Fina."

"Okay, doctor," she says and turns around and leaves.

"So, Mr. Valenti, you are of Italian descent but come from America?"

"Yes, from New York City," I say. I am starting to wonder what is going on here.

"You told them at reception that you are Elena's friend," Isabella says.

"Yes, I am a friend," I say. "Soon as I heard about this, I came over here to see how she is doing."

"I see," she says.

"So, how is she doing?"

Isabella sits back in her chair and sighs. "She came in here Code Red, Mr. Valenti. She is in serious trouble. I'd like to know how she got that way."

"Please call me Bobby," I say.

"Okay, Bobby, do you know what happened to her?"

I am starting to get nervous here. Could she be thinking that I did this? "I was told about this by her neighbor. She told me that she was the one who found her and called 112."

"Well, we have no information up until this moment," Isabella says. She lifts a file from her desk. "According to the report we have, an anonymous call came in about a woman in serious condition. They were given an address and flat number, but that is all. Who is this neighbor you're talking about?"

"Well, I went and knocked on Elena's door today," I say, not wanting to get Carla into trouble even though she deserves it. "The neighbor was coming down the hallway and told me what happened."

"How did you know to come here?" Isabella asks with a raised eyebrow.

I think quicky. "I used my phone to look up the nearest emergency room, and I came directly here."

"Okay, I see," Isabella says, putting down the file and folding her hands on top of it. "My concern is that this young woman has been severely beaten. She has needed surgery for internal injuries and, if she survives, she is going to need multiple procedures for the damage to her face."

"Multiple procedures?" I ask as if I am in a brain fog.

"Yes, of course," Isabella says, "this will involve several stages since the damage is quite severe."

I am overwhelmed by what I am hearing. I blurt out, "If needed, I can help pay for any surgery or anything like that."

"Oh, that is not necessary, Bobby," Isabella says with a serious expression as if she still has doubts about me. "Elena happened to have her health care card and I.D. card in her wallet that was found at the scene. There are no financial worries, but I would like to find the person who is responsible."

I glance out the window and see a fat seagull on the ledge. "Yeah, so would I."

Isabella leans forward and asks, "Bobby, are you Elena's boyfriend."

I shake my head. "Oh, no, I am just a friend."

"Bobby, a friend would want to find the person who did this, no?"

"Yes, I do want to find the person who did this," I whisper, thinking about how I want to beat up Nino worse than what he did to Elena. "Am I able to see her?"

"I would advise against that," Isabella says. "It is difficult to look at her the way she is right now."

I sit forward and say, "I can handle it. I need to see her."

Isabella stands up and walks in a regal manner toward me. I stand up and she looks me in the eye. "Five minutes. She is in and out of consciousness."

We walk down another hallway, and she hands me scrubs, a hat, and gloves. I dress quicky, and then I am in another room looking at Elena in a big bed. The left side of her head and eye are completely covered by bandages, as are both arms. She has a cast on her left ankle, and there are lines connected to her arms; machines beep next to her and behind her.

I stand there as if I am paralyzed. Elena looks so small in the big bed, and her beautiful face and lovely body have been battered beyond reason. I move to the right side of the bed, take her hand, and squeeze it. "Elena, it is Bobby," I say. I glance at Isabella who takes a deep breath and then walks away.

Elena opens her right eye that is black and blue. She whispers, "Bobby?"

"What happened?" I ask. "Why did he do this to you?"

She is struggling to speak. "*Orgasmo*," she whispers.

"You told him about the orgasm?"

She tries to smile and whispers, "Very angry."

I squeeze her hand tighter. "I'm going to make him pay, Elena."

"No, he's crazy," she says.

"I can get crazy too," I say.

She struggles to speak. "Take me away."

Her eye shuts. I lean closer to her ear and whisper, "When you get out of here, I'll take you away. Don't give up, Elena."

I start to cry and kiss the back of her hand. Suddenly, I feel a hand on my shoulder. Isabella says, "You have to go now."

In the hallway, I take off my scrubs and throw them in a big bin with other used ones. I look at Isabella, and she hands me a tissue from a box on the counter. "I see that you care about her," she says.

I wipe my cheeks dry and blow my nose. "Yes, I do care about her."

"Prove it!" Isabella says. "Find the guy who did this to her."

I start walking down the hall, but I turn around and say, "I'm going to find the guy who did it, and he will pay."

"I am talking about doing it the legal way, Bobby," Isabella says with her arms flailing, "not some sort of New York street justice."

"I'm sorry, Isabella, but sometimes that's the best kind of justice," I say as I walk down the hallway, throw open the doors, and make my way to the elevator.

Outside, I start to cross a bridge over a canal and look back at the hospital. I did not notice before in my rush to get here, but it is a big beautiful building with ornate columns, magnificently intricate metal windows, and statues all over it – it looks like a grand church or palace – I learn later that it used to be a monastery. I am so sad that Elena is in there in such a terrible condition.

I am not sure what I am going to do, but I must do something. I take the phone out of my pocket and call Adamu. He answers and says, "Hey, man, what's up?"

"Adamu, remember that creep from the bar who was bothering the young girl?"

"Indeed, I do," Adamu says.

"Well, he just almost killed someone I care about. I need to get into fighting shape as quickly as possible."

"Okay, Bobby," he says, "let's go to the gym."

I look out over the water and see seagulls swooping over a gondola. "Okay," I say. I think I can take Nino as I am now, but it will not hurt to get back into the ring again.

CHAPTER FIFTEEN – Working Out

For the eighth time over the last two weeks, I finish a workout with Adamu in a gym near where he stays with his father in Dorsoduro. We spend about two hours sparring, hitting the heavy bag, the speed bag, running on the treadmill, and lifting on the weight machines. Today, we spent more time on sparring.

I come out of the shower and head for my locker. Adamu is already standing at his locker and getting dressed. I have a towel around my waist as I open my locker. I glance at him and ask, "How do you think I did today?"

Adamu slips on his shorts and smiles. "I think you're gonna knock Nino's block off, my friend."

I nod my head and say, "I felt like I was really throwing nice, heavy punches today."

We finish getting dressed and go outside carrying our backpacks. "Are we getting lunch?" Adamu asks.

I adjust the Mets baseball cap on my head and say, "Yeah, you pick the place."

After a ten-minute walk, we reach a café situated with a view of the lagoon, where vaporetti and other watercraft are going by in different directions. Adamu holds the menu in his hands and says, "This place has the best ravioli in Venice."

I laugh. "You know my friend; your Italian blood seems to override your Ethiopian appetite."

"Well, when I was younger, my mother always cooked Italian food to please dad and us kids," Adamu says with big smile.

I nod my head and say, "My Polish mother did the same thing for my Italian father. I have no idea what Polish food tastes like – except one time when my Uncle Casmir came to our house and brought kielbasa with him. I didn't want to tell my father that I liked Polish sausage better than Italian sausage."

We both order spinach ravioli with grilled chicken. The waiter also brings us two big bottles of still water. After working out, we are both rather thirsty. Adamu asks, "Isn't that ravioli great?"

"Uh, yeah, spectacular," I say.

"How's Elena doing?" he asks.

"It's been really slow," I say. "Sometimes it seems like she is improving, and then there is another setback." It hurts me to see her in that bed looking like a broken vase that is slowly being put back together, but the glue is not setting quickly enough.

Adamu slips a ravioli into his mouth and chews vigorously. He stares at me and says, "You know, you're looking great in the ring, but the big thing is the ring has its rules. You don't think that Nino guy cares about rules."

"Yeah, I know that," I say.

"When you do confront him, he could have a knife or a gun," Adamu says. "Then it doesn't matter that you have a killer left hook."

I sip some water and say, "I've thought about that a lot, and I don't really have a game plan yet."

Adamu chews a piece of chicken and asks, "Well, what are you planning to do? Kill him or incapacitate him or what?"

I sit back and sigh as I look out over the lagoon. "At first, I wanted to kill him, but I've had time to think. I think Dr. Iannelli is right. He needs to face legal justice."

"Oh, so now you're listening to the pretty doc who seems to like you," Adamu says with a chuckle.

"Hey, she doesn't give me any thought," I say. "She's just interested in me to find the guy who hurt Elena. Besides, I have promised Elena that I am going to take her away, and I am going to keep that promise."

"You're really still doing that?"

"When I learned she was hurt and left for dead, I realized I had feelings for her," I say. This is the truth – I did not realize how much I cared about Elena until I thought she was going to die. I do not love her, but I feel responsible for her condition. I guess that will have to be enough.

"You're gonna run away with a hooker?"

"She is a victim, Adamu. She came here innocently and wanted to start a better life," I say. I eat another ravioli, and it is damn good. "Wow, you're right about these."

"I don't think you're thinking straight, Bobby. Didn't you say she's 21 or 22? She's kind of young for you."

"She's 21," I say. I hear what he is saying, and I sit back and take a sip of water. "Yeah, I know, but someone has to take care of her. She can't go back to her family in Milan. Her uncle will put her to work in the factory job that killed her mother."

Adamu shakes his head. "I don't know, man; I don't think you're thinking straight anymore."

In some ways I agree with him. "Yeah, maybe you're right, but I got this protective feeling for Elena. I just want to make sure she is safe."

"Yeah, I…I understand," Adamu says and then sucks up another ravioli and hums. "Man, I'm glad that I found this place. It's going to be hard to go home next week."

"Oh, you're going back to the real world?" I ask.

"Yeah, I've got to go back to work and pay some bills," Adamu says. "I still help my mom and sister out."

I eat another ravioli and stare at him. "I'm gonna miss you, man. With you here it felt a little more like home."

"Yeah, I felt the same way." He leans toward me and says, "But you've got to figure out what you're doing with this Nino dude."

I take a sip of water. "I know that. I've looked in the mirror, and I know I'm not a killer. So, I guess I have to find a way to beat the crap out of him and then call the cops."

"Be careful, man," Adamu says. "That guy is bad to the bone. If he can beat Elena like that, you don't know what he will do."

"Yeah, I know," I say. "But right now he is a ghost. I don't know if I'll ever find the bastard."

Adamu grins and says, "Knowing you, you're gonna find him."

Right now, I am hoping Carla will help me find him. "I'm doing my best."

*

I go to the hospital for my daily visit with Elena. She is no longer in ICU, but she is in the plastic surgery department where she will undergo the first of many operations to repair her face. Elena is sitting up in her bed drinking juice through a paper straw.

"Hey, how are you doing today?" I ask as I sit down next to her. The left side of her head and left eye are still covered with bandages.

"I'm doing okay," she says, forcing a brave little smile.

"So, when is the first operation being done?" I ask.

"Dr. Iannelli was here before," she says. "I think it will be either tomorrow or on Thursday."

"Oh, that's great," I say.

"She says it's the first of a number surgeries to put my face back together," Elena says. "She said something about bone grafts and soft tissue repair. I'm not sure what all of this means."

"Well, they can do wonderful things today," I say. "Eventually, you will look as beautiful as you did before this happened."

Elena sits forward and whispers, "You thought I was beautiful?"

I touch her hand and smile. "Yes, you are beautiful – inside and out. Don't worry about anything. They will do a great job, and you'll be as good as new."

"Carla came to visit me this morning," Elena says happily. "It was good to see her after all this time."

"Carla?" I ask. Now I am worried. "What did she want?"

"She was checking on me," Elena says rather innocently.

I think it is more than that. "I think she was checking on you for Nino. I'm sure he is worried about what you're going to say about him to the authorities."

Elena sucks on the straw, looking like a little girl who is in the hospital and badly hurt. "I don't think he is worried. I haven't told anyone – even Dr Iannelli – anything. I just want to get out of here."

"I know," I say, squeezing her hand again.

"Remember when you said you were going to take me away?" she asks.

I nod my head. "Yes, and I am going to take you away. Where would you like to go when you get out?"

"Can we go to New York?" she asks. "I mean, from watching TV shows and the movies, I've always wanted to go there."

"Elena, I left there and came here because I needed to get away from things," I say. "It's a great big world. Let's go anywhere but there."

"Oh, okay. I would like to go to London and see some shows," she says. "Can we go to London, Bobby?"

"Yes, of course," I say. "London is wonderful."

"Carla was asking me about when I was coming home," Elena says.

"What did you tell her?" I ask.

"I said that I was never going home," Elena says with a smile. "I told her I was going away with you."

This worries me, and I take a deep breath. "Elena, Carla has not always had your best interests in mind. She lured you here to be basically enslaved by Nino. I'm sure she is asking these questions on his behalf."

"Maybe you're right," Elena says. "Hey, there's nothing to worry about because you're going to take me away."

"Yes, okay," I say, "just don't tell anything about your progress or anything else to Carla anymore. I don't trust her."

"Okay," Elena says with a smile, "I won't."

*

As I am walking down the hallway toward the elevator, Dr. Iannelli stops me and asks, "So, you are still coming around to see her."

"Yes, Isabella, I am," I say.

"I guess there is no new information about her attacker," she says.

"No, Elena says that she can't identify him," I say, nervously pushing the button for the elevator.

"I'm trying to figure you out, Bobby," she says. "You seem to care about Elena, but you don't want justice."

She is starting to make me feel angry. "I do care about justice, Isabella. And I'm going to make sure that it happens one way or another."

Isabella touches my arm. "Any man that could do what he did to Elena – he is an animal. I don't think you can stoop to that level. Do you?"

The elevator doors open, and I go inside and push the button for the lobby. "I guess we'll have to see about that." I see the genuine concern on her beautiful face as the elevator doors close.

*

On my way home, I stop in my local *supermercado* to get a few things. Old Marco is smoking his stinky cigarette and drinking a Moretti. "Where have you been?" he asks. "I don't see you for a long time!"

I am throwing a few things in my basket and look up at him. "I've just been busy. I've been eating out a lot."

"That is too expensive," he says, throwing away the nub of his cigarette and taking a swig of beer. "It's cheaper to eat at home."

I go up to the register to check out and say, "You're probably right about that, Marco. Sometimes, I'm too lazy to make my own meals,"

As he is scanning my items, he looks up at me with weary old eyes and says, "There was a guy in here today asking about you."

"A guy? What guy?" I ask, starting to worry about Nino.

"He was an angry man with beady eyes," Marco says. *That sounds like Nino.*

I try to stay calm and ask, "What did he want?"

"He wanted to know where you live," Marco says. "I didn't trust him, so I said I didn't know."

"Thank you," I say.

I carry my food and beer up the 62 steps, put everything away, and then stand at the window and stare out at the Campanile as it becomes illuminated in the dusk. Maybe it was Nino looking for me at the market today, and maybe it was not. I sip my beer and know I must be ready for anything from now on.

CHAPTER SIXTEEN – A Friend in Need

Pietro called me and asked to meet at the taverna where Paula tends bar. Since I have not been there in a while, I agree to meet him. He says that what he wants to talk about is of the utmost importance.

It is Thursday evening, and I saw Elena earlier in the day after her surgery. Her face was rather puffy, and she said that she felt "weak and sore." She still is improving rapidly and walking all around the hospital floor to get exercise because she is feeling much better.

I am standing at the bar with my exquisite martini made by Paula. There are people scattered around the place at tables, contemporary music is playing, and Paula is wiping down the bar in front of me. "You've been busy," she says.

"Sorry, I've been taking care of things," I say and sip the nectar of the vodka gods.

Paula leans on the bar so that I can see her seahorse tattoo. "You still nursing that poor little injured sparrow?"

"Yeah, but she is doing better every day," I say.

"I'm no psychiatrist – although I hear my share of looney cases – but I reckon that you have a need for this – this caring for someone," Paula says.

I sip my drink and feel my face reddening. "Perhaps, but I just feel like she has no one else who cares about her."

"Yes, but you're also taking on a responsibility for her," Paula says. "My question is can this be love or some sort of assuaging of a guilty conscience because, by paying for her services for months, you kind of contributed to her condition."

I am shocked by the accuracy of Paula's diagnosis. "Hey, you sound a lot like a psychiatrist to me."

"Am I on target or what?" she asks.

"The truth is that I have thought about this," I say. Although I have not really thought too much about it, Paula is right that by paying for Elena's services I was indeed actually empowering Nino by default. "At the time, Dr. Paula, I was too needy and lonely to think more deeply about what I was doing."

"And too horny," Paula says with a lovely smile.

"Yeah, that too," I admit. "I guess I am trying to make up for the error of my ways by helping her."

Paula whispers, "But do you really love her? Or is it that your guilt is making you feel something else?"

I do feel something for Elena and care about her, but I am not *in love* with her. I did feel love for Mireille, but she disappeared from my life, and then there is the unattainable Paula. "I have complicated feelings," I say, "and I'm not sure about how I really feel. I just know I care about her."

"Perhaps sometimes that is enough," Paula says.

"Yeah, perhaps," I say.

Pietro comes into the place wearing untucked button-down blue shirt and gray shorts. He is usually dressed in a suit for our writers' group because he comes there right after work, so this is a new look for him. I turn to Paula and say, "My friend is here."

"I remember that bloke," she says, "he's the one who drinks the wine and thinks that he's too good to stand at my bar."

"Bingo!" I say with a chuckle. "You got his number. See you later!"

I walk up to him and say, "Hi, Pete," and shake his hand.

"Hello, Robert," he says.

"There are plenty of tables available," I say. "You want to pick one out?"

Pietro looks around and sees a table in the corner. "Let's sit there because what I have to talk about is difficult."

We sit down at the table, and he is looking around as if he wants to be sure that no one is in earshot of us. Almost immediately, a waitress comes up to us and asks us, "What are you drinking?"

I lift my half-finished martini and say, "I'll have another."

Pietro says, "I'll have Johnny Walker Black over ice, please."

I stare at him and ask, "Are you hitting the hard stuff now?"

"Yes, I need liquid courage," he says.

I can see Pietro is very nervous. His possum like whiskers are very twitchy, and his hands are all over the place as he is rubbing them across the table. "Is everything okay, Pete?"

"No, everything is not okay," he says.

The waitress brings our drinks, and he grabs his and takes a big gulp. "Wow, something really big must be going on."

"Robert, I am at a crossroads," he says, his eyebrows skewing and his face contorting as he speaks. "I need some advice."

"About what?" I ask, then finish my first martini.

"This thing with Brian and me is falling apart," he says. "I am between a rock and a hard place."

"The old Scylla and Charybdis situation, huh?" I ask.

"Exactly!" he says pointing at me as if we were playing charades.

"Is this about you having a civil ceremony?" I ask.

"Yes! And the huge party Brian wants afterward. He wants to invite family and friends from London, and he expects me to invite my family and friends," Pietro says in a flustered manner.

"Well, the question is do you love him enough to do this?" I ask.

"I don't know how to do it – to come out! I don't think I can do it."

I sip my new martini. "I can't help you in that department." I glance back at the bar and say, "But I do think I know someone who can."

"Oh, no, not that snarky seahorse woman," Pietro says with his nose twitching.

"Hey, she is a lovely person," I say, "and she is in a successful relationship with her *female* lover. I think she can help you."

He sips his drink. "I…I guess it won't hurt to talk with her."

"Wait right here," I say. I go up to the bar and call Paula over to me. "Hey, it's not such a busy night. Do you think you could come over to our table for a few minutes?"

"What's up?" she asks.

"My friend is having trouble – trouble *coming out* to his friends and family," I say. "He needs help."

"Paula scrunches her nose and says, "Well, I have experience in this area, so I guess I can talk to your mate if you like." She turns around and says, "Gina, please cover the bar for me for a few minutes." A darkhaired young woman puts down her serving tray and runs behind the bar. "*Grazie!*" Paula says as she comes out from behind the bar and walks with me over to where Pietro is sitting impatiently. She sits down on the other side of the table across from Pietro and me and stares at him. "How can I help you?"

Pietro looks at me as his upper lip quivers. He then turns to Paula and says, "This isn't easy for me."

Paula puts her hand on his arm and says, "It's not easy for anyone." She folds her hands and presses them on the table. "What's happening with you?"

Pietro glances at me and then looks back at her. "Look, my partner wants to make things official – legally official."

"Well, that makes sense," Paula says, "My partner Viv and I did that a few weeks ago. It gives us both protection we deserve."

Pietro puts up a hand like a crossing guard stopping a car. "I have no trouble with doing the legal thing; my problem is having the big ceremony – he wants something much bigger than a wedding, almost like a coronation!"

Paula looks at me and then back at him. "As Bobby knows, we did have a little party, but nothing that big or spectacular."

"I was honored to be invited to that little gathering," I say, remembering that day and feeling happy that Paula has someone like Viv who loves her, even though it is not me.

"Well, that is not what he wants. He wants a big party, and he wants me to invite my family and friends from back home," Pietro says, "but I don't want to do that because I haven't come out to them yet, and I'm not sure that I ever want that."

Paula sits back in her chair and sighs. "There is no one way to go for coming out. What works for me might not

work for you. In my case, I told my parents when I was 18 –
as soon as I was old enough to do things my way."

Pietro shivers like ice cubes were dropped down his
back. "Oh, I'm twice that age, and I still don't think I can do
it."

"Pete," she leans toward him and asks, "your name is
Pete, right?"

He looks at me and nods his head quickly. "Yes,
yes!"

"Okay, Pete, it comes down to how much you love
him. Do you love him so much that you're willing to do what
is very difficult?"

Pietro stares at her with wide eyes. "I…I don't
know."

"The other question is, does he love you enough to let
this pass, to have the ceremony without your family and
friends from home? These are the two questions that need
answers."

Pietro rubs his chin a couple of times. "I know. You are right. These two questions do need answering."

Paula glances over at the bar where Gina seems to be very busy. "My work is done here," Paula says as she stands up.

Pietro looks up at her and says, "*Grazie mille!*"

Paula gives him a thumbs up and glances at me. I say, "Thanks, Paula." She flashes that beautiful smile and walks away, a once happy seahorse enjoying her human life.

I look at Pietro and sip my martini. "Well, I hope that helps you in some way, but now it's up to you, my friend."

Pietro downs the rest of his drink and signals the waitress. "Another round, please!"

"Getting drunk isn't going to give you the answers to those questions," I say.

"I know, but at least I can feel good even when things are so bad." Pietro takes a deep breath and exhales. "You know, everything was going so well for us. I thought Brian and I were happy. I am very content with the way things are. I don't know why he has to keep pestering me about this so much."

I sip my martini as the waitress brings another round. "Sometimes people aren't satisfied with the status quo."

Pietro lifts his drink and looks at me over his hand. "Well, I like the status quo. I don't know why Brian wants to change things."

"Why don't you ask him?"

Pietro sips his drink and says, "I will. I'm going to ask him when I go home tonight."

I lean forward and say, "Just prepare yourself, Pete. You may not like what Brian has to say."

Pietro nods his head and sips his drink. "That's what I'm worried about."

For the first time since I know him, I feel sorry for

Pietro. I wonder if Brian and he will work things out. I lift

my drink and say, "Here's a toast to everything working out

between you two."

Pietro clinks his glass against mine and says, "I hope

so."

*

As I walk home, I pass the illuminated Gallery of

Modern Art overlooking the Grand Canal; its Baroque

marble majesty is perhaps even more impressive at night than

during the day. In fact, all of Venice is more beautiful at

night. When the sun slips away and the heat dissipates, the

lights along the canals glow like entities, watching everything

and knowing all. The buildings' arches and windows glow in

sharper and luminous magnificence. The gondolas float along

glittering dark water, and music drifts across the streets as if

from a place that is just as close to heaven as any place on

Earth can be.

I wander in and out of narrow lanes, turn a corner, and see the fork where I will turn to go to my building. I am wondering about Pete, thinking about how he does not seem certain about what to do. He reminds me of myself when I started resenting Beth when she got to take all those business trips for the firm. I guess I should have brought it up to her, but instead I let it fester in my mind and felt slighted for not being considered for the opportunity.

The worst thing I did was getting drunk at the office Christmas party while she was away, and I had a stupid one-night stand with a woman who meant nothing to me. That cost me my marriage and my career. I hope that Pietro has better luck than I did when speaking a truth that Brian may not want to hear.

CHAPTER SEVENTEEN – The Ghost Comes Out of Her Shell

I wake up to the sound of my phone ringing. In my life right now, I rarely get a phone call. I live in the world of texting, and I have the few people in my life like Elena, Pietro, Paula, Adamu, and Serge who text me regularly – but none of them call me.

It is early – my windows are just starting to brighten with the dawn of a new day. I grab my phone from the night table and look at it. Probie's picture is there with a weird expression, so I tap the phone and say, "Hello, Probie. What the hell are you calling me for so early in the morning?"

"Hey, pal, it's late in the evening here," he says, slurring his words a bit.

"Are you a little drunk, Probie?"

"I am a little tight if you have to know," he says. I hear pounding music in the background.

"Where the hell are you?"

"I'm in a club," he says. "I took the client from Milan out tonight. We are just about winding down if he ever stops dancing with the young lady he met."

"So, why are you calling me, Probie?"

"I miss you, you big lug," he says.

"Yeah, okay, I know you a long time," I say. "You must want something."

"Oh, no, I have to tell you something good," Probst says.

I sit up in bed, resigned to the fact that I am now up earlier than I want to be. "Okay, what's going on?"

"I told the client about how when I saw you in Milan and that you came in from Venice," Probst says.

"Why would you tell the client about that?"

"Oh, well, he was talking fondly about his holidays in Venice," Probst says. "I told him that you're a writer living there now!"

"I'm not a writer yet, Probie; I'm trying to become one though," I say.

"Well, he wants to know if you can write a book about living in Venice and working as a writer there."

Now, I know that Probie is bombed out of his mind. "I told you I am trying to write a book – a book about growing up in our old neighborhood!"

"Yeah, I know, but has something changed? When I was there, you told me you had barely been able to write ten pages."

I pinch my nose between my eyes and say, "Yeah, I'm still stalled."

"Hey, why not think about it," Probie said. "I'll get together what he wants, and I'll email it to you. He says he's willing to make it worthwhile. What do you have to lose?"

"Okay, fine, I'll check it out," I say.

"Gotta go; love you, man!" Probie says before hanging up.

I push myself out of bed, go into the kitchen, and get myself a bottle of water from the fridge. I am fairly dehydrated from my night out with Pietro. I walk over to the window, pull up the shade, and see San Marco's bell tower against the clear blue sky. Another beautiful, hot day awaits me in the old city.

*

After breakfast, I sit on my couch and scroll through some news apps on my phone – *New York Times, USA Today*, and CNN – so I am caught up with what is happening out there in the world that I basically ignore most of the time. I check my email, but I have nothing from Probie yet. Perhaps he was so drunk he will forget about even making that call.

Elena texts me like she does every morning.

"*Buongiorno*, Bobby. *Come stai?*"

"Okay," I text. "How are you?"

"I'm doing okay. Dr. Iannelli says I'm making great progress."

"Great!" I text. "I'll be over later today."

"Okay, I'll see you later. *Ti amo!*"

I take a deep breath and text back, "Yeah, me too." Do I really? I put down my phone and stare out the window.

I go into the bathroom, where I shave and take a shower. Afterwards, I stare at myself in the steamed-up mirror. I wonder how I got here; who is this guy looking back at me? I do know why I am here – meaning being divorced and living in Venice – but I do not understand how it all happened. I am not sure I could even explain anything to my younger self. If I could go back in time, what would I say to the 18-year-old me to help him avoid my mistakes? Where would I even begin?

After getting dressed, I figure it is time to take my walk before it gets too hot. I go down the 62 steps, which is much better than coming up them, and go out into a day that is already scorching. I walk over the surprisingly uncrowded Rialto Bridge and purposely wander the streets north of Piazza San Marco to avoid the tourist crowd.

Going down a narrow street, I discover an old bookstore – Acqua Alta – that is nestled in a quiet nook away from the frenzy of it all. Many savvy book lovers are congregating outside the store in a narrow courtyard where stacks of books are available. A hand painted sign featuring a cat proclaims entrance is free, and there is a water fountain for thirsty travelers to fill up their empty bottles.

Inside there are hundreds of books everywhere, including piles of them inside a gondola on the floor, and there is even a staircase completely made from stacked books. Cats roam the store freely – on shelves, tables, and walking across the floor – and customers are socializing as much as they are shopping. There is also the smell of the place: the sacred odor of ancient texts mingling with cat smells. It is an interesting atmosphere for bibliophiles to be sure.

As I exit the place, I hear a text ping on my phone. When I pull it out of my pocket, I am surprised to see a message from Mireille. She writes, "Just got back in town. Can you meet me for lunch?"

I am shocked because I have not heard from her in almost a month. I am giddy but also apprehensive. Should I even bother with responding due to my situation with Elena? Of course, some of the things Paula said to me last night have me thinking about everything I am doing. Am I up to taking on Elena? Caring for her? I am very confused by everything.

Going down to the Grand Canal, I lean on a railing with a view of the Rialto – now teeming with tourists. Should I even respond to her? Of course, I would like to know why she ghosted me. I start typing a text, and then I stop. What the hell am I doing? I defiantly shove my phone into my pocket and start walking rapidly to not think about anything.

Eventually, I find myself wandering through the covered Rialto Market where it is cooler in the shade. The fish vendors are there in full vigor, with the seagulls' call filling the air as they swoop in and land near the carts to see what scraps they can get. It is packed with tourists, but I head away from the steps off the bridge to go down to where old Tinno is selling his high-quality fruits and vegetables.

"Hey, Bobby," he says. "Haven't seen you in a while."

"I've been busy," I say as I buy a shiny apple.

"How is life?" the old man asks.

"*Complicato!*" I say as I bite into the apple.

"Ah, all of you – young people who are crazy," he says with a wave of his arthritic hand. "With your phones and computers and everything."

"Yeah, we are a mess," I say and take another bite of the delicious apple.

"For me it was simple," he says. "I found a good girl; I married her, then I worked hard, and she had children. This is how I found happiness."

I stare at him, and though he is old and his face is worn and wrinkled, I can tell by the way he speaks that he has lived a genuinely happy life. "Good for you, Tinno. You're a lucky man."

*

I come across a small, old church that I have not seen before, and I go inside where it is cool and the lights are low. A few people are sitting in the pews; others are lighting candles and praying. I genuflect and make a sign of the cross – recalling my Catholic school days – and slide into a pew near the back of the church.

Although it is a small church, the walls are covered with beautiful artwork featuring scenes from the life of Jesus. There are marble Stations of the Cross along both side walls, and lovely statues are in nooks high up near a mosaic ceiling.

I close my eyes and pray, "Dear God, help me today. I need your help in all things big and small."

A few people standing in the aisle near where I am sitting are stopping to take photos with their phones even though a sign by the back door has an advisory not to do so. I feel saddened that there is no respect for anything sacred.

God must have heard my prayers because I feel a rush of inspiration to contact Mireille. I take out my phone and text her back. "Sure, where do you want to meet for lunch?"

*

In a café not far from the Rialto, I see Mireille sitting at a table under a big Campari umbrella fluttering in the breeze. She is dressed in her business attire just as when she came to the writers' meetings. Her usually pale skin seems darker, almost as if she has been on a beach vacation. I walk over to her and, for some strange reason, I shake her hand. A large bottle of still water is on the table with two glasses filled halfway with ice.

"How are you?" I ask as I pour myself some water and replenish her glass as well.

"I am sorry that I have not been in touch," she whispers. "I had to go home."

"Is everything okay?" I ask and sip some cold water.

"Yes and no," she says.

"Oh, what's going on?"

"I had to see my sister Colette," she says. "She asked for me to come home because she was having problems."

"Are they serious?"

Mireille sips her water. "Yes, it was about her fiancé."

"What about him?"

"She was having doubts and wanted me to meet him," Mireille says. The waiter comes over to the table with a margherita pizza and places it on the table with two plates. I look up at her, and she smiles. "I know you like this."

"Yeah, sure," I say. I take a slice and look up to see her lips quivering.

"What is wrong, Mireille?"

"Jan is Dutch and she wanted me to meet him because some of his ways are strange," Mireille says. "She was having doubts about him after the engagement."

"So, did you meet him?" I ask and then take a bite of pizza, which has a thin crust and is delicious.

"Yes, several times," Mireille says and takes another sip of water. "He seemed nice at first, but there was something in his eyes."

"Well, sometimes we can tell a lot from a person's eyes," I say.

"Something wasn't right about him," Mireille says. "Eventually, after many days of us being together and talking, Colette decided to break it off with him."

"Oh, I am sorry," I say because I am not sure what else to say.

"It is fine now," Mireille says.

"You look great like you got a lot of sun," I say and eat some more pizza.

She smiles and takes a slice of pizza and puts it on her plate. "Yes, I decided to cheer Colette up, so I treated her to a trip to Nice. My uncle said to take as much time off as I needed – he knew I was helping Colette."

"Oh, how wonderful," I say with a smile.

"She is okay now," Mireille says. "She has moved out of his place in Amsterdam and back in with my parents for now."

"I am happy for her," I say.

"I really was so involved with her and everything back home, so that is why I didn't contact you," Mireille says. "I'm sorry if it seemed like I disappeared or something."

"I totally understand," I say, though I really do not. How hard is it to respond to my text messages?

"Also, I didn't want you thinking that I forgot about our time together. I want you to know I care about *us*!"

Us? She has been gone for a month, and now she is talking about us. I would have loved to hear this a month ago. I do not know what to say, so I blurt out, "That's good to know."

"What have you been doing while I was gone," she asks and then takes a bite of pizza.

I think about Elena and say, "I've been helping a friend out who is in a bad way. It's taken up a lot of my time."

"Oh, well I can't imagine having a better friend than you," she says with a big smile. "I know how you were there for me."

I look out over the canal at the gondolas and vaporetti going by. I have no idea what I am going to do, but I figure that I should have prayed a lot more back in that church. I need guidance divine or otherwise right now.

CHAPTER EIGHTEEN – The Vanishing

After lunch with Mireille, she goes back to work, and I wander the streets in a fog, even on this sunny, cloudless day. I realize I am near the canal, and I must have been unintentionally moving in the direction of the hospital.

I glance at my watch, and it is almost three o'clock, which is my usual time to visit Elena. I take a deep breath, turn around, and head for the hospital. As I go around a corner, I see the building up ahead and feel sick to my stomach with guilt for having lunch with Mireille. What am I going to do? I do not know yet, but I'll think of something by the time I see Elena.

They know me at reception now, and they look up my name and print my pass quickly. Once I am in the elevator, I feel my heart pounding in my chest like I had just run a marathon. The doors open, and I see the swinging doors that lead to a hallway and Elena's room.

I stop to take a few deep breaths to try to calm myself down. When I feel I am ready, I go through the swinging doors, pass a few rooms, and then go into her room. There is a male orderly in there mopping the floor with a powerful disinfectant. I ask, "Where is Elena?"

He keeps mopping and mumbles, "*Niente inglese!*"

I turn around and go up to the nurse's station. I see Fina, the nurse whom I have met before, and I ask, "Where is Elena Gallo?"

Fina recognizes me and says, "I think you should see Dr. Iannelli."

I follow Fina down the hallway, and Isabella is coming out of another patient's room. When she sees me, there is an intense expression on her face. "Thanks, Fina, I'll take it from here."

Fina walks away, and I ask, "Where is Elena?"

"I believe I should be asking you that question," Isabella says with a tinge of anger in her voice. "Let's go into my office."

I follow her down the hallway as she walks with such poise, noting how statuesque she is. I bet she could carry a stack of books on top of her head across a stage and not drop one. She sits behind her desk and stares at me. I ask, "So, where is she?"

"She is gone," Isabella says. "A young woman came here, brought her some things, and Elena signed herself out."

"A young woman with red hair?" I ask.

"Yes, she seemed to get along with Elena. She helped her complete the paperwork for her discharge, and then they left."

I feel like the wind has been knocked out of me, so I fall into a chair and say, "I don't understand."

"So, you're telling me that you know nothing about this?"

"Yes, I'm completely shocked," I say. "Why didn't you stop her?"

"Well, she is an adult, and there were no medical reasons to keep her. She is fully recovered," Isabella says.

"What about her face?" I ask.

Isabella leans forward on her desk. "She has another surgery scheduled for next week; are you going to make sure she comes back for it?"

"I…I definitely will make certain that she makes that appointment," I say with no idea about how I will do that.

Isabella sits back in her chair and folds her arms. "I don't know what to think about you, Mr. Valenti."

"Please, call me Bobby."

"I don't know what to think about you, Bobby. You appear to be earnest and to care about Elena, but you seem to have not tried to find her attacker."

I am insulted by her accusation. "I...I have tried to find the attacker. Elena tells me what she has told you – she didn't know him." Now even the lies I tell are worse lies.

"Well, now she is back out there, *Bobby*. Is she safe?"

She scares me by saying this. I jump up and say, "I have to go and find her."

I head toward the door. "Bobby," Isabella says, and I turn around. "Be careful out there."

I nod my head and say, "I will."

*

I make my way quickly along the Grand Canal, rushing over a busy Scalzi Bridge, going past the park and down the street to the building where Elena lives. When I come out of the stairwell, I am surprised to see the door to Elena's flat wide open. I am wondering if I will encounter Nino and feel the hairs stand up on my back as I prepare for an attack.

When I go through the doorway, I notice that all her belongings are gone – all that remains is the stark furniture and the bare kitchen counter. I open the closet door, and her clothes are gone. The drawers in the bedroom are empty. It is like she never lived here.

I go into the bathroom in hopes that my wedding band would be where I left it, but the shelves above the sink and toilet are bare. Whoever cleaned out this place made certain to take everything.

Isabella said a woman with red hair came to get Elena, so it had to be Carla. I go out in the hallway and pound on her door. I hear mumbling behind the door, and Carla, wearing her yellow robe, opens the door slightly and says, "Go away, Bobby."

I shove the door and push my way inside. The apartment is arranged the same as Elena's place. There is a customer on the sofa bed covering up his naked body with a sheet. I point at him and say, "Stay there!"

"Look, Bobby, you have to go," Carla says.

I grab her by the arms and squeeze them hard. "You helped Elena check out of the hospital today. Where is she?"

"Just let her go," Carla says. "For her sake, please."

"Did Nino take her?" I ask.

She nervously nods her head. "Yes. He took her somewhere, and I don't know where she is."

I release Carla's arms and try to control my anger. "She still needs surgeries on her face that are scheduled."

"I don't know anything about that," Carla says.

"*Per favore, signore,*" says the man cowering behind the sheet.

I point at him again. "Shut up!"

"Look, I heard him tell her that she can't see you ever again or he will kill her," Carla says. "He took away her phone and told me that he was bringing her somewhere that you could never find her."

I hold the sides of my head with my hands trying to control my anger. "If you find out where she is, you have to promise you will text me and tell me."

Carla nods her head and starts crying. "I will; I promise," she says as she puts her number into my phone.

I turn around and leave the flat. I go out into the street and feel like the world is spinning the wrong way. If only I had acted that night in taverna, if only I had taken Nino out that night; he would have been the one in the hospital.

*

After wandering aimlessly for hours, I make my way to the taverna and walk up to the bar where Paula is staring at me like she is seeing a ghost. "What happened to you?" she asks.

"I look that bad, huh?" I ask.

"Yeah, you look ghastly," she says. Paula grabs a clean bar towel, runs water over it, and hands it to me.

"Thank you," I say as I place the towel on my face. After I have cooled down, I take the towel and wipe my neck and arms with it.

"Can I get you anything?" she asks.

"Yeah," I say, longing for a cold one. "A cold beer, please!"

Paula comes back with a bottle of Moretti and a glass, but I drink it straight from the bottle. "Take it easy, Bobby. You probably need something to eat. Would you like some *cicchetti*?"

I nod my head. "Yeah, that would be great." Paula goes off to get my food. I look up and see myself in the mirror, and I look like one of the living dead. I hate to admit it, but I feel like one of them too!

Gina the waitress comes over to me with a plate with little fried meatballs, small fried ravioli, and miniature panini on it. She says, "Come sit at a table."

I take my beer and follow her, collapsing onto the chair. "*Grazie*, Gina," I manage to say.

"*Prego!*" Gina says. "Would you like anything else?"

"Yeah, another beer, please," I say. I start to devour the food, like a man lost at sea and having a first meal after being rescued.

Paula walks over to me and puts a hand on my shoulder. "How are you doing?"

I swallow a meatball and say, "I'm better now."

She sits down and stares at me. "You're acting like you have the weight of the world on your shoulders."

I sit back, finish my beer, and sigh. "Let's say it has been one of those days."

"Bobby, you have to take care of yourself before you can take care of anyone else," Paula says.

I nod my head. "Yeah, I'm sort of learning that today."

Gina brings me another bottle of beer. Paula leans her head sideways and says, "I thought I had you figured out, but I guess I'm still puzzled by you."

"I was just trying to do the right thing," I say and then take a little panino, bite off half of it, and chew quickly.

"Sometimes the right thing isn't what we think it is," Paula says.

She is sitting so that I can see the seahorse tattoo. "Yeah, I would like to go back to when I first met Elena and do things differently."

"What would you do differently?"

"I would stop myself," I say. "I never had been with a prostitute before. I guess I should have just left, but when she asked for the money, I gave it to her because she said Nino would hurt her if I didn't pay."

Paula puts her hand on my arm. "Don't be so hard on yourself. Maybe you were just trying to get a little affection."

I pop another meatball into my mouth. "I kept telling myself that. I even told Elena that. I think that's when we started getting into trouble."

"How so?"

"Well, I was starting to care for her, and then we had a session and she had an orgasm – the first one she ever had."

"Bobby," Paula says placing her hands in her lap, "you gave her something special."

"Yeah, but then she told her pimp about it," I say, "and that landed her in the hospital because he beat her up when she told him."

"I know that despicable Nino character," Paula says as she shakes her head. "I guess you were too much competition for the guy."

"I don't know, but I regret ever going to her," I say. "Now he has taken her away, and I don't know what to do."

"Bobby," Paula says, again placing a firm hand on my arm. "People are going to live their lives, and we cannot change that to be the way we want it to be."

"What are you saying?"

"Maybe, just maybe, Elena wanted to go with the guy," Paula says as she stands up. The place is getting busy, and so my time with her must end.

"I…I can't believe that," I say.

"Let her go, Bobby," she says as she walks away.

I pop another meatball into my mouth and take a sip of beer. I think about it, and Paula is right – I am trying to control a situation that is out of my hands. If I were not involved with Elena, she would be okay and her face would not need surgeries. I am the one to blame.

*

Almost a week after Elena disappeared, I sit alone in my flat drinking beer and eating a slice of pizza. My phone pings, and I take it out of my pocket. Mireille texts me. "Just want to say goodnight."

It is almost midnight, so I text back, "Thanks. Goodnight!" I cannot think about Mireille tonight. That is a situation I am going to leave to tomorrow.

She calls me and I answer the phone tentatively. "It's going to be a beautiful day tomorrow," Mireille says. "Would you like to go to the beach with me?

"Beach?" I ask. "I didn't know Venice even had a beach; I thought it was all canals."

Mireille laughs. "Oh, we have one of the best beaches."

I must get my mind off everything, so I say, "Yeah, I'd like to go to the beach tomorrow." After I hang up, I am wondering where this thing is going with Mireille, and I am still worried about Elena, but there has been no news from Carla about her whereabouts.

I go to the fridge and grab another beer. I fall onto the couch and watch some Italian TV show with no subtitles. At this moment, I like it that way because it reflects the way I am living right now – I am at a place in my life where I do not understand anything that is happening to me.

CHAPTER NINETEEN – Lido

When Mireille told me that we would be going to go Lido for a beach day, I thought about Lido Beach back home out on Long Island. Here in Venice, Lido is a long barrier island that catches the waves from the Adriatic Sea on its east coast, creating the natural Venetian Lagoon on its west coast that flows into the canals of Venice.

It is a quick 15-minute ride on the vaporetto to get there, and Mireille is wearing a little sundress with colorful flowers on it and pink sandals. She is carrying a beach bag and wearing a wide brimmed pink hat. She keeps glancing out the window and then looking at me and smiling. Somehow, I feel rather peaceful being with her.

Over a week has come and gone since Elena vanished. I have thought about filing a police report, but what would I say in it? She voluntarily signed herself out of the hospital. That is on record, so how is she missing? As I walk around town or go to the taverna, I have been looking for Nino, but he is nowhere to be found.

So, I must let go, as Paula has told me to do, and I am trying to get back to a normal life. I skipped the writers' group this week because I was feeling very emotional, and I am not sure what I am going to tell Serge and Pietro about Elena. Perhaps I will say nothing at all to them.

For now, I am trying to enjoy my day with Mireille. I thought it was over for us, but perhaps this a second chance. The boat is very crowded because it is a beautiful day and the last Sunday in August. Everyone is trying to enjoy what is left of the summer season.

We get off at the vaporetto stop and cross over the street. To my surprise I see traffic – cars, buses, and trucks – unlike back in car-free Venice. Once we are on the other side of the busy street, Mireille points to an intersecting street and says, "This is Viale Santa Maria Elisabetta. We will use it to cross over the island to the beaches on the other side."

The tree-lined street – the only trees I have seen in Venice are the ones in the park in near Elena's flat – has ice cream shops, retail stores, restaurants, beach supply stores, and cafés with umbrellas over tables. We pass one woman's clothing store with dresses in the window that impress her. She looks at me and smiles. "How do you feel about my doing a little shopping on the way back?"

I do not like shopping, but I say, "If that will make you happy."

She suddenly reaches out told hold my hand, and we continue walking down this long, busy street. She says, "You know, the Venice Film Festival will be held here the next two weeks. If you want to see Hollywood stars, we can come back if you like."

I answer truthfully. "No, I'm not a crazy fan like that. I enjoy movies and TV shows, but I'd rather see the stars on a screen and not in person."

Mireille stops walking and looks at me. "You are always surprising me, Bobby. I really like that!"

"Good to know," I say.

We finally reach the beach area where there are various beach clubs, and Mireille says, "We're going to this one," she says pointing to a blue gate. "When my cousin came to visit last summer, we went here. It has a snack bar, pool, showers and, of course, the beach."

After I buy tickets, we go through a hallway and walk into a courtyard where we can get our towels. An attendant leads us down to the beach and our two lounges and a large blue umbrella. I take off my backpack and sit on a lounge. "I guess it's time to put on the sunscreen," I say.

Mireille smiles and takes a long tube out of her bag. "This is a natural tanning lotion. I got it when I was in Nice." She puts it on the lounge and pulls her dress over her head, revealing her pink bikini and a model-like body that is already tan. I have only seen her in business attire or demure clothing – I am amazed by her lovely appearance.

We rest on the lounges for a while, listening to the waves and the indistinct chatter of people on lounges all around us. Very large seagulls are swooping overhead and above the sea. The sand is pristine white and the water a deep blue under the cloudless sky.

"This is like paradise," I say.

She reaches over to hold my hand, and I take it. "This *is* paradise, Bobby."

Later, we go into the water to cool off. She swims way out beyond the waves, like she could have been an Olympian. While I did my fair share of swimming at Rockaway Beach back home, I am not so adventurous because we had a bad undertow in those days. She beckons me with a wave of her hand, so I fight my inhibitions and swim over the waves until I reach her.

"Isn't this perfect?" she asks; her wet hair is pushed back, and her lovely face glistens in the sunlight.

"Yeah, it is," I say.

"Did you swim a lot back home?" she asks.

"Yeah, I did swim when I could get to the beach on the subway," I say. "I'm not as good a swimmer as you are."

"Colette and I were always on swimming teams," she says with a big smile. "She is even a better swimmer than I am."

"How is she doing?" I ask.

"She is getting by each day," Mireille says with a suddenly serious expression. "It is difficult when you realize the man you love isn't who you thought him to be."

I know how I sadly fit that description because of Elena, and I am not sure if Mireille loves me, but I am feeling love for her. I am just worried that somehow, I could end up disappointing her one day. I have to say something, so I say, "I guess it is a good thing that you went home."

"Yes, Bobby, I am very glad that I did. She had to get away from Jan."

*

After swimming our bodies glisten as we dry off on our lounges. She turns to me and says, "I have never been in a serious relationship, and I know that you were married, so I am not sure about what you are feeling."

I keep looking up at the blue umbrella rattling slightly in the wind coming off the water. I want to be careful here, so I say, "I'm feeling very attracted to you. I was feeling that for you before, but then you went away, and then I was uncertain about everything."

Mireille sits up and looks at me. "I am sorry I did that, but I had to help my sister. Now that I am back, I want you to know how much I care about you."

I sit up, turn my body to face her, and put my feet on the sand. I know that Mireille is too good for me, but I am hoping that she will save me just like she saved Colette. "I care a lot about you too, Mireille."

She reaches over and touches my hand. "I've never been close with a man because I've not trusted anyone. I feel like I can trust you."

I squeeze her hand and say what I feel. "I want to be worthy of your trust."

Mireille's eyes are filled with warmth as she stares into my eyes. "I believe you, Bobby. I believe you."

I had been so depressed when I did not know where Mireille was, but now that I am with her, I feel a joy I have not known in years. Perhaps things are on track for me now. I want to do my best to be the man Mireille needs me to be.

*

We have lunch at the beach front café at a table under a blue umbrella with a view of the beach. I get a chicken club sandwich, and Mireille has a Greek salad. We share a big bottle of still water. Mireille looks out at the scene before us and smiles. "This is very relaxing, isn't it?"

I swallow my food and nod my head. "It truly is wonderful."

She leans back and looks up at the sky. "One day I would like life to be like this every day." Mireille looks at me and asks, "Is that just a crazy dream?"

I like this idea too. "No, it's not a crazy dream at all. If you believe in the dream, sometimes it will come true."

"Then I will believe," she says and stabs her fork into her salad.

I have a question that has been on my mind. "Mireille, can I ask you a question?"

She prepares to put a forkful of salad into her mouth and nods. "Of course."

This has been bothering me, so I go ahead and ask, "Why did you leave when your father came back home years ago? Don't you love him?"

Mireille puts down her fork and sits back. "It is not about love. I love my father, but I don't like him."

"Why?"

"He is a believer in that a woman's place is in the home," she says and takes a sip of water. "He allows my mother no room for her opinion and does not want to hear anything but what he wants."

"I guess what I am asking," and this will get to what I worry about, "is if your father ever was cruel to you?"

Mireille smiles and shakes her head. "No, he doted on Colette and me. We were his little angels. And, in turn, we loved him without asking questions. His behavior toward our mother was routine – it is how we grew up."

"So, what changed?"

"When I was older, I recognized this treatment of my mother was wrong," she says. "I knew it wouldn't change because Mother would never change; she would always allow my father to rule with an iron fist."

I sip my water and ask, "How were things when you went home to help Colette?"

"Fine," she says, stabbing at her salad again, "mostly because I stayed in a hotel. When I saw my father, it was briefly as I came to pick up Colette. Mother came out to lunch with us one day, and it was on this day that she helped Colette decide about Jan."

"Really? What did she do?"

"Mother held Colette's hand, glanced at me, and said, 'Mireille tells me Jan is like your father, and you know how he and I have been all these years. I don't think you want to live as I have lived; please choose to be a free woman who does things her own way.' And Mother did it! Colette decided to leave him.

"I went with her on the train. She used her key, and she knew that Jan would be at work. We cleaned out all her belongings, including my grandmother's teapot, and she left him a note. I do not know what it said, but let's just say she has never heard from Jan again."

"Good for her!" I say and take a bite of my sandwich. "Now what is Colette going to do?"

"Thankfully," Mireille says grabbing her hat because of a gust of wind, "she had kept her French job working online in Amsterdam, so she is waiting to find the right flat, and then she will move out."

"I'm glad the story has a happy ending," I say. "Except I guess for your mother."

Mireille shakes her fork at me. "No, my mother has her happy ending believe it or not."

"How? With your father?"

"Yes! Because, despite all his faults and all his toxic masculinity, my mother loves him. I envy her in the sense that she loves him so much that she will withstand all his weaknesses for that love. I don't how she does it, but she does."

"I guess that's what they call unconditional love," I say and bite into my sandwich.

"Yes, Bobby, and I love her because she is the only woman in the world who could love that man, and without her he would crumble. He would perish without her. That's why he came back home; he was falling apart without her."

"I guess they are actually good for each other," I say.

Mireille nods her head, "Exactly!"

*

After a long, lovely day on the beach, we are going along the avenue to get back to the vaporetto stop to go home. We are walking hand in hand, and Mireille stops to look at different store windows. When we reach the store with the dresses she admired earlier in the day, she turns to me and says, "I think it is time to try on these dresses."

I tip my Mets cap and say, "Take all the time you need."

She hands me her beach bag and walks elegantly into the store like a model ready for the runway. I find a bench, sit down, and am willing to wait as long as she wants to be in that store. For the first time since my good times with Beth, I realize that there is no place I would rather be, and no one I would rather be with.

I am giddy as a kid on the last day of school, and I wonder how long this feeling of ecstasy can last. Mireille is genuinely a beautiful soul inside and out, and that may seem cliché, but it applies here. I am not sure what I have done to deserve being with her, but perhaps my parents up in heaven are working some kind of magic. I know they would not want to see me living alone for the rest of my life.

I look up at the sky that is a lovely crimson as the sun begins to set, and I say, "Thanks, Mom and Dad." I hope they can hear me.

CHAPTER TWENTY – Here Comes the Rain Again

As I get up and look out my window, it is raining again. It has been raining every day in this second week of September, but Mireille has been busy with work, and I am getting somewhere with a story about the glassmakers we met during our visit to Murano. I am hoping it will be ready for the writing group this Friday afternoon.

I sit staring out the window watching San Marco's bell tower through the sheets of rain coming down. The weather matches my mood right now, as I wonder about what is happening with Elena and worry about what has become of her. I checked in with Isabella at the hospital, and Nino has not allowed her to return for her follow up surgeries. I have no idea how she will look without them.

Carla says she that she does not know where Nino and Elena are. She has moved out of her old flat and into another one in Dorsoduro. Carla is working in the Prada store near Piazza San Marco and trying to live a normal life, and I am happy for her.

The morning goes by quickly as I work on the story, trying to capture the beauty of the glassmakers' craft. I wonder if reading a story with Mireille in it is even appropriate. Surely, Pietro will make a snarky remark about it. I guess I will change her name to make things easier for me.

Shortly after noon, I go into the bathroom and shave and brush my teeth. I have an appointment to meet Serge in a place in Piazza San Marco for lunch. I notice my windows brightening, and I look outside to see that the rain has stopped, and the bell tower glistens in the sunshine.

I feel chilly when I go outside and walk down the street – this is the first time I have not felt warm in Venice. I see Marco standing outside of his store smoking a cigarette. I wave to him, and he waves back. I continue walking with my sunglasses on and my Mets cap pulled down over them. Now, in the cooler weather, I wear cargo pants instead of shorts and a jacket over my polo shirt.

Before I cross over the bridge into San Marco, I see people coming over the bridge wearing different colored, just below knee-high, rubber boots. I stop a guy who happens to be British who is wearing plastic yellow boots, and his girlfriend's boots are orange. I ask about them, and he says, "You need them on the other side; there is water in the streets."

I go into the market and notice they are being sold in several shops. I opt for a blue pair, sit on a bench, take off my sneakers, and pull them on. As I start walking in them, they seem fine and comfortable enough, and I have my sneakers in the boots' bag. As I come down on the other side of the bridge, everyone is walking around in similar boots or more expensive ones, plowing through a few inches of water in the streets. Some tourists in regular shoes or sneakers are laughing and happy enough to be walking through the water because they are in Venice.

I splish-splash as I walk and make my way to the square. Serge is already there, sitting at the table wearing expensive looking black boots. He is dressed impeccably as always. We shake hands, and I take a seat. The waiters are going back and forth through the water as if nothing is unusual.

"Sorry about the water," Serge says. "I guess I should have called you when I heard the sirens earlier."

"Sirens?" I ask. "I did think I heard something this morning."

"Yes, they are set off around the city when the tide is above the measure line," he says with a deadpan expression. "This way we know to wear our boots."

"The streets in San Polo are dry," I say. I remember that as being a selling point when I bought the flat.

"Yes, our lovely, elevated San Polo," he says.

The waiter walks toward our table in his fancy jacket, sloshing through the water. Serge orders a bowl of *pasta e fasioi* soup, and I order a chicken panino. We ask for a tall bottle of still water.

"It's kind of crazy they have to work in these conditions," I say.

"They and their predecessors adjusted to it," Serge says. "The *acqua alta* is a fact of life in Venice. We don't let it interfere in our plans. Though in the hotels it may be suggested to guests to wait it out until the tide goes down."

"That's what I love about this place," I say. "There is a resiliency that makes it quite unique."

"Yes," Serge says, "indeed Venetians are intrepid to say the least."

Our food and drink come courtesy of the waiter pushing through the water. He smiles valiantly as he serves us. I smell Serge's delicious soup and say, "Hey, that soup smells so good."

Serge tastes a little bit of soup, keeping the spoon in his mouth and closing his eyes. He removes the spoon and says, "This version of the soup is quite good, but my old cook when I was a boy used to add a little radicchio that was a nice touch. It is great on a winter's day."

"I can imagine," I say. "Looks like a hearty soup."

"There is a chill in the air today, so this soup is *apropos*," Serge says.

"So, you made this sound important. What's going on?" I ask, then take a bite of my sandwich, which tastes wonderful.

"The countess and I are going to take a cruise on my yacht," Serge says.

"Good for you," I say. "Where are you going?"

"We're going to see the pyramids," he says. "She has never been and asked me to take her."

"Well, that sounds great," I say, "but I'm not sure why you're telling me."

"If I tried to do this as a child, I would have been scolded." Serge takes a piece of bread, dips it into the soup, and then eats it with his eyes closed. "Such are memories that are bittersweet." He looks at me and says, "Oh, yes, I wanted to ask you for a favor."

"Well, I'll try, if possible," I say.

"I will miss one writer's meeting while I am away this Friday," Serge says. "Would you be able to hold it in your place?"

I am very shocked about this request. I try to stay calm and say, "We usually have 10 to 15 people in the group each week – I can probably squeeze five of them into my flat if you want them to be comfortable."

Serge slightly slurps his soup and then dips another piece of bread into it. "Who says writers need to be comfortable?"

"Well, there is also your wonderful spread of food," I say.

Serge smirks as he says, "I'm sure that you can provide something."

"Yeah, beer and potato chips are what I'd have for them," I say with a slight chuckle.

Serge shakes his head. "Oh, that will not suffice. Not at all."

"Listen, Serge, I think you can skip a week, and no one will mind," I say.

Serge stares at me with widened eyes. "There are certain people – like Anna and Pietro – who live for that meeting. Missing it will be something upsetting for them."

"Well, I certainly don't want to upset anyone, but I can't get 15 people into my flat or provide adequate food for them," I say.

"Oh, Bobby, I do understand," Serge says. "Can we think of some other option for a location?"

I suddenly think about Paula and her taverna. "Serge, I am going to ask a friend of mine who runs a taverna near

Campo Erberia. She has some backroom space there, and we might be able to use it."

Serge sucks some more soup from the spoon.

"*Brillante!* That sounds like a wonderful idea, my friend."

"They would have to pay for their drinks and some *cicchetti*, which is quite delicious there," I say.

"No, we can't have that." Serge reaches into his pocket and pulls out a wad of euros. He counts out five hundreds and looks up at me. "Will this be sufficient?"

"I think that will cover things," I say.

He hands me the bills, thinks about something, and hands me two more hundreds. "Please give this to the manager as a sign of my gratitude."

I take the bills and say, "I'm sure that she'll appreciate your business and generosity."

Serge dips another piece of bread into his soup. "Perhaps, if this goes well, we will keep this as a permanent venue for our meetings, pending the group's approval."

I shrug my shoulders. "It would give her more business, and if the members are okay with it, why not?"

"How is our dear Mireille?" Serge asks. His soup is gone, and he is using his bread to soak up what is left in the bowl.

"She is doing well," I say without divulging any details about us. "She has taken up lacemaking as a creative pursuit."

Serge finishes his bread and sits back in the chair. As the water flows around our feet, Serge acts like there is nothing extraordinary happening to us or to everyone else in the square. "She is a lovely girl; I hope you two will work it out."

"We're taking it slowly," I say. "I am there for her if she needs me."

"Well, she is a fine young lady," Serge says. "Try not to let her go, but also, don't break her heart."

"I'm trying my best," I say as I sit back and sip my water. I think I am trying each day, and I am hopeful it will all work out between Mireille and me.

*

That evening, I walk into the taverna, and see a large man standing by the front door. Gina the waitress is walking by with an empty tray and turns to the man and says, "That's Bobby! He's a regular, Lorenzo. He's good."

"Thanks, Gina," I say. I turn to the man and say, "I'm Paula's friend. Is everything okay."

Lorenzo looks like a wrestler, but he has a big smile, light blue eyes, and curly blond hair. "Paula hired me to watch the door; there have been a few issues recently."

"Well, looks like you can handle anything. Nice to meet you, Lorenzo," I say. I go up to the bar, and Paula is coming through the swinging out door from the kitchen. I put a thumb over my shoulder and say, "I met your muscle man. What's going on?"

Paula leans on the bar and frowns. "We've had some ugly incidents recently. Occasionally, we'd get a rowdy drunk, but these guys were trying to start fights, and I don't want any customers getting hurt."

"I'm sorry to hear that," I say.

"Any news about Elena?" she asks.

"Nothing as of now," I say. "It's like she disappeared off the face of the Earth."

"Bad guys like that Nino can do something like that," Paula says. "What can I get you?"

"Tanqueray on the rocks please," I say.

I look around the room, and there is some business, but it is quiet for an early evening. The music is playing, Lorenzo is at the door, and all seems right with the world. Paula places my drink on the bar. "And as for the other lass?" she asks with a smile.

"We're doing okay," I say, feeling my face flushing.

"Oh, I think someone is in love," Paula says.

"We're getting there," I say. I think about Serge and ask, "Do you ever use the backroom?"

"Sometimes for parties," she says with her hands on her hips.

"My writing group needs a place to meet this Friday around four o'clock," I say. "Is it possible?"

"Sure, it would be empty otherwise," she says with a smile.

"If they can order drinks and have a some *cicchetti* that would be perfect," I say.

Paula starts putting some glasses from the under the bar into a tray for cleaning. "What do the people write about?"

"Loss, love, sadness, loneliness, and joy," I say. "But mostly a lot about loss and loneliness."

She stops what she is doing and asks, "Can we blame society? Who do we blame for unhappy and lonely people?"

I think for a moment and say, "Perhaps it is human nature. We want the best but expect the worst. Maybe we only have ourselves to blame."

Paula is finished filling the rack and says, "That's a little profound, hey?"

"I have my moments," I say. I watch her go back through the other swinging door into the kitchen. I turn around and lean my left elbow on the bar. Customers are starting to come in. They must show an I.D. to Lorenzo. Some of the regulars probably will not like this at first, but they will get used to it.

I take out my phone and text Serge. "We're all set for the next meeting at the bar."

"*Bellissimo!*" Serge texts back quickly. "Send me the address of the taverna, and I will forward the information in our group text."

I quickly text the information to Serge. "I hope it will go well," I text.

"With you in charge, what can go wrong?" Serge texts back.

I stare at the phone in my hand and think, "Plenty!" But I will leave him to his belief in me for now.

I turn around and look at myself in the mirror behind the bar. I wonder about the wisdom of having a mirror there. It is like that in many bars back home as well. Perhaps the mirror is there to shatter any illusions about yourself – I do not like how I look when I get drunk, and I do not feel that much better about my sober image either, although Beth always told me I was handsome. I turn away and look at the happy customers – at least they appear to be happy. Perhaps we are all fooling ourselves. I guess I want to hold on to my illusions, at least for now.

CHAPTER TWENTY-ONE – The Meeting at the Taverna

The writers' meeting is a success in the back room of the taverna. The drinks flow and the *cicchetti* is eaten, and everyone seems happy. Even Pietro – who usually finds something wrong in everything – claims it is a hit. The last person to read is Anna, who stands there defiantly with cane in one hand and a piece of paper in the other. Her thick white hair is in a tight bun on top of her head.

Anna writes in pencil to enable multiple edits right up until the time of the meeting. She smiles and says, "Good evening. I wrote this for my mother, who came to me in a dream last night. The title is 'Sotto Voce.'

"My mother always spoke in a quiet voice,

As if she did not want anyone else to hear.

I often asked her about this odd choice,

But she claimed that her reasons were clear.

My words are for you to whom I am speaking,

No one else has a right or a need to know.

You are the one my special words are seeking,

Because it has been such a joy watching you grow.

I want you to know that I will always love you

Things I've done for you have been done with love

No matter where you go or whatever you do

I am with you, and you're the one I'm thinking of."

Anna looks up from her paper, and there is complete

silence in the room. I glance at Pietro, who is emotional.

Anna says, "I wrote this for my mother because in the dream

she said that she will see me soon. I didn't want to go my

whole life without writing something for her. This is it."

Everyone starts clapping. In Serge's absence, I have

been the master of ceremonies. I walk up to the front of the

room, and I have the inclination to hug Anna who has tears

on her face. I whisper in the ear, "That was lovely." She smells like cinnamon.

Pietro comes running up to Anna and grabs her hand. "It was so lovely, signora. Brava!"

"Thank you," she says.

Paula has been in the room for most of the meeting, and she walks up to us and says, "You are all such talented people!"

Everyone is congratulating one another for great writing that was shared this evening. I lean toward Paula and say, "I was afraid about how it would go here, but it went very well thanks to you."

Paula smiles. "I'll take you and your literary types anytime." She points toward the Three Germans as they hover over the *cicchetti* on platters. "What's up with those guys?"

"They come to the meetings but never speak or read any poems or stories," I say. "They just eat."

Paula laughs. "Well, they obviously do that well."

After most of the group leaves, Pietro and Anna go out into the public area and sit at a table as Paula's crew starts cleaning up the backroom. I have not had a drink yet as to remain a sober master of ceremonies, so I ask Gina at the bar to give me Smirnoff Red on the rocks. I get a glass of wine for Pietro, and a cherry brandy for Anna. I bring the drinks over to the table and say, "Great poem, Anna."

"Anna," Pietro asks, "your mother must be smiling in heaven right now."

Anna sips the brandy and smiles. "I should have written something much sooner for her, but it is better late than never."

"I thought it was lovely," I say. "It also seems like the meeting was a great success. A few of the members were grumbling at the beginning, but by the end everyone seemed okay about having it here."

Pietro sips his wine and wiggles his whiskers. "I like it very much, but I did hear some complaints about this place from some of the others. The Three Germans were not pleased and will let Serge know."

"Okay," I say, "let's see what happens."

Pietro turns to Anna. "You said that your mother said something about seeing you soon. My dear, it was only a dream."

"Oh, I know," Anna says as she sips her brandy. "It is just that I remember my mother telling me that her mother came to her in a dream and said the same thing."

"Really?" I ask.

"Yes, and mamma was dead in a few days," Anna says.

"Oh, I am sure you have many more days to come," Pietro says.

Anna leans forward, and in her *sotto voce* says, "The way I see it, I was inside my mother when she was inside my grandmother before my mother was born."

"What are you saying?" Pietro says.

"When my mother was a fetus, she already had all her eggs in her ovaries. This gives me a connection to my grandmother and my mother. The message is being passed down for generations."

"Well, that is very interesting," I say.

Anna sips her brandy. "So, my daughter was inside my mother as well when she was pregnant with me. See how the connection just keeps going." She seems to stare off at a faraway place. "I imagine one day my daughter will come to my granddaughter in a dream. I know she will be welcomed into heaven, just as my mother is welcoming me."

Pietro sits back and sighs. "Well, this evening went from joyous to depressing rather quickly."

I shake my head. "No, Pete, Anna is sharing a beautiful thing with us." I turn to her and say, "Thank you, Anna."

"It was nice to see that young man – Rolando – read tonight," Anna says. "He usually just sits there and listens."

"I found his story rather pedestrian," Pietro says.

I think about Rolando – 30 years old, rather handsome, with a slight build – and the story that he read was about working on his family's farm in Tuscany. It was not a great story, but it was a good start for him.

When I get up for another drink, I see Rolando sitting at a table alone drinking a beer. I walk over to him and say, "Hey, Rolando, why don't you join us?"

Rolando looks up at me. "Oh, I did not want to intrude."

"It is no intrusion; in fact, we were just talking about how happy we were that you read tonight," I say.

"Oh, *grazie, signor*," he says.

"Please call me Bobby," I say. "I'm going to get another round for our table. Do you want another Moretti?"

"That is very kind of you," Rolando says.

I go up to the bar and order the drinks as Rolando walks over to our table. As Paula pours our drinks, she says, "You're bringing me new customers and business. I am grateful, Bobby. And please thank Serge for my tip."

"Of course," I say. "It was well deserved!"

Once back at the table, everyone seems to be getting along well. Rolando turns to Pietro and says, "I was very touched by your story, Pietro. Is it a true one?"

Pietro has shared a story about the trouble in his relationship with Brian, and it is a very moving piece. "Sadly, it is true. It was very therapeutic to write it."

"Oh, I imagine it was," Rolando says.

Anna looks at her watch and says, "It is getting late for me; I'm usually in bed by now."

I get up and say, "I will walk you to the vaporetto stop."

"Oh, don't be silly, Bobby," Anna says.

"No, it's late, and I want to make sure that you get there safely," I say.

"Well, okay, thank you, Bobby." Anna struggles to stand up, puts the strap of her purse over her shoulder, and grabs her cane.

As we walk toward the exit, Anna looks at Lorenzo who smiles at us. "I hope you had a good time," he says.

"It was wonderful," Anna says.

I look at him and say, "I'm just walking her to the vaporetto stop. I'll be back."

*

When I return from helping Anna, Pietro is sitting alone at the table sipping his wine. I ask, "Where did Rolando go?"

"Oh, he was a bore," Pietro says.

"Pete, what did you do?" I ask.

"Nothing," Pietro says and sips his wine. I stare at him, and he looks away from me. "I did absolutely nothing wrong."

I go up to the bar to get another drink, and Paula grabs a glass and fills it with some ice. "Does your mate there always start a row?" she asks.

As she pours the vodka into my glass, I say, "He tends to ruffle feathers. What happened?"

"He and that young lad got into a bit," she says as she puts my drink in front of me. "Lorenzo had to come over and say something to them."

I sip my drink. "Did Rolando leave?"

"Yes, he rushed out of here," Paula says.

I look at Pietro sitting with his crooked halo over his head. "I'll see what happened. Sorry about that, Paula."

"No worries," she says. "These things happen in a pub, but that Pete is an oddball."

"Yeah, you could say that," I say with a smile. I go over to the table and sit down. "Paula tells me that you and Rolando got into an argument."

"Oh, it was no such thing," Pietro says.

"What did you say or do?" I ask.

"Look, he asked me if I liked his story. What was I supposed to do? Lie to him?" Pietro says with wide eyes.

"Pete, have you learned nothing since the debacle with Mireille?" I ask.

He sits back and acts as if he is flabbergasted. "Oh, come on, Robert. Her poem was awful. At least I responded with honesty and was not swayed by a so-called pretty face."

I sip my drink and try to contain my anger. "Pete, we have a group here that is meant to encourage writers. I believe the bylaws state that we are supposed to be supportive and use kindness in responses to work that is shared in the group."

"By-laws?" Pietro asks with a wave of his hand. "I am not sitting there every week listening to drivel."

"What did you say to Rolando?" I ask.

Pietro crosses his legs and sips his wine. "I'd rather not say."

"Pete, I need to know what you said."

"Why, so you can report back to Serge, so that he can admonish me yet again," Pietro says with a slap of his hand on the table.

"No, I need to know how bad it was since I was in charge this evening," I say in a slightly elevated voice.

"Okay, all I said was that the story didn't interest me. I said writing about life on a Tuscan farm is rather boring, and that he should write about something else. That's all I said."

"That's all? Pete, this is so embarrassing," I say. I am at a point that I do not know what do about him and wonder if he is trying to sabotage his membership in the group.

"Listen, I bring a well-crafted story each week," he says tapping the table with his fingers. "It's not my fault if some people don't put in the same effort."

I am angry now, but I am trying to contain it. Through gritted teeth I say, "Serge has said that he wants new blood in the group. Rolando is a young writer, and he should be encouraged and not subjected to your negativity. You're no Kafka, my friend."

Pietro sits up straight and stares at me. "What are you saying?"

"Look, I enjoy your stories, but none of us here are literary greats," I say. "We're all working on our stories and poems and trying to get better."

"How dare you! I had a story published in *TheFLR*!"

"Okay," I say, "how many years ago was that?"

Pietro stands up, grabs his battered binder, and says, "I'm not staying here and listening to your insults." He turns around and storms past Lorenzo and out the door.

I get up and go over to the bar, where I catch Paula laughing as she dries her hands on a towel. "He is quite hysterical," she says.

I nod my head. "He is a character to be sure. He thinks he's a great writer, but his work is just decent. He said he had a story in a magazine that probably isn't published anymore, so I'm not sure if it is true or not," I say. "No one in the group is published except Serge. I believe he has a book of poems out there, but I'm not certain about it."

"Isn't your group just for fun and comradery?" Paula asks.

"It should be," I say. "Pete just takes it all too seriously. Serge dismisses his behavior because he is a Florentine."

"What does that mean?" she asks.

"I have no idea," I say.

"You have a lot of drama in your life, Bobby," she says with a smile. "Imagine blaming Florence?"

"Yeah," I say, "I recall Iago rejecting Michael Cassio for a similar reason."

Paula's face becomes animated. "I see you know *Othello*," she says with a smile.

"Yeah, but we are just acquaintances," I laugh.

She winks at me and says, "You're a clever one!"

Paula goes off to handle some customers at the other end of the bar. I sip my drink and look at myself in the mirror. I could be anywhere right now. The mirror does not betray time and place – it is rather anonymous and yet somehow intimate. As I stare at my reflection, I feel like someone else is looking back at me – someone who can see through my veneer and knows me better than I know myself.

CHAPTER TWENTY-TWO – The Inevitable

After having breakfast, I sit down to do some work and, about an hour later, Mireille calls me. I grab my phone and say, "Hello?"

"*Bonjour*, Bobby; *ça va?*"

I laugh and say, "Who is this?"

"Oh, you are too silly," Mireille says.

"How is work?" I ask.

"It's just the same," she whispers. "Always the same every day!"

"Sorry," I say. "I wish it could be better."

"Oh, it is better now talking to you," she says.

I think about what she is saying and want to cheer her up. "Hey, what about dinner tonight?"

"Oh, that will be wonderful," Mireille says. "It's just sometimes things seem so tedious here. I have so many appointments and a meeting this morning. It feels like a long time until I'll see you for dinner."

"Look, you have an important job there," I say – she is the general manager of a beautiful old four-star hotel close to the Rialto – "so you're going to have those Mondays where it gets difficult."

"Right now, it feels like every day is Monday in this job," she sighs.

"I'm sorry, but how about we go to that nice trattoria with the view of the Rialto where we went to for lunch last week. They had that great risotto and salmon dish that we liked," I say.

"Oh, yes," she says, "that's where I had that perfect Bellini."

"Yes, that's the place," I say as I glance out the window. "It's a beautiful day. It should be a lovely evening."

"Okay," Mireille says, "that sounds good. I must go to my meeting now."

"Goodbye, Mireille," I say, "I'll see you later."

I try to get back to my work, but I cannot stop thinking about Mireille, and that lovely day outside my window is beckoning me. I put on my Mets cap, jacket, cargo pants, and sunglasses. I slip my feet into my sneakers and head out the door. When I go outside, I feel a refreshingly cool breeze, wave to Marco who is smoking outside his store, and head up the street toward the Grand Canal.

Making my way around the maze of streets and alleys, I enjoy seeing familiar places and things I have never seen before, until I find a mask shop with a large grim reaper statue outside its door – wearing a black robe, eerie skeletal mask, and holding a large scythe in its bony fingers. I stop for a moment, and it seems to be staring directly at me with its glowing red eyes, making me feel uncomfortable.

I rush away from the shop and end up at the Rialto, where the market is teeming with tourists pouring down the steps from the bridge in the bright sunshine. It is late September, and I am wondering when does this tourist thing ever let up?

Feeling like a delicious apple from Tinno's cart, I find him smoking a cigarette and talking to an older woman. He sees me, and a smile lights up his sunburnt face. "Bobby! *Buongiorno*! Good to see you."

"*Buongiorno*, Tinno," I say.

He turns to the woman and says, "This is my sister Rosa." As he looks back at me, he says, "Rosa, this is my best customer."

"Oh, I wouldn't say that," I chuckle.

Rosa holds my arm and says, "My husband died last month, so I've come to stay with Tinno and cook for him and care for him."

"She was caring for her husband until he died," Tinno says.

"I'm sorry for your loss," I say to Rosa.

"He was old, sick, and it was his time to die," she says. "I was all alone, but Tinno needed me."

Tinno shakes his head. "I was getting by."

Rosa pinches his cheek. "I have to care for my little brother."

"I'm glad neither one of you is alone now," I say.

"It is terrible to die alone, especially in Venice," Tinno says.

Rosa nods her head. "Dying anywhere is not good, but to die alone here where the canals keep flowing, with the gondolas passing by, and the tourists keep coming, you may be just forgotten."

"Yes," Tinno says, "and maybe they find your body a year later and dump you in the canal and take your things."

"Oh," I say being a little surprised by this, "I can't believe that."

"Do you live alone?" Rosa asks me.

"Uh, yeah, I do," I say, suddenly feeling uncomfortable.

She leans forward and whispers, "Don't die here alone."

I feel my head spinning and just walk away from them as Rosa's words echo in my mind. I had not thought that if I lived here long enough, I would die alone someday. I believe they are two old people who are exaggerating, but they have unsettled me. When I stop walking, I am standing in front of St. Mary's Basilica. I lean against a wall, catch my breath, and think about last night.

Mireille and I were watching Stranger Things *while sitting on my couch, and I had my arm around her shoulder. When the episode ended, she took the remote and hit STOP on it. She turned to me, put her hand on my cheek, leaned forward, and started kissing me.*

We kissed softly, as if our lips were exploring a new frontier. We had kissed before, but this tentative and then more aggressive interaction felt different. With another woman, after this had gone on for ten minutes, I probably would have started becoming a little more passionate. However, Mireille revealed that she was a virgin, so I wanted to be very careful about not going too fast with her. I thought, what was the rush? We have all the time in the world.

Mireille stopped kissing me and put her head on my chest. She whispered, "I know you're being careful with me and kind."

I caressed the back of her head. "I enjoy being with you, Mireille. There is no time span to any of this."

She lifted her head and looked up at me. "I was raised by the nuns and almost became a nun. I may dress like other women my age, but I am in some ways a regular

clothes nun in my heart and mind."

    I touched her cheek. "It is okay." I was being more

honest with her than I had been with any other woman. "We

will just take things slowly. There is nothing to worry about."

    "But you were a married man – used to

having his needs met," she says, placing her head on

my shoulder.

    Once again, I caressed her hair. "I told you about

how I messed up my marriage," I said. "I was a fool. I don't

want to make any mistakes like that again."

    "Please just hold me," she said.

    I wrapped my arms around her, and she put her head

on my chest. "Isn't this nice?" I asked. "I could sit this way

all night." Amazingly, I meant every word that I said.

    Looking up at the lovely Gothic church glistening in

the sunshine, I wonder why I have read that some critics call

its exterior plain or drab. It also has a distinctive bell tower at the rear on its left side. I have gotten my awareness and senses back. Tinno and his sister "threw me for a loop" as my father used to say when something rattled him.

I turn around and start walking back toward my building. I want to get some work done and then get ready for dinner with Mireille. I am hoping to take her mind off work and the troubles of her day.

*

It is a lovely early evening as the sky turns orange-red beyond the Rialto as the sun slips out of the sky, and the lights over the now closed umbrellas illuminate above the sidewalk tables. Gondolas with passengers in them drift by in the canal beyond the low wall next to our table. Mireille glances at a young couple holding hands as a stoic gondolier pushes them toward the Rialto.

"They look so in love," Mireille says and sips her Bellini through a straw.

"Yes," they do, "I say."

She finishes her drink and pokes at her risotto with her fork. "How do you know when you are in love, Bobby?"

I stare at Mireille, her face glowing in the light from the candles flickering on our table. I am awed by the innocence of this question because – even at 38 plus years old – I do not have the definitive answer for this, so I say, "I think it is a feeling that you want to be with the other person as much as possible."

Mireille nods her head, takes a forkful of risotto, and eats it. I can see she is processing what I have just said. "So, then, when you are not with this person, does it cause you discomfort?"

I sit back and touch my wine glass as I contemplate my answer. "Uh, I think, yes, you do feel anxiety or longing for the person when you're not with them. That is a normal feeling I believe when you care for someone."

She sips her wine and smiles. "It is just that I used to love my job. I didn't mind the customers and the meetings, but now I am distracted all the time. I keep thinking of moments like this, and wish I didn't have to be at work and could instead be with you."

I chew a mouthful of risotto and nod my head. "I felt the same way today. I had to take a walk and clear my mind because I didn't want to do any work after your phone call."

"So," Mireille leans toward me, "are we in love?"

I want to be careful now and take a deep breath and say, "I would say we are at the kindling stage."

She looks a little confused. "*Kindling stage?*"

I laugh. "I'm sorry – *kindling* is used to start a fire."

"Ah, so we are at the beginning stage of love. Yes?"

I nod my head. "Yes, I believe so."

"How many times have you been in love?" she asks.

I do not have to think very hard about this. "Twice! Once with my high school girlfriend Bonnie – but I'm not sure if that was real love or just infatuation."

Mireille laughs and sips her wine. "What about the second time?"

"With my wife," I say as I cut a piece of salmon and then eat it.

Mirelle stares at me. "Do you still love her?"

I take a sip of wine. "It's been almost a year now. I think I still care about her, but the love part is no longer with me."

"And now, I will be number three, if this *kindling* stage moves ahead for us. Is this correct?" she asks.

I put down my knife and fork and reach over and hold her hand. "Yes, I think that is correct."

We finish our meal and, after our plates are taken away, we sit drinking our wine. "You know, Bobby, I stopped the lacemaking. It is too tedious for me."

"Really?" I am surprised by this.

"I have been trying to write again," she says with a smile. "It feels easier to me now."

I know this a touchy subject with her, but I want to be supportive. "Oh, great, what made this happen?

Mirelle giggles. "You did?"

"*Moi*?" I ask and sip my wine.

"Yes, you have made such an impact on my life that I felt inspired to write something about you."

I sit back and take a deep breath. "Wow! Now I'm an inspiration for your creativity!"

"So far, it is only two pages," Mireille says, "but I'm happy to be writing again."

"Will I ever get to see it?"

"Maybe someday," she says with a little smirk, "when I think it is ready."

Suddenly, there is a commotion in the street behind us. There is yelling and then the rushing of a person coming quickly in between the tables where we are sitting. I turn around and see Elena – dressed in black jeans, combat boots, and a long sweater with a black patch over her left eye. She pulls away from a waiter and runs up to our table. I look over Elena's shoulder and see Nino standing there with his arms folded and his beady eyes watching us.

Mireille is staring at Elena with a horrified expression because her hair – now turning back to her natural brown color – is a mess, and she is catching her breath. Mireille looks at me hoping for answers.

"Has he had sex with you yet?" Elena asks a shocked Mirelle. Elena turns to me and snarls, "He likes to come for sex once a week! Right, Bobby?"

I am more than speechless – I just stare at her and do not know what to say except, "Please, stop this."

Elena digs into her pants pocket, pulls something out, and slams it on the table. "You forgot this in my flat. You took it off when we took a shower together."

"Bobby?" Mireille asks, her lips quivering.

I notice that the left side of Elena's face is damaged, though mostly covered by her hair. Elena is staring at me, and then Nino pushes a waiter with a towel over his arm out of his way, grabs Elena's hand, and screams, "*Andiamo!*" He drags her away as she keeps looking back and staring at me with one solemn eye.

"How do you know this person?" Mireille asks with tears running down her cheeks.

"I…I met her in a bar," I say, which certainly has truth to it, "but before I knew you."

Mireille is shaken as she picks up the ring. "I remember you wearing this. This…this *is* your ring."

"Mireille, I can explain," I say.

"You told me that you take it off when you take a shower," Mireille says. "And you were wearing this after I met you – so that means you showered with her after you and I were seeing each other."

"It happened when you were in Paris," I say. "At the time, I didn't think that I would ever see you again."

"That person – *that kind of person* – how could you be with that kind of person?"

"I…I was lonely and…"

She gets up and throws the ring at me, hitting me on my forehead. "I never want to see you again!" Mireille grabs her purse and walks quickly away from the table. Everyone at the other tables is staring at me.

I bend down, pick up the ring, and my hands are shaking. The waiter with a towel over his arm stands by the doorway looking at me. I reach into my pocket, take out 200 euros, and I hand it to him. "I'm sorry for what happened."

I get up and start walking like a man with paper legs. I finally get into step as I am moving quickly like I had someplace to go. My mind is racing, and my heart is pounding. Did Nino make Elena do this? Why were they fighting before she ran up to the table? I do not know what I am thinking, but it feels like the world has just ended for me. My life as I know it is nothing now.

*

Walking into the taverna, I see Lorenzo and wave to him. It is fairly crowded for a Monday evening. Music is playing, and Gina walks past me with drinks on a tray and says, "Hi, Bobby."

I nod my head and stagger to the bar. Paula is at the other end handing drinks to a young couple who look so happy. I do not know what happy is anymore. I am lost and will never be found. How could I have been so stupid? How could I think that I could just do whatever I wanted and not be caught in my lies?

Paula leans on the bar in front of me and asks, "What happened to your forehead?"

I touch the spot where the ring hit me, and it feels sore. "I got hit with my wedding band."

"Oh, you've found it!"

"Yeah, lucky me."

"You look like a boy who just lost his little puppy."

"It's much worse than that," I whisper.

"Reckon you could use a drink," she says.

"Smirnoff Red on the rocks, and keep them coming," I say.

I watch Paula pouring my drink, and I wonder how cruel the world can be to take me from a moment where new love was starting to the dregs of hopelessness in less than five minutes.

She places the drink in front of me and asks, "Does it involve one of the two women in your life?

I sip my drink and say, "I have three women in my life," and wink at her. I take a piece of ice from my drink and apply it to my forehead.

"Yeah, but I'm your bartender," Paula says with a big smile as she hands me a few napkins. "What's wrong, Romeo? Did Juliet not come out onto the balcony?"

"It actually involves both women in my life," I say. "Elena crashed my dinner with Mireille tonight."

I have seen Paula's face remain stoic in many situations, but she seems genuinely shocked this time. She holds her hand over her heart and asks, "Elena is, okay?"

"No," I say as I slurp my drink, "Elena is definitely not okay. She looks like a mess, has a patch over her damaged eye, and she was with Nino."

"Hmm. Lorenzo threw him out of here the other night," Paula says. "He said that he was looking for you, but I told Lorenzo you were no friend of that pig."

I sip my drink and say, "This has been all part of a plan. I think Nino was scouting out my flat a while back. Then he was coming here to look for me." I finish my drink and hold up my glass as I dry my forehead with the napkins.

Paula snatches my glass, dumps out the old ice, and puts fresh ice into it. She pours the vodka and hands the glass to me. "I thought you said Nino took Elena away?"

"That's what her friend Carla told me," I say. I sip my drink and my hands are shaking. I use my left hand to guide my right hand to put the glass down on the bar.

"Bobby," Paula says, "are you okay?"

I lean my elbow on the bar and my head on my hand. "I just lost the most lovely, delicate person I have ever known. I have lost her, and now I will die alone in that flat, and they will dump my body in a canal and take my things."

"What?" asks Paula.

I shake my head and say, "I'm just repeating a story an old man told me today."

"Bobby," Paula says as she puts a hand on my arm, "you have to calm down. Try to take deep breaths." She walks away to handle the waiters' drink orders at the other end of the bar.

I hold the bar rail with both hands and take several deep breaths. I am feeling better, although I still feel my heart racing. The song "I Want to Know What Love Is" by Foreigner starts playing, and I shiver as I remember sitting on a swing at recess listening to this song on my Walkman and staring at beautiful blonde Bonnie who was talking with her friends. We were in seventh grade then, but I waited until freshman year in high school to get enough courage to ask her to go out with me. All these years later, and I realize that I still do not have a clue about what love is.

I think of my pathetic attempt to explain what being in love is like to Mireille, and how Elena appeared like a specter from out of nowhere to slap my wedding ring down on the table in front of Mireille to remind me that I am a miserable failure in trying to love Bonnie, Beth, and now Mireille. I wait until the song is finished, gulp the rest of my drink, and stagger out of the bar like a straw man whose legs are moving out of control.

*

I stumble up the 62 steps to my flat, unlock the door, and stagger into the room, shutting and locking the door behind me. I turn on the lights, grab a beer from the fridge, and fall onto a chair in front of the TV. I turn it on and the lovely blonde woman is doing the weather report again.

Sipping my beer, I look at my phone – no message from Mireille – and I look at my wedding band on my hand. I drop the phone and start to cry – I have not cried since my mother died – not even when Beth left me. I am feeling so much sorrow that it is overwhelming, and all this sobbing takes a good deal of energy out of me.

After I stop crying, I sip my beer and stare vacantly at the TV. I glance over at the couch, where only the night before Mireille and I sat hugging and kissing. My life is like a doomed rollercoaster – from the highs of last night to going off the rails tonight. I do not think I have ever been at a lower point than this.

I get up, take my vodka bottle from the freezer, and pour myself a drink. I go over to the window and alternately sip the vodka and the beer as I sit staring at San Marco's illuminated bell tower.

This city of romance is dead to me now, and all the possibilities I thought about for Mireille and me are ghastly illusions. There is no looking forward to tomorrow, no hope for marriage and children and a normal life. I will be awaiting nothing but emptiness and sorrow now.

I only have myself to blame. I cannot make excuses for myself anymore. I kept thinking that I could take any actions – like having sex with Elena while I was seeing Mireille – and justify them because I had needs that had to be met no matter what.

Now I am alone again, and I remember what Tinno and his sister said to me. I must prepare myself to exist in this city – now my mausoleum – for the rest of my life until I die alone in this flat with walls that are as bare as my heart.

CHAPTER TWENTY-THREE – Aftermath

I wake up on my couch, swinging my arm that had fallen asleep out from under my body and knocking over a beer can on the corner of the table. I watch the little beer left in it run across my tile floor. For whatever reason, the TV is still on, and Barney the Dinosaur is on the screen dancing around with little kids and singing in Italian. For a moment, I figure this is my own circle of hell.

My phone is ringing somewhere, and I feel around for it until I realize it is in my cargo pants pocket. I pull it out and see Serge's face on the screen. While I know he means well, I am still not answering my phone. It has been three weeks since the incident with Elena, and I have only ventured out to my local market to get beer, booze, and food.

Pushing myself up from the couch, I stagger into the bathroom to relieve myself. Afterwards, I splash my face with cold water, stand up, and see myself in the mirror. I have three weeks' worth of beard on my face, my hair is a scraggy mess, and my eyes are watery red pools. No wonder I do not want to see anyone.

I manage to find Nonna's Moka pot and start the coffee. I glance in my fridge to see I have two eggs left, one old croissant, and a little butter. I guess I will be visiting Marco's store today.

After frying the eggs, warming the croissant, and making coffee, I sit at my table and eat. Glancing at my phone, I have 72 text messages – none of them from Mireille. I suppose hoping for one is beyond foolish, but we had just reached such a sweet place in our relationship, and to have it snatched away from us like that is beyond unbearable.

In the beginning, I tried to text and call Mireille, but she apparently changed her number. I know where she works, and a few times I walked past the hotel and contemplated going inside, but I figured that would not be fair to her – she has enough stress there. I do not know where she lives, so there is no opportunity for me to try to visit her. Once I realized she had cut me off cold, I went into hermit mode.

As I eat my eggs and sip my coffee, I scroll through the text messages. Pietro has sent me 39 of the 72; 14 are from Serge, and the rest are from Paula. They are reaching out to me and are worried about me, but I am sick of their questions. Why am I am missing the writers' meetings? What am I doing to myself? Why am I not coming to the taverna? They are also 51 voicemails – again from Pietro, Serge, and Paula. It is nice to know these people care about me, but I just cannot deal with any of them right now.

I put the dishes in the sink, finish my coffee, and decide to get ready to go to the store. Also, it is about time to take my overflowing garbage downstairs and across the street to put in the appropriate bins. Somehow or other, I must try to get back to the living again; I just do not think that I am ready yet.

As I am getting dressed, someone is ringing my doorbell. This has happened several times over the last three weeks. At first, I believed it was people visiting someone else and trying all the buttons just to see if anyone buzzed them in, but then I got to thinking it was Pietro because I foolishly gave him my address when he wanted to drop off a copy of *TheFLR*, the magazine with his story in it. At that time, he left the magazine in my mailbox in the downstairs outer hallway, but now I think he is coming to check on me.

Waiting a long time after the bell was rung, I shove my shopping bags into my jacket pockets and carry two big garbage bags down the stairs. When dealing with the 62 steps, I try to make as few trips as possible when carrying things.

I go across the street to the big garbage bins. There are four of them for different kinds of trash. There is always some trash that belongs in a different bin shoved into the wrong one. That is not my concern as I make certain to put my trash into the correct bins.

Going down the block, I look over my shoulder to see if anyone is following me. I believe stalking is something that Pietro would be quite adept at doing. I reach Marco's store, and he grunts to acknowledge my presence as he smokes and reads his newspaper.

I open my bags and take five pre-prepared meals, a few bags of various chips, 12 cans of cold beer, a six pack of brown eggs, and two bottles of Smirnoff Red. I will get my croissants from the baker later. As he scans my items, Marco glances up and then looks me over from head to toe.

"What?" I ask.

"Are you okay, Bobby?" he asks.

Oh, Marco, I did not know that you cared. I nod my head and say, "Yeah, I'm okay."

I trudge back down the block and, as I get to my building, I see Pietro with his arms folded standing there in a long coat and leaning against my front door. "Well, well, well," Pietro says, "no wonder you don't want to be seen."

"I don't have time for this, Pete," I say as I take out my keys and open the front door.

"It looks like you have nothing but time, Robert," he says as he holds the door so that I can pass through with my groceries.

"Pete, I don't want to talk about anything," I yell as I start pounding my way up the stairs.

Pietro is following me and says, "Serge and I have been very concerned about you. We didn't know if you were dead in the street somewhere."

I finally reach my flat door, and Pietro is out of breath from the climb up. I unlock my door and turn to Pietro, "Get out of here, Pete?"

Pietro stares at me and asks, "What are you going to do? Punch me?"

I push my way into the flat with him following me, and Pietro closes the door after he is inside. I put my bags on the kitchen counter and shake my head. "I'm not going to punch you." I start taking things out of my bags and putting them away.

"You look terrible, Robert," he says as he takes off his coat and hangs it on the rack near the door.

"Oh, you're making yourself at home I see," I say.

"We have to talk," Pietro says.

I shake my head as I shove the beer cans into the fridge and then put my vodka bottles into the freezer. "No, we don't have to talk."

"Look at you," he says with a dramatic outstretching of his arms. "You're a mess!"

I put the last of my things away, take off my jacket, and throw my sunglasses and Mets cap onto the hall table. "Yeah, I'm a mess. Why does Serge care? And why do you for that matter?"

"Because, you are our friend," Pietro says. He looks around the room and says, "I find it interesting that you have nothing hanging on your walls. You have done nothing to make this place yours. I think that says something. What are you doing to yourself?"

I flop into a chair across from Pietro and say, "Look, I'm just handling things in my own way. And as for my walls, I like them this way!"

His face becomes very animated, and he motions to me with both hands. "But this is not handling anything. You look like a mountain man or hermit!"

I shake my head, lean it back against the chair, and stare at the ceiling. "Please let me just do this my way."

"Serge and I think it would be good for you to come back to the group," Pietro says. "At least you can get out and socialize."

I lean forward in the chair and stare at him. "I cannot bring myself to write two sentences much less write anything that would be acceptable to read."

"Remember our young friend Rolando who just sat there and never read? And what about your friends the Three Germans?"

"My friends?" I ask shaking my head. "Yeah, sure."

"Rolando has been bringing something to read each week now," Pietro says. "But he sat there for weeks and just listened. You could certainly do the same."

"I'm not good company for anyone – even myself!"

Pietro folds his hands and sits forward to study me more closely. "Paula told me about what happened. She is worried about you too."

"Please tell everyone that there is nothing to worry about. I am fine!" I take a deep breath and exhale loudly. "I just want to be alone and suffer in silence."

Pietro sits back in the chair and shakes his head. "I'm sorry, Robert, but the way you look is anything but fine. I know you're hurting because of losing Mireille, but you can't keep doing this to yourself."

"It was all going so well with Mireille and me," I say. "We were slowly falling in love. I was trying not to rush things, to let everything happen naturally."

"But meanwhile, you were screwing the prostitute on the side," Pietro says with a little smirk.

"No, that is not true," I say as I stand up and walk to the window where I can see San Marco's bell tower under a clear blue sky. "It was when Mireille went away for a month, and I didn't know where she was, that I saw Elena again."

"You were horny and why not?" Pietro says. "If you could have just waited for Mireille, but you had to get your comfort visit in to satisfy your urges!"

I keep looking out the window like I did when I saw Beth leave me and get into a taxi to never be seen again. "It's not like that, Pete. Not like that at all."

Pietro gets up and walks over to me. "Hey, what a view. I guess that's why you don't mind all those steps."

I turn to him and say, "I did go to Elena because I had a need, but as soon as Mireille came back, I stopped seeing Elena."

"But Elena didn't forget about you," Pietro says. "She saw you with this beautiful girl and felt jealous. She had your ring, and that was your undoing."

I turn to look out the window again. "The last time I saw Elena, we took a shower together. Unfortunately, I always take off my wedding ring when I take a shower, but this time I forgot to put it back on."

"And she used it when she came to your table to show Mireille that she had showered with you!" Pete slaps his hands together. "Boy, you put the nail in your own coffin!"

"Yes, I have myself to blame," I whisper, "but you have to remember that her pimp beat the crap out of her in between," I say. "I believe Nino put her up to this."

"Well, there is nothing you can do about that," Pietro says.

I turn away from the window and walk toward the kitchen. "It doesn't matter anymore. I lost that gentle person, and I'm done. Just done."

"What does that mean, Robert?" he asks.

"The whole charade – trying to do things the right way and being the way people want me to be," I say, being very honest and surprising myself. "It is over for me."

"Maybe if you give yourself some time?"

I shake my head. "There is no more time, Pete. None! Now, will you please get the hell out of here!"

Pietro turns, picks up his coat, and puts it on. "We are always a text or a phone call away, Robert. Please remember that."

I say nothing as he goes out and quietly shuts the door behind him. I take a beer from the fridge, go over to the window, and sit on the chair. A pigeon flies by my window and sets down on the railing of a balcony in the house across the street. Even that bird is freer than I am. I am hopelessly trapped now by my actions.

Since I came to Venice, I was trying to live my life free from everything I left behind in New York. The problem is that the past does not go away – my actions follow me like clinging spirits that cannot be exorcised. I am destined to be forever haunted by what was and what might have been – not a very pleasant place to be. I am not sure how long I can go on like this because I feel dead inside right now.

CHAPTER TWENTY-FOUR – *Sotto Voce*

I am in and out of sleep in the early morning hours, as dawn starts inching its gray tendrils around the edges of my window shades. Between asleep and awake, I alternately have dreams about Elena and Mireille. I am not sure what they are about, but they are disturbing nonetheless, and then I hear a ping on my phone, forcing me to sit up and be awake.

Before I look at the phone, I realize it has been another week since Pietro came to visit me and tried to force me into the land of the living. I have been a hermit for a month now, and I am not sure if I like it or not. I just do not think I am ready for interactions with other people yet.

I pick up the phone and look at my texts. "Anna is dead!" reads the text message from Pietro. At first, I think this is a clever ploy, something an obnoxious Pietro has dreamt up to pry me out of my hibernation.

I wipe the sleep from my eyes, fall back onto my pillow, and figure I will play his game for now. I write back, "What happened?"

"Oh, it's alive!" Pietro writes back.

"Okay, not funny, Pete; tell me about Anna." Suddenly my phone is ringing, so Pietro has broken my code of silence with no respect for it. I have told him that I am only willing to accept texts, but now he is calling me. Such sacrilege! I answer only because I want to know if something has really happened to Anna and ask, "What happened?"

"Her granddaughter called Serge," Pietro says. "The poor thing died in her sleep last night."

"Oh, well, that is sad to hear," I say.

"Details are to follow," Pietro says.

"Details?" What is Pete talking about?

"Arabella, Anna's granddaughter, told Serge that she would like to talk to him about the arrangements."

"Oh, well, I will send flowers or something," I say without thinking.

"Wow!" Pietro gushes.

"*Wow*? What does that mean?"

"Anna dies, and you show no sorrow," Pietro says.

"Oh, give me a break, Pete."

"Arabella called Serge for a reason – the group was a very important part of her life," Pietro says.

I liked Anna very much, which was why I was protective of her. I miss my own grandmothers, so I guess she was a substitute in a way. "Oh, I'm sorry, Pete. I did like her and care about her."

"I'm just telling you in advance," he says.

"What do you mean?"

"Well, you cannot show up looking like that! We are meeting with Serge and her later today. Apparently, Serge wants us there for support because Arabella mentioned you and me, and she wants us to be there. I'll text when I know the time!" Pietro says and hangs up.

I stare at the phone and then toss it aside. No matter how depressed I am, I cannot ignore Anna's loss. There is some sort of cosmic intervention at work here – only Anna's death would shake me up and snap me out of my funk.

Getting up and going to the bathroom, I relieve myself and then stare at my reflection in the mirror. I would scare myself if I saw me coming down the street. I grab a pair of scissors and get to work on my shaggy hair.

*

With my hair cut, face shaved, and my body showered, I get dressed to face the world of the living, I make my way to Serge's home to meet with Arabella. Pietro was very vague on the phone about what we are meeting about, but he said something about the arrangements and other matters for the funeral.

As I walk into Serge's rear street entrance, I see Serge's majordomo Whitman standing in the foyer. Whitman is tall, thin, and has a head of wavy gray hair and piercing blue eyes. "Good afternoon, Signor Valenti."

"Hello, Whitman," I say.

"Please follow me, sir," he says. I am promptly escorted down a long hallway that I have never entered before. Whitman opens a dark wooden door, and I walk into a magnificent library with crystal chandeliers, walls lined with seemingly ancient texts in bookshelves, and large old Queen Anne style furniture. Serge is sitting at a desk with a laptop and papers on it under the glow of a banker's lamp.

He rises from his chair and shakes my hand vigorously. "Based on Pietro's description, I was expecting something like a mountain man coming through those doors, but you look like a proper gentleman this afternoon."

I laugh. "No, I can clean up pretty quickly when I have to do so."

"Arabella is coming here soon to discuss matters of her grandmother's funeral," Serge says as he sticks an unlit pipe in his mouth.

"What about the rest of her big family?" I ask.

"I have no idea," Serge says as he walks over to a portable bar. "Can I get you anything?"

It is a little early in the day for me, so I say, "No, I'm fine."

Serge fills a snifter with a dark liquid and swirls it around. "100-year-old brandy from my grandfather's vineyard on the mainland. It has such great legs."

We sit down just as Pietro is shown into the room. He is dressed like a Wall Street banker as he is coming straight from his office in the museum. He rushes in sniffing the air and moving those whiskers. He looks down at me in the chair and says, "Well, it is good to see you in your human form again, Robert."

"Thanks, Pete, nice seeing you in your work attire," I say, thinking maybe I will have that drink now.

Serge motions to another chair for Pietro, who sits down and looks at us and says, "Well, what are we expecting here?"

"It seems," Serge says rather seriously, "that Arabella needs our help in planning the funeral."

"But Anna wrote about her big family and many grandchildren; where are they now when she needs them?" Pietro asks.

"I have no idea," Serge says.

I am thinking about what is going on and say out loud, "I wonder if Anna's depiction of family in her stories is a bit too idyllic when you think about it."

Pietro rubs his chin and says, "That is very interesting, but her stories seemed so realistic and happy, like they were the stuff from her life."

Serge sips his drink and says, "Mere speculation on our part."

Suddenly the library doors open, and in walks this lovely young version of Anna. She has her grandmother's face, with bouncing long blonde hair and bright blue eyes that sparkle with youthful energy. Like Anna, she is quite short – probably five feet tall at best. She is dressed in black and walks toward us with a confidence that is impressive.

Serge takes Arabella by both hands and kisses her on both cheeks. "Welcome, I am Serge, and this is Pietro and Bobby."

Arabella beams a big smile as she looks at Pietro and then at me. "It is a pleasure to meet you all – Nonna's good friends who she thought of as family! I know about all of you from the stories that she told."

"It is wonderful to meet you despite the unfortunate circumstances," Pietro says, grabbing her hands and kissing her on both cheeks.

I extend my hand, and she shakes it. "Forgive me, I'm an American."

"Oh, Bobby, it's okay," she says. "Nonna always talked about you. She was very fond of you."

I feel happy to hear this and say, "I am honored to have known her."

Serge motions towards a chair. "Please sit down, Arabella."

"Thank you," she says as she takes a seat.

We all sit down, and Serge asks, "Can I get you anything?"

"Coffee – American coffee – would be nice," she says.

Serge lifts the phone on his desk and requests coffee to be brought into the room. He then turns to Arabella, leans his elbows on his desk, and asks, "So, how can I help you?"

Arabella takes a deep breath and says, "I would like you to help me plan the funeral for my Nonna."

Serge looks at Pietro and me and then says, "We are happy to help, but what about your large, wonderful family?"

Arabella laughs and says, "Nonna and I were the only ones left of my family. Nonna was 94 and outlived everyone, even my mother."

Pietro leans forward and says, "But she wrote so lovingly about all her grandchildren and her time with them."

A butler I have not seen before enters the room with a silver coffee pot on a silver tray with white cups, saucers, sugar bowl, and milk pitcher. We all watch him quickly prepare the coffee and hand the cup and saucer to Arabella.

"Would anyone else like coffee?" Serge asks. Pietro and I decline, the butler leaves, and Serge turns to Arabella and says, "Please, let us know what happened?"

Arabella holds the saucer, lifts the cup, and takes a sip of coffee. "Nonna died in her sleep in hospital last night. I took her there two days before because she was having trouble breathing. I had visited her yesterday after work, and she was on oxygen but seemed to be doing well. I was shocked when they called and told me that she had passed away in her sleep."

"Oh, at least she died peacefully," Pietro says.

"Yes, she did," Arabella says with a little smile.

"So, Arabella, how can we help you plan the funeral?" Serge asks.

"Gentlemen, first let me say that my Nonna was a very good writer. Unfortunately, all these wonderful stories are fiction. She made them all up.

She had one child that was a surprise at 45 – my mother –

and only one grandchild – me!"

We all look at each other with shocked expressions. I

say, "Your grandmother had us all believing these were true

stories."

"No, they are fiction. Perhaps, she had hoped for a big

family. There are other stories that she never shared with

you," Arabella says. "They are all about your group – that is

why I feel like I know all of you."

Pietro glances at me and says, "I would like to have a

chance to read these stories."

"Yes," I say, "so would I."

"Of course, I will arrange that," says Arabella. "Now,

as to the funeral – I have no ability to give Nonna the

services she deserves. I work in a bank, and while it is a good

job, I have no savings, and Nonna had a small pension from

my Nonno. So, I am not sure what to do."

Serge sips his cognac. "So, are you saying that we are the only ones who will be there for you during this time?"

"Yes, I have no other family," she says.

Serge looks at us and says, "Well, we will happily assist you. We can have the visitation here in my home, and did your grandmother have a church she attended?"

"Nonna always went to Sunday Mass at St. Mary's Basilica until this week," Arabella says.

"I know the pastor," Serge says, "I will handle scheduling the funeral Mass. What about a cemetery, my dear?"

"There is a place for her to be buried with my Nonno in a cemetery on the mainland," she says. She puts down her coffee cup, reaches into her purse, and pulls out some papers. "I have the documents you will need."

"Very good," Serge says. "Is there anything else that you would like to add?"

"'*Sotto Voce*,'" Arabella says.

"Her poem?" Pietro asks.

"Yes," Arabella says, "Nonna wrote that poem for her mother, but I would like it read for Nonna because she always spoke in a soft voice, and all the love I know in my life was because of her."

Serge stands up and says, "I will be honored to read that poem for her at the service."

*

Serge, Pietro, and I stand on the dock with Arabella as we watch the men load Anna's dark brown coffin onto the blue and white funeral boat. Flowers from the church adorn the coffin that shines brightly in the sunshine. The priest says a final prayer and makes the sign of the cross.

Arabella starts to cry and buries her head on Serge's shoulder. He pats the back of her head and looks stoically at the boat as the engine starts. One of the men unhooks the rope from the dock, and the boat starts making its way through the glittering canal water.

I glance at Pietro and ask, "What happens now?"

"They will take the coffin to the parking island, where it will be transferred into a van and driven to the cemetery on the mainland." Pietro stares at the funeral boat as it slowly fades in the distance, and I notice a tear on his cheek. He whispers, "I loved that old woman."

*

After the solemn final moments on the dock, Serge invites the whole group back to his home for a lavish luncheon that features every delicacy with wine and drink flowing. We are once again in the ballroom where the writing meetings take place, and an enormous portrait of Anna is on an easel next to the buffet table.

I am standing on line for the buffet behind the Three Germans. I must wait as they take a long time to load up their plates. Pietro is behind me and says with a smirk, "They big men – they need much food!"

I put some shrimp and pasta on my plate, and take a glass of wine and sit at a table with Rolando and Pietro. I glance at Anna's huge portrait in the front of the room and say, "I think she is here with us today."

"I didn't know her long," Rolando says, "but she was very kind to me."

"I am glad she is at peace," Pietro says. "But I will miss her."

"I too will miss her," I say. "She managed to touch each of us in a special way."

Pietro motions to the front of the room where Serge and Arabella are sitting and eating at a table near Anna's portrait. "I think Serge is taking her under his wing."

I look at them as they are talking and eating and say, "Well, he was very moved to learn Arabella has no other family."

"I hope the countess won't be jealous," Pietro chuckles.

Even in this moment he cannot miss taking a swipe at someone. "Come on, Pete. This is not the time and place."

"What are you guys talking about? Rolando asks.

"Pete is just being Pete," I say.

"Uh, okay!" says Rolando as he looks puzzled, but he sips his wine and pops a meatball into his mouth.

Suddenly, there is the sound of "Twinkle, Twinkle, Little Star" being played not very well on a piano. I look up and see Arabella sitting at the grand piano in the corner. Serge stands behind her and glances at her approvingly like a proud parent.

Pietro puts a hand to his cheek and gushes, "He said something about adopting her earlier today."

"How old is she?" I ask.

"20, I believe," Pietro says.

Arabella finishes playing, stands up, and says loudly, "This was Nonna's favorite song. I would play it for her every night before she went to bed."

"Perhaps we now know what killed her," Pietro says.

Rolando laughs, but I look at him, and he stops. "You can never refrain from saying these hurtful things, Pete."

He sips his wine and smiles. "That is my forte!"

"Yeah, we know," I say.

Rolando takes a sip of wine and asks, "Are you doing okay, Bobby? You haven't been to a meeting in a long time."

I glance at Pietro and then look at him. "I've been going through some issues, and I had to deal with them."

Pietro snickers. "He had a bad breakup with Mireille, and he was locking himself up inside his flat."

"I don't think it's funny, Pete," I say and then chew my food.

"Oh, I didn't mean to disparage you in any way," Pietro says. "I'm just noting that it is sort of a teenage way to solve your problem."

Rolando is shocked. "Pietro? What are you saying?"

"Well, isn't it like a teenager to wallow in their problems and sulk alone in their room?" Pietro asks.

"Okay, Pete, we get it," I say.

"I hope you do," Pietro says. "I'm just saying to be an adult about it. You keep calm and carry on."

"That's so British of you, Pete," I say.

"Quite," he snickers.

Arabella walks over to our table and says, "Thank you for being here." She hands us each a flash drive. "These have all Nonna's stories about the group. I hope you enjoy them."

We all look at one another and Pietro says, "Why, thank you, Arabella. How thoughtful."

*

Later that day, I walk along the streets with my tie loosened and my coat over my arm because it is a warm October afternoon. On my way back to my flat, I stand looking out over the Grand Canal and wonder about Anna's husband. He was lovingly depicted in her stories, and now they are together in eternity.

I envy them but not in a negative way – I wish I could have had a love like that. I thought I did have a special love when Beth and I got married, but lost sight of our union by getting jealous of her opportunities to advance in the company when I was stagnating. Instead of learning from her, I allowed my weaknesses to get the best of me.

I then had a second chance with Mireille, and perhaps that would have been an even more lasting love story. We had a unique connection, but once again my weaknesses – going to see Elena even when I was getting to know Mireille – was my undoing.

When I think of it, how stupid and arrogant I was. How did I think I could have my panino and eat it too? I wish I could go back in time, slap myself in the face, and say, "What the hell are you doing?" Alas, I cannot, and I have suffered the consequences.

Now, as I stare at the water near the Rialto where gondolas filled with couples and tourists go on by. For now, I am alone again. Perhaps I will be this way for the rest of my life. I look up at the sky and whisper, "Rest in peace, Anna. I wish I could have what you and your husband had." I turn around and slowly walk back toward my building.

CHAPTER TWENTY-FIVE – The Break Up

As the first writers' meeting that I have attended in over a month ends, I stand up and walk over to Serge. "Where was Pete tonight?"

Serge rolls his eyes. "I don't know, but he should have followed the protocol and at least let me know that he was not coming."

"I know he was upset about losing Anna," I say. "He was crying on the pier as the funeral boat moved away."

"Pietro crying?" Serge asks. "I have known him many years, and I have never known him to cry about anything – even when his little dog died."

"Well, he obviously cared about Anna," I say.

"I texted him before the meeting," Serge says as he glances at his phone. "Still no response."

A side door opens, and Arabella appears in a short red dress and matching heels. She waves to me and runs up to

Serge, who puts his arm around her. I feel uncomfortable and turn away from them.

Rolando walks up to me and says, "The meeting was not the same without Anna."

"Yeah, I know."

Suddenly, "Twinkle, Twinkle, Little Star" is being played on the piano by Arabella, and I turn and see Serge nodding and smiling as she plays.

"That damn song again," I whisper, surprising myself for saying what I was thinking out loud.

"Serge seems to like it," Rolando says.

"Maybe he should get her lessons," I say, again surprising myself with the candor of my words. It is almost like I have lost control.

"And it was weird without Pietro here too," Rolando says. He looks at Serge clapping and Arabella running over and hugging him. "What's going on with them?"

I shake my head. "I have no idea." My phone rings, and I take it out of my pocket and see that Paula is calling me. I answer, "Hello. What's up, Paula?"

"Bobby, your mate is here, and he is getting drunk," Paula says, talking loudly over the music in the background.

"Pete?" I ask. "What's happening?"

"I don't know, but he is depressed and drunk – not a good combination for anyone," she says. "I don't think he can be allowed to go home like this."

"Okay, I'm on my way," I say.

"What's up?" Rolando asks.

"I've got to go," I say, "Pete's in trouble."

*

I walk into the bustling taverna filled with music and people, wave to Lorenzo, and head toward a table in the corner where Pietro is sitting with a drink in his hand and his face is contorted by alcohol. He looks up at me and says, "Bobby?"

Now, I know he is in a bad way; he has never called me "Bobby" before. I see Paula coming toward me and she says, "Thanks for coming, Bobby."

"Do you know what's going on?" I ask.

"When he ordered his first drink, he said he was celebrating tonight," Paula says. "I don't know anything more than that. Do you want something to drink?"

I look at Pietro and say, "I don't think I have a chance to catch up to him, but bring me a gin and tonic."

"Okay, Bobby," she says and walks toward the bar.

I sit down across from Pietro, touch his arm, and ask, "Hey, Pete, what's going on here?"

"What does it look like – I'm celebrating!" Pietro slurs his words as he raises his glass and drinks from it.

"Paula called me," I say, "she was concerned about you."

Pietro looks over at the bar and shakes his head. "She should stop playing mother hen and mind her own business."

Paula returns with my drink. "How's he doing?" she asks.

Pietro slaps his hand on the table and says, "I'm fooing dine!"

"Oh, brother," I say, knowing he is bombed.

"You're cut off, Pete," Paula says and turns around and walks away.

Pietro points at me and says, "You *finishhh that*, and we can go someplace else."

I sip my drink and say, "The only place you're going is home."

Pietro sits back in the chair and looks at me with a crooked stare. "It's over!"

"What's over?"

"Brian and me – we are over!" he says.

"*That's* what you're celebrating?" I ask.

He points at me. "*Yeshhh!* That's it!"

"What happened, Pete?"

"He left me – he left me!"

"I'm sorry, man," I say and sip my drink and watch as he slithers back in the chair, shuts his eyes, and slides down onto the floor.

*

Lorenzo helps me get Pietro out to a water taxi – this is a more expensive way to get a ride directly to where you want to go. I know where Pietro lives in a flat near Campo Santa Marina because he once invited me to have dinner with Brian and him, but when I showed up, he sent me home because they were having an argument.

Luckily, Pietro lives on the second floor in the building and not higher up, so I throw him over my right shoulder and fireman carry his dead weight up two flights of 15 steps each. I take the keys out of his pocket, and with some difficulty, manage to get the door open.

I bring Pietro into the living room, struggle to get his coat off, and drop him onto the couch. I look around the room, and it seems like a hurricane came through the windows that are open with curtains flowing in the cool October breeze.

Shutting the windows, I see picture frames on the floor. I pick one up, and it is a portrait of Brian and Pietro in their happier days; the glass over their faces is shattered. Talk about a breakup!

*

The next morning, I wake up in the chair across from Pietro, who is snoring loudly on the couch. I decided to stay here in case something happened. I did not want him to die choking on his vomit or some other issue.

I go into the kitchen and notice that Pietro has a fancy Italian espresso machine that I have no idea how to operate. Instead, I boil water and make some tea for myself. I sit there sipping tea, but Pietro continues to snore.

Another hour passes, and I decide to wake him. I shove his arm and say, "Pete, hey, Pete, wake up."

His eyes blink, and he sits up halfway and starts to cough. I pat him on the back, and he moans, "What are you doing here?"

"Paula called me to let me know you needed help," I say.

"You have violated my *Sanctum Sanctorum*," he says and then yawns.

"It looks like Brian beat me to it," I say.

He looks around at the mess, nods, and yawns again. "Indeed, he has – I suffered living with him for years, hoping I could change him."

"You know that never works out," I say.

Pietro stares at me. "I found out the hard way. How did I end up on the couch?" Pietro says with another yawn.

"So, I got you out of the taverna, put you in a water taxi, and brought you home last night," I say.

He sits up straight on the couch and leans his hands on his knees. "Did you take advantage of me?"

Even while suffering, Pietro cannot avoid an attempt at humor. I chuckle and go over and sit in the chair. "You told me about what happened with Brian."

"Oh, yes, that," he says as he sits back and stares at the ceiling. "He left me!"

"I know," I say and sip my tea.

"He insisted that we go to Florence this weekend, and I would come out to my family, so that we could then plan a big celebration for our civil union," Pietro says. "But I can never do that as long as my father is alive – never!"

"I…I guess I understand that," I say.

Pietro seems suddenly aware of the magnitude of the mess in the flat. "Oh, look how Brian took his anger out on this place!"

"It must have been ugly," I say.

He sniffs the air and says, "You didn't make coffee?"

"I have no idea how to use that contraption in the kitchen," I say.

Pietro struggles to stand and then staggers toward the kitchen. "It's a La Marzocco and made in my hometown – it makes the best espresso! If you looked in the cabinet, I have a Bialetti. Even you could use that I assume."

"Yes, I still use my Italian grandmother's Moka pot," I say, fondly remembering my Nonna making coffee to have with the cake after Sunday dinners.

Soon, Pietro has the coffee made, and the room has the heavenly smell of a corner café in Paris. He puts out a spread of scones, croissants, and biscuits on the table. I sit down, sip the cappuccino, and nod my head. "Excellent!"

Pietro smiles. "Even with a hangover, I can bring Italian civilization to you."

I grab a croissant and sniff it. "So fresh – how did you do this when we didn't go to the bakery?"

"The freezer and microwave are wonderful things," he says.

"How are you feeling?"

"Like I got hit by a train in my head," he says.

"Paula was very worried about you," I say.

Pietro smirks and says, "See, she does love me."

"We all care about you," I say.

"Robert, I'm touched," he chuckles.

"You called me 'Bobby' last night," I laugh.

"Now, you know I was stoned," he says.

I cut open a croissant and put a little strawberry jam inside. I bite into it and sip my coffee. This is probably the best Italian breakfast I have had since I came to Venice. "Why did you get so drunk like that?"

He shakes his head and sips his espresso. "It's just so hard, so very hard, to make a relationship work."

I nod my head. "I know that firsthand."

"Robert, I know you have had issues, but imagine how much harder it is for *us*. Despite all the pretenses, the world is stacked against us. I guess it would have been a miracle if Brian and I were successful."

"You seemed to be going well there for a long time," I say.

Pietro sips his espresso. "The truth is that we often argued. Remember that night you were supposed to come for dinner?" I nod my head. "Even on that night we had a fight, and I had to ask you to go home."

"I remember," I say.

"Relationships are not easy," Pietro says with a frown, "but everything was amplified in our relationship because we would even argue about how gay we were, or in my case, that I was not gay enough."

"Oh," I say, "is that even something to fight about?"

"Apparently, it was an issue for Brian," Pietro says and then sips his coffee.

"Did you always, like, know you were gay?"

Pietro nods his head somberly. "Since I was a kid in school. My friends were talking about girls and obsessing about their bodies and going out on dates with them. Me – I was only interested in other guys. How they walked, how they dressed, how they smelled, and everything else."

"Must have been difficult," I say.

Pietro pops a biscuit into his mouth and chews. "You have no idea!"

"And you kept it all to yourself?"

"Yes, of course, until after high school. I left Florence to come here to attend Università Ca' Foscari! It was my salvation. I could finally be the person I was born to be."

I nod my head. "Good for you, Pete."

"I met Brian there in my second year. We seemed so attuned to one another back then. I really didn't pick up on any of his many idiosyncrasies as we dated." He sits back and sips his espresso. "Then he went back to the U.K. after graduation for many years, but we stayed in touch. Then I went on holiday to London a few years ago and we reconnected. His job allowed him to work remotely, so he moved here, and we started to live together. I told him that it had to be on my terms, and Brian accepted that for a long time. We were okay until we weren't okay."

"Isn't that true about most relationships?"

"Yes, Robert, that's true, but it is overcoming all the other obstacles that Brian and I faced. He was just lucky to have a very supportive family. My family, though wonderful, is very old fashioned and very Catholic. I guess I should have known it would turn out this way inevitably."

"Again, I'm sorry," I say. Despite how cruel Pietro had recently been to me when I was down and out over losing Mireille, I will not stoop to his level and hit the poor guy while he is down and almost out.

"I know you are," Pietro says. "Thanks for taking care of me last night."

"Of course, what are friends for," I say.

"How was last night's meeting without me?"

"It just wasn't the same without you and Anna. Serge was a little annoyed with you for not letting him know you were missing it in advance."

"Of course, he was," Pietro says rolling his eyes. "He's so concerned with all his many protocols."

"Oh, and then there is Arabella – she played the piano again last night."

"Oh, my, not the same song?" I nod my head, and Pietro looks up at the ceiling. "There is no God."

"Oh, and there is a rumor that Serge wants to do more than adopt her," I say. "They are being rather affectionate and not in the way of a father and daughter."

"Hmm. I wonder what the contessa will think about that?"

"It should be an interesting meeting next week," I say.

Pietro puts down his cup and stares at me solemnly. "You know, I wouldn't choose to be this way."

"I think I understand," I say.

"But to be this way is one thing," he says as he puts a little jam on a croissant, "telling the world is quite another."

"But you are quite open about it in our group and when you were with Brian in public," I say.

"Yes, Venice is my heaven because I get to be the *real me* here," Pietro says. "But, when I go home, I'm just like the boy back in school who pretended to like girls just like my friends did."

"I guess that makes sense," I say.

"I have no other choice," he says with a deadpan expression. "If you met my father, you would understand why."

I think about my father and say, "In a different way, I had issues with my dad, but he was a good guy and always fair to me."

"Oh, please," Pietro says, "my father is a veritable saint." I widen my eyes as he says, "I'm telling you, he is such a good man, such a devout Catholic, that he must be hiding his halo. That is also why I can't do this to him – it would destroy him."

I sip my coffee and say, "Then you're a good man as well, Pete. There might even be a sainthood in it for you too."

"Ha! Ha!" he laughs, "that will be the day!

*

After I leave Pietro's flat, I wander along the Grand Canal on a busy Saturday morning. It is chilly with a slight breeze. I watch the gondolas and the vaporetti, and the occasional water taxi, go by. The world just keeps moving here – Anna's death, Serge's suddenly awkward interest in Arabella, and Pietro's breakup with Brian – nothing interferes with the way of things, making our joys and woes seem inconsequential. I accept this reality rather reluctantly.

As I turn and start walking back over the Rialto, I wonder why the world is so cruel and how God allows it to be. Perhaps I am indifferent to things because the world has made me this way. I am not certain anymore.

As I go through the web of narrow streets to get back to my building, I think about my little flat with its bare walls and a beautiful view of San Marco's bell tower. It is the quiet and rather lonely place that I call home.

CHAPTER TWENTY-SIX – Halloween in Venice

October 31 is tomorrow, and I have seen some evidence that people celebrate the holiday in a meaningful way here in Venice. There are paper jack-o-lanterns pasted in the local shop windows and carved pumpkins on front steps here and there, and there are typical costumes available in the mask shops and other stores. I am happy to see that they embrace my favorite holiday here in Venice.

As I wake up and go into the living room and look out my window, there is a thick fog hovering above the streets after last night's rain. For the first time since I have lived here, my view of San Marco's bell tower is obscured. The streets seem appropriately eerie for the day before Halloween – what they call Devil's Night back home – when all sorts of mayhem can occur in preparation for the big night to come.

I scramble a couple of eggs, toast some bread from the bakery, and make my coffee in my Moka pot. As I sit down to enjoy my food, my phone buzzes. It is a text from Arabella – somehow, I now live in a world where I am getting text messages from Anna's granddaughter in a group that includes, Serge, Pietro, and Rolando.

"Hi, guys," she writes, "I want to have a Halloween party tomorrow night."

"That is fine, my dear," Serge texts back. He went to Milan for a business meeting a few days ago, but is supposed to be home later today.

"Halloween?" Pietro writes. "I don't celebrate that American holiday."

"Oh, Pete," Rolando writes, "it is so much fun! You should be enjoying Halloween; it is a cool thing for us to celebrate."

"A thing?" Pete writes. "I don't do a THING!"

Serge writes, "I think it would be splendid to give Arabella the party that she wants. Please text me separately, my dear, about this."

I think about it, and I feel like I can use some fun. I type, "I'm in!"

"Of course, you are!" Pietro writes.

"Okay, guys, so start looking for your costumes," Arabella writes accompanied by smiling and thumbs up emojis.

"We will get back to you about everything after I come home today and plan it with Arabella," Serge writes.

After we are all done texting, I realize that it is odd that I was thinking about Halloween and then Arabella texts about a party. The universe works in mysterious ways.

*

When I go out, I know exactly where I am going to get a costume – Emilio Ceccato – the official gondolier supply store right by the Rialto. When I enter the store, there are several customers rummaging through the items on the shelves.

I ask one of the clerks, "What's the difference between the blue striped and the red striped gondolier shirts?"

"Ah, signor," the tall, thin fellow says, "that is a good question. It used to be that gondoliers on the right side of the canal wore blue stripes, and it was red stripes for the other side."

"But I see a gondolier with red stripes sometimes right next to one with blue stripes in the canals," I say.

"It has changed now," the fellow says. "Gondoliers are offered a choice of one or the other – they are both the official uniform along with the matching straw hat and black pants. Which color is for you?"

I have seen that most gondoliers seem to wear the blue striped shirts, so I opt to purchase a red striped shirt with official gondolier emblem on it and a straw hat with a matching red ribbon. I walk back to my building with a smile on my face, and I make it back just as it starts to rain.

Standing before my long bathroom mirror, I like the way I look in the shirt and hat. I have a pair of black pants – which are an important part of the official uniform – and there is a broom in the closet that with a little creativity will make a perfect oar.

Now that I have my costume, I want to get to work on a story that came into my head as I was getting into the Halloween spirit. I am going to write a story about the Halloween night when I first watched the film *Halloween* as a kid with a babysitter while my parents went out to a party – the same scenario from the movie – and how much it scared me.

*

As I walk through the streets on the way to Serge's palace on the Grand Canal, I see groups of little kids walking in costumes with their parents. Perhaps they are on the way to parties. Rolando called and told me that – if we did not have Serge's party – that there are many more opportunities to celebrate Halloween here like haunted palace tours and spooky costume parties. No one gives me a second look because I am in my gondolier gear carrying a broom with a brown bag stapled to the bristles to make it look like an oar.

When I enter Serge's foyer, I am greeted by majordomo Whitman who looks me up and down. "Well, at least that costume is something recognizable," he says.

"Thank you, Whitman," I say.

"Good choice, sir," Whitman chirps back.

I enter the ballroom where large black and orange ballons are floating along the walls. The music is pounding in the room – one Taylor Swift song after another – making me assume Arabella is a Swiftie because I doubt this music is Serge's preference.

At the bar I see a werewolf, mermaid, and a Viking getting drinks. I ask for a Smirnoff Red on the rocks. I get a tap on the shoulder, and I turn around to see Rolando dressed as a zombie – complete with ears hanging from threads and blood running from his eyes. "Very creative," I yell over the music.

"I've been wanting to be a zombie for years," Rolando says. "I'm a big fan of *The Walking Dead*!"

"Yeah," I yell over the music, "I like it too."

Rolando grabs a beer, and we walk across the dance floor where nurses are dancing with Freddy Krueger, an astronaut, and the Frankenstein monster. In the corner near the DJ booth, Serge and Arabella are dressed as Dracula and one of his wives. Serge has the perfect and classic Bela Lugosi look complete with fangs, and he drinks his cocktail through an appropriately black straw. Arabella has on a black wig, white makeup, and very red lipstick. Her powder white breasts are oozing out of the top of her long black gown.

"Good evening," Serge says with a Lugosi accent.

"This is great," Rolando gushes.

Arabella glances at Serge and says, "He gave me carte blanche, so we went all out."

"Who are all these people?" I ask.

"Well," Arabella says, "there are some friends of mine from work here."

"About two dozen of them," Serge notes with a smirk.

"There are also members of the writing group and some of our neighbors," Arabella says with a toothy vampire grin.

"Where the hell is Pietro?" I ask.

"I don't know if our friend will be coming," Serge says. "Apparently it is not his *thing*."

"Enjoy the party, guys," Arabella says as three girls dressed as different incarnations of Barbie – the toy doll – run over to her and start screaming about their costumes.

Rolando and I head back across the dance floor to the buffet, where Michael Myers, a mummy, and ninja are getting some food. There is a wide variety of *cicchetti* available and American favorites like potato chips, pretzels, and popcorn. I grab a few fried meatballs and some small panini, while Rolando loads his plate up with potato chips and pretzels. I glance at him and he says, "I never get to eat these kinds of things."

"When in Rome," I chuckle.

"You mean Venice, right?"

I laugh and say, "Yeah, sure."

Suddenly, I get a tap on the shoulder, and I turn around to see someone in a Yoda costume saying in muffled words, "Size matters not."

I glance at Rolando and then say, "May the Force be with you!"

The person struggles to take the mask off, and it is Pietro with his hair all sweaty. "I decided life is short, so here I am."

"Good to see you, Pete," I say. "I didn't know you were a *Star Wars* fan."

"Well, I am," he says with his whiskers fluttering. "Yoda is my favorite character because he is small like me."

"I like *Star Wars* too," Rolando says. "But I haven't really seen the old films yet."

Pietro grabs his arm and says, "You have to watch them in order to fully understand anything."

"So, Yoda is your favorite character just because he is small?" Rolando asks.

"Of course not, Rolando. Without Yoda none of the rest of the stuff makes sense. I got this costume in college and thought it was time to break it out again." He notices the buffet and says, "Time it is to eat!"

Rolando and I watch him scurry off toward the buffet. Rolando looks at me and says, "You have to admire him staying in character."

"Yeah," I say as I pop a meatball into my mouth, "he is quite a character!"

Three big guys dressed as trolls walk up to us. "You guys look like Shrek," Rolando exclaims like a happy child.

"We are *trolls*," the biggest of the three says. "Shrek is an ogre!"

I notice the German accent and realize these are the Three Germans, as Pietro always calls them, from our writers' group. The only one who ever speaks is a big guy named Heinrich, so I ask, "Is that you, Heinrich?"

"Yes, it is I," he says. "You look good, Bobby."

"Thank you," I say. "You too!"

Heinrich spies the buffet and hits the other two trolls on the arms. "Let's eat!"

As they walk away, Rolando looks up at me and asks, "Why do those German guys come to our meetings?"

"I don't know," I say. "Maybe they like Serge's food, or maybe they like to hear our stories."

"Yeah, I guess," Rolando says.

"Pietro is always suspicious of them," I say, "but I think they mean no harm."

"Serge says he knows them from *the war*," Rolando says as he crunches a chip.

"What war?"

Rolando shakes his head. "I don't know."

"Sometimes I wonder about Serge's life history," I say. "He's in his late thirties, so he's been around the block a few times."

"Around the block?" Rolando asks.

"Means he's had a lot of experience," I say.

"Oh!" Rolando smiles and nods his head.

One of my old favorite Halloween songs – "Monster Mash" – starts playing, and Arabella grabs a microphone and yells, "Everybody dance!"

Soon I am on the floor with Rolando dancing with the nurses; they are cute but too young for me. Serge and Arabella are dancing madly around one another, and the three trolls are going strong dancing in a circle. Suddenly, Yoda comes through the crowd, doing a pirouette that is appreciated with loud applause. This is probably the best time I have had since I came to live here.

*

It is getting late, but the party keeps going on. I am sitting at a table with Rolando and Pietro – sans mask – and having a Smirnoff Red on the rocks. I look at them both and say, "This has been quite a party."

"Arabella has changed Serge immeasurably," Pietro says.

Rolando sips a beer and says, "I've noticed that too."

"Really?" I ask. "He seems to be the same suave, sophisticated fellow that I have come to call my friend."

"But look at him," Pietro says, "he has a buoyancy to him; look how he is dancing with her. He seems to have forgotten all the dark times."

"Dark times?" I ask.

"When his parents were ill and dying," Pietro says. "They had all the money in the world, but it could not save them."

"That's a shame," says Rolando.

"And the contessa seems to be yesterday's news," Pietro says with a smirk.

The DJ announces, "This will be the last song ladies and gentlemen. Please get up and dance."

"Careless Whisper" by Wham! starts playing, and I get transported to those clubs back home that usually played this song last, encouraging couples to have that last dance. Serge and Arabella are dancing close together. The nurses are dancing with the trolls, the mermaid with the werewolf, and the Barbies with Freddy Krueger, the ninja, and the mummy.

As the song plays on, Pietro gasps. "Oh my God!" I look up, and Serge and Arabella are in the middle of a deep, passionate kiss. "I guess the adoption is off now."

I surprise myself and say, "I guess they have moved up to the engagement stage."

"I would be shocked if Serge ever remarried," Pietro says.

"Remarried?" I ask.

"Yes, in his early twenties he married a German woman. They had a child together – a son he named Sergio – but they fought all the time," Pietro says.

"Maybe that's what he meant about during the war," Rolando says.

"Yeah, that makes sense. Are those German guys connected to his ex-wife?" I ask.

Pietro sips his drink. "I believe they are Frieda's brothers or cousins or something familial."

The lights come on, the music stops, and suddenly everyone is talking and laughing.

I get up and say, "I think I'll thank our host and be on my way."

Pietro stands up and stretches his arms. "I guess I will do the same."

*

After saying our goodbyes, everyone departs the palace on the Grand Canal and heads for home. As I am walking down the street, a young couple comes running up to me. The man asks, "Do you speak English?" with a British accent.

I say, "Yes, I do."

"I know it's late," he says, "but could we please have a gondola ride? I'm willing to pay extra because of the time."

I remember that I am wearing my gondolier costume and laugh. "Oh, I'm sorry, this is just a Halloween costume. I'm not a gondolier." They both seem drunk and look at one another, start laughing, and stagger away.

Once I am home, I take off my costume and hang it lovingly in my closet – it is a souvenir that I will cherish. I put on a pair of shorts and a Mets T-shirt, grab a beer from the fridge, and turn on the TV.

As I am flipping through the channels, I feel my phone buzzing in my pocket, and I take it out and see that I have a text from the lovely Dr. Isabella Ianelli. It says, "Please call me right away."

I look at the time, and it is almost midnight. I call Isabella and get her voicemail. I say, "Hi, just got your message. I'm available now if you want to call back."

As luck would have it, I come across the 1978 version of *Halloween* starring Jamie Lee Curtis – the film that scared the crap out of me when I was a kid. I am enjoying it even more now as an adult.

My phone rings in my pocket, and I see that it is Isabella calling me back. "Hello, Isabella," I say.

"Bobby, I just came out of surgery – Elena is back in the hospital."

"What happened?" I ask as I sit up.

"They brought her in with multiple stab wounds," Isabella says.

I stand up and look around the room with so many things racing through my brain. "But she's gonna be okay, right?"

"I…I don't know for certain; her condition is critical," Isabella says. "I think you better come if you want to see her."

I unfortunately have heard this before – each time one of my parents lay dying. I take a deep breath and say, "Okay, I'll be there as soon as I can."

CHAPTER TWENTY-SEVEN – Il Giorno Dei Morti

I wake up and realize that I am in the hospital waiting room all alone. It is six o'clock in the morning, and I sit up straight and take a deep breath. I last saw Isabella around one o'clock, and she let me briefly see Elena before she was taken for surgery.

Elena was very still in the bed and covered with bandages and tubes running into her body. She was receiving oxygen, and she seemed so battered and bruised – much worse than the last time.

"Elena," I said, squeezing her hand." I'm here, Elena!"

Isabella was standing behind me. "She can hear you, Bobby. It's good to let her know you're here."

"How did she get here?" I ask.

"Her friend with the red hair called it in," Isabella said. *"She was here for a while, but then she left."*

"She saved her life," I said.

"Yes, she did!"

"I'll be here after your surgery, Elena," I said, squeezing her hand again.

Isabella put a hand on my shoulder. *"The bandages have a hemostatic agent that helps stop the bleeding."*

"So, why does she need surgery?"

"Unfortunately, some of the wounds are deep and involve organ damage; she was stabbed at least 30 times," Isabella said. *"The many minor lacerations have been sutured. Her hands and fingers had many cuts and gashes – she tried to fight off her attacker."*

I saw Nino's ugly face in my mind. "I know that she would fight back."

Two orderlies came in to take Elena to surgery. Isabella said, "I have to go now."

"Save her, Isabella – please!"

"I'm going to do everything I can," she said as she left the ER.

I walked down the hallway to the waiting room. I felt exhausted and crashed into a chair. A few people were sitting there and looked up at me, no doubt wondering why I made so much noise.

I shut my eyes and thought, "I'm going to kill that bastard!" I did not how I was going to find Nino, but I was determined to turn over every rock until he finally slithered out from under one. Due to the long day and even longer night with the party going on so late, I quicky fell asleep.

The sun starts rising over the buildings on the other side of the Grand Canal. I glance at my watch and realize that it has been a long time since I saw Elena.

I go into the hallway, and there are nurses and doctors rushing to go somewhere and orderlies pushing gurneys. I walk down the hallway, feeling as if I am in a daze, and I find a cafeteria where people are eating breakfast like it is just another day in a building where children are born, patients are very ill, and some of them die.

I buy a coffee and a plain croissant and go back to the waiting room. I bite into the croissant, but it seems like tasteless cardboard. I am hungry, so I eat it anyway. Sleep has not brought me anymore clarity. I am trying to process what has happened, to understand that Elena is in seriously bad shape. I believe Isabella is a good doctor and that she will do everything she can to help her.

My phone rings, and I see it is Carla calling me. I had left her a message last night. "Hello," I say.

"Bobby, I'm sorry I didn't call last night," Carla says. "I was sleeping and had to get up for work early today."

"Thank you for saving Elena's life," I say.

"She called me moaning and crying," Carla says. "Luckily, I don't live far from where she was staying."

"Was she staying with Nino?" I ask.

"Yes, but he was gone when I got there," Carla says. "There was blood everywhere, and Elena was covered with blood."

"Nino is worse than an animal," I say. "Do you know why he did this?"

"Elena said he became angry about something," Carla says, "she could barely speak when we were waiting for the ambulance."

"Do you have any idea where I can find that pig?"

"No, I only knew where she was staying because I brought her some stuff she wanted and some food," Carla says. "He was not feeding her much."

"That bastard!" I say, noticing Isabella coming into the room. "I'll call you later; I have to go!"

"Bye, Bobby," Carla says.

I stand up, and Isabella says, "Let's go to where will have more privacy." I follow her down the hallway, and we go into a consultation room. She closes the door and whispers, "Let's sit down."

I am feeling anxiety now and my hands are shaking as I sit down. "What happened in surgery?"

"Everything went well, but there was more damage than we realized. She was stabbed in the stomach, the left kidney and lung, and we had to remove her spleen."

I hold my head in my hands and say, "Oh, my God!"

"She was also eight to ten weeks pregnant," Isabella says, and I look up at her in shock. "The fetus was killed by the stabs into the womb."

I remember Elena telling me that I was the only one with whom she had sex without condom. "A baby?" I start crying, and I cannot stop.

"I'm sorry, Bobby," she says.

I look up at Isabella who hands me a tissue box. I blow my nose, wipe my face, and sit back and take a deep breath. "I…I think that baby was mine."

Isabella nods her head and looks at me with compassionate blue eyes. "I was wondering if it was or not. I'm truly sorry."

I forget about the baby and think about Elena. "Is she going to be, okay?"

Isabella sits back and grips the arms of her chair. "She has lost a lot of blood, and we must treat her with antibiotics now because there is infection. She is in intensive care, and there is not much more we can do now but wait."

I am not sure what to do or say. "What should I do now?"

Isabella puts her hand on my hand. "Go home – you are exhausted. Get some sleep. You can't help her if you get yourself sick, and pray if you believe in God."

*

I reluctantly leave the hospital on a sunny but cool day. I came running here in my shorts and Mets T-shirt, so I am not dressed for the weather. Once I get home, I go into my bedroom and flop on the bed. As I am drifting off to sleep, I think about Beth.

"I'm pregnant!" Beth said joyfully as she came out of the bathroom with the pregnancy test in her hand.

I stared at her at first in disbelief and then happiness. "We did it!" I said.

We hugged and kissed each other. Beth stared at me.

"We have so much to do."

"Yeah," I said. We lived in my small one-bedroom

apartment. "I guess it is time to look for a house."

"Oh, Bobby, this is so exciting," Beth said.

"What about names – Elizabeth if it is a girl and

Robert if it is a boy!"

"Bobby, I'm Jewish – we don't name babies after

ourselves," Beth said. "We usually name them for relatives

who have passed away."

"Oh, that sucks," I say.

Beth's eyebrows skewed. "It doesn't suck. It is a

Jewish tradition. If it is a boy, we could name him after your

father."

I thought about it and said, "Oh, okay."

I wake up and it is dark outside. I quickly check my

phone, and there are no calls or text messages. As my mother

always used to say, "No news is good news."

As I am getting dressed, I wonder if Nino has left the city. I cannot even think about him until I know Elena is going to be okay. I go down the block and get two slices of pizza. The only thing I ate today was that stale croissant. After eating, I make my way back to the hospital in hopes of seeing Elena.

In the lobby, I am told that Isabella has left for the day, Elena is still in intensive care, and visitors are not allowed to see her. If Isabella is not there, I figure I should just leave. The person at the desk says I should call before I come back tomorrow.

As I am walking home, my phone rings, and I see that it is Serge calling. "Hi, Serge," I say.

"Bobby, I am inviting you to come to a luncheon with us tomorrow," Serge says. "We are going to celebrate The Day of the Dead and honor Anna's memory."

I do not want to tell Serge about Elena at this point, so I say, "Okay, I guess I can do that."

"Excellent, Bobby," Serge says. "We'll see you at one o'clock, okay?

"One o'clock it is," I say.

*

The next day, Isabella calls me early in the morning. "I heard that you were here last night."

"Yes, I came back hoping to see Elena," I say.

"Bobby, she is still in critical condition."

"How is she doing?"

"She's a fighter, and we are doing everything we can to help her," Isabella says.

"Will you let me know when I can see her," I ask.

"Yes, I will call you later today."

"Thanks, Isabella," I say.

Since I cannot see Elena, I shave, take a shower, and get dressed in a gray blazer, white dress shirt, black slacks, and my good shoes. I am interested to see what they are doing on this Day of the Dead – what we called All Souls

Day back when I was in Catholic school, and this will be better than sitting all alone at home waiting for Isabella to call me.

When I get to Serge's home, Whitman lets me in and says, "Please wait here in the portego."

"Thank you, Whitman," I say. I sit in one of the red velvet chairs, and look around at this space that I usually just walk through quickly. There are numerous doorways with elaborate frescoes above each one. The marble floor sparkles in the sunlight coming through one of higher windows.

"Beth called 911," my brother Vinny said when he called me.

"How do you know?" I asked

"Mom called me because she couldn't reach you."

"I was in a meeting," I said.

"Mom is driving behind the ambulance," Vinny said, "they're heading to North Shore."

"What's wrong?" I asked.

"Beth had some stomach pain," he said.

"Okay, thanks," I said as I started running out the door. I took the train back to Manhasset Station where my car was parked, and then I quicky drove to the hospital with my heart beating fast.

I was directed to go to the ER, and Mom was in the waiting room. "Hey, Ma, what's happening?"

She kissed me on the cheek as she always had done since I was a little followed by a pat of her hand on my arm. Mom was still beautiful now – her eyes glowing with love. "She called me and told me she had pain. I drove over to your house and we called 911."

Later, I drove Beth home – to the new house we had bought for the baby – and she said nothing in the car; she just stared out the passenger window.

At home Beth sat crying on the edge of the bed. I sat next to her, and she buried her face on my chest. I touched the back of her head. "Everything is going to be okay," I said.

She lifted her head and looked at me with tears on her cheeks. "We lost the baby – <u>our baby</u>. I don't know how to live with this."

I whispered, "We'll just take it one day at a time."

She stared at me with glassy eyes. "And they don't know if I can have more children," she said.

I tried to put my arms around her, but she got up and walked out of the room. We never talked about the subject ever again.

"Bobby…Bobby," Serge says as he taps my shoulder.

I snap out of it and say, "Oh, I'm sorry, Serge." I get up and shake his hand. I notice that

Pietro, Rolando, and Arabella are all standing behind him.

"Arabella and I just got back from the cemetery to visit Anna," Serge says.

"We are supposed to clean up the gravesite," Arabella says, her blonde hair glowing in the sunlight. She is wearing a short black dress and matching heels and looks lovely. "But there wasn't much to do with the grave having just been opened and closed."

"That is tradition," Serge says. "We also stopped in St. Mary's on the way home to light a candle and pray."

"And when do we get to the luncheon part?" asks Pietro. Everyone looks at him and starts laughing.

*

We sit around the table in the grand dining room that has gilt chandeliers and Baroque furnishings including the magnificent dining table and chairs. The artwork on the walls reflects the luxury of that era.

As we sit around the right side of the table that could fit at least 50 people, Serge stops the conversation and directs us to look at the place laid with a glass of water in front of it. "This place is set for our beloved Anna, who is here with us today in spirit."

Pietro raises his glass of wine and says, "For our dear Anna!"

We all raise our glasses and say, "For Anna!"

I turn to Serge. "What a wonderful tradition."

"We believe that on this day there is a strong bond between the living and the dead," Serge says.

"Yes," Arabella says, "I could feel Nonna standing beside me at the gravesite today – she was there!"

"And she is with us here now," Serge says, "sitting in that chair and enjoying the fact that we honor her memory."

Whitman leads several butlers into the room carrying trays. Just as the food is being served, my phone rings in my pocket. I get up and excuse myself from the table. I go out into the hallway and see that Isabella is calling me.

"Yes, Isabella," I say, feeling anxiety about hearing her voice.

"Bobby, I am deeply sorry to have to tell you like this over the phone," Isabella says, "but Elena passed away a few moments ago."

I feel like someone punched me in the stomach. I crumple over and fall onto my knees. I say, "No, no, no!!" My voice is echoing in the long hallway.

"We did everything we could," Isabella says, "but she never regained consciousness. If it helps, she didn't suffer at the end."

I stare at a Renaissance painting on the wall in front of me of a man and woman holding hands blissfully in another time and place. In my sadness I wonder why life cannot replicate such bliss. "She didn't suffer?" I ask.

"She was on morphine," Isabella says. "We knew we were losing her. If you want to come here, I will be available to talk, or we could…"

"No, thanks Isabella, I just want to be alone now," I say as I get up and start shuffling down the hallway.

Whitman runs after me and asks, "Is everything all right, sir?"

"I…I just learned someone I care about died in the hospital," I say. "I have to go."

Once outside I wander along streets and canals. I watch the motion of the city – the people, the gondolas, the vaporetti, and the busy bridges – Elena is dead and nothing changes. Anna died and nothing changed. The world keeps spinning and we all matter not – it is relentless in its indifference.

I lean on a railing and stare at the busy Rialto Bridge packed with people. I picture Elena's face when she would look up at me. She was too beautiful to be trapped in that life, too fragile to be put under such pressure, too good to have been sucked into that ugly business by an evil man who ended up killing her.

When Nino found out that she was pregnant, he must have killed her in a rage. A pregnant woman would be no use to him in his dirty world. He killed the baby – he killed *our baby*! I am going to make him pay for what he has done. I keep walking along the Grand Canal, ignoring everyone and everything around me. I feel enveloped in a fog of mourning that overwhelms me.

Elena has died on the Day of the Dead. Another lost soul in a world of lost souls. When I regain my senses, I lean on a railing by Campo di San Silvestro looking out over the Grand Canal as the sun goes down behind me. Serge said that on this day the dead had a strong connection with the living, and I want to connect with Elena, but I cannot feel anything.

Perhaps Elena does not even know that she is dead yet. Her soul is too new on the other side; she is probably running around looking for a way out, but then an angel appears holding our baby. Elena will hold that baby in her arms, and I am glad they are together over on the other side. No more suffering for them, no more pain of any kind. They are together in a peaceful eternity – and that gives me some comfort.

But I am here alone to pick up the pieces – the detritus of a life Nino shattered beyond repair. I cannot allow Nino to escape punishment for his crimes. When I find him, he is going to wish that he had never been born.

CHAPTER TWENTY-EIGHT – Dig Two Graves

Pietro and I are sitting at a table in the taverna drinking and eating, the music is playing, and there are many customers in the place on this night. Instead of going home after an intense workout at the gym, I came here to eat, drink, and to think. I am surprised to see Pietro in this place on his own.

"I thought you could use some company," Pietro says.

"How did you know I was even here?" I ask.

"She told me about Elena." He points to Paula at the bar. "Our guardian angel is always looking out for us you know."

"She knows what I have to do," I say, thinking about Nino.

"You don't *have* to do anything," Pietro says and sips his drink. "You *want* to do this thing!"

"Nino murdered Elena and our baby," I say. "I have to do something. They have to be avenged!"

"Look, Robert, you are a decent chap," Pietro says. "Have you ever killed anything or anyone?"

I stare at him. He is sincerely trying to help me. After all this time, I realize that Pietro is a good friend. "Do the cockroaches in my apartment back in NYC count?" I ask, picking up the last fried ravioli and popping it into my mouth.

"No, they do not," Pietro says. "You're not like Nino – you're not a killer!"

In the gym I was hitting the speedbag hard, and Coco – the gray haired manager of the gym – asked me if I wanted to spar with someone. "Hey, you look like you have some fighting to do."

"Yeah, sure," I said.

He led me to the ring where a young, buff guy was walking around with his gloves and headgear on. Coco introduced me to him. "This is Rollo; Rollo, this is Bobby."

"I hear you're a good boxer," Rollo said.

"I can handle myself," I said.

Coco put a hand on my shoulder. "Rollo has won ten fights with no losses."

Rollo grinned and said, "I'll go easy on you."

I looked him over. He was a natural light heavyweight like I was. Perhaps he bulked up a bit using weights like I had done, but he was young and a little cocky. I put on the gloves and headgear, Coco slipped in my mouthguard, and I climbed into the ring.

As we began to spar, I realized that Rollo was a lefty. He caught me with a quick head shot, and then tried again, but I ducked it and popped him on the chin. He did not like that. We danced around a bit, and then he came at me and got another head shot in that stung. I went backwards into the ropes, and I started seeing Nino's face instead of Rollo's,

and I plowed forward throwing punches.

Next thing I know, Coco was pulling me away from

the center of the ring toward the ropes, and I looked back

and saw Rollo on the canvas. "What are you doing?" he

screamed. "You are only sparring."

I did not remember it, but Coco later told me that I

sent a barrage of punches into Rollo's chest and head,

knocking him down and out. In the locker room as I was

changing, Coco came over to me. I looked at him and said,

"I'm sorry."

"He's going to be okay," Coco said, "but you looked

like you wanted to kill him."

I got dressed and left the gym, but as I was walking

over the completely wooden Accademia Bridge – an anomaly

compared to the other bridges of brick and stone over the

Grand Canal – to go home, I was thinking Coco was right,

except I was not trying to kill Rollo. It was Nino I wanted to kill.

Paula comes over to the table to collect our plates. "Feeling better, Bobby?"

I look up at her and say. "Not so good," I say. "I have an ache in my mind and body that will not go away."

"It is going to take time," she says, walking away with a tray filled with dirty plates and glasses.

Pietro sits back and sips his drink. "When Brian left me, I felt like it was the end of the world, and I wanted to die. But now, with some time passing, I'm doing better."

"I'm happy for you, my friend," I say. "At least you know Brian is living and breathing somewhere. Elena is dead and so is our baby. I don't know how I ever get over that." The truth is that I believe that I will never be the same.

"I understand," Pietro says, "but you cannot look for revenge. You know what Confucius said: 'He who seeks revenge should dig two graves.'"

"Confucius? Really?" I ask, with my head spinning from my thoughts and the drinks.

"Take some time, Robert," Pietro says. He looks at his watch. "I've got to get going. Have to be at work early tomorrow. Remember, you are not a barbarian! I know that you are not a killer!"

"Take care, Pete," I say as he gets up and leaves.

Paula returns and sits down at the table with a bottle of Smirnoff. She pours some into my glass and says, "Bobby, you are a good man, despite all the self deprecating things you say about yourself."

"Thanks, Paula," I say. "But I don't have good thoughts in my head right now. I keep picturing myself killing Nino in different ways."

"Let the police handle it," she says.

"When he beat her up the first time, they couldn't find him," I say. "Now, they can't doing anything because I gave them a description, but I don't even know his last name. He's out there thinking he got away with it."

"He will get his justice," Paula says. "It's the way the universe works."

I look at her and honestly say, "But the universe is too slow. I want justice now."

"Why are you so impatient?"

"The truth is," I say and sip my drink, "is that I'm guilty for being a customer. I'm guilty for not taking her away when she asked me to, and I'm guilty for not acting the first time that this happened. If I went after him then, Elena and the baby would be alive, so I do blame myself for this."

Paula puts her hand on my arm and says, "Go easy on yourself, Bobby. You did nothing wrong. Give yourself a break."

I look up at her and say, "I can't rest until I make things right."

She gets up, refreshes my drink, and says, "Then get ready to be restless a long, long time."

As she walks away, I close my eyes, and wonder when I will find peace. I really need to find some peace.

*

My phone is ringing, and I wake up and feel around the bed for it – somehow it is inside my pillowcase. I answer it. "Hello?"

"Bobby, this is Carla."

"Hey, Carla. Is everything okay?"

"Yes, but I saw someone today at the Rialto Market who maybe knows where to find Nino," Carla says.

"Really? Is this an old customer of yours?"

"No, no. He came to my flat a few times when Nino was there," Carla says. "He is Nino's cousin Franco. He is a good man who works hard. He always came to get paid back money Nino owed him."

"Okay," I say getting up, "where can I find this guy."

"He's very fat with a bald head," Clara says. "He only sells watermelons, so you cannot miss him."

"Thanks a lot, Carla," I say. "I really appreciate this."

"Good luck!" Carla says.

I get dressed and stick a pair of leather gloves into my jacket pockets to protect my hands for when I do find Nino. I rush out into the street and make my way toward the market on a beautiful but slightly chilly day.

When I arrive at the market, it is a busy Friday with a horde of shoppers; the seagulls are squawking, and indistinct chattering is all around me. I pass Tinno, wave to him, and say, "*Buongiorno!*" but keep walking fast.

Then I find Franco; he looks just like Carla described him, his bald head shiny in the sunlight. He has watermelons of all sizes, including pre-cut watermelons, on a long table. He has a scale hanging above the table, and a cash box on a counter behind him. I walk up to him and say, "Do you have a minute?"

He looks up at me with a furrowed brow, reminding me of an overweight Mr. Freeze from the *Batman* comics. "Yes, what is it?"

"I'm looking for someone you know."

"Yes, who?"

"Your cousin Nino," I say. "I need to find him."

Franco looks both ways and whispers, "I don't want any trouble, and I know with Nino there is always trouble."

"And I don't want to cause you any trouble, but I need to find him." I try to think quickly and say something he can appreciate. "He owes me a lot of money."

Franco shakes his head. "He always owes people money. Nino is always gambling and losing money. He has a bad temper and causes nothing but trouble."

"Where is he?" I ask. "You tell me and, if I find him, I'll never come back here again. If I don't find him, then I'm coming back and causing you trouble."

Franco takes a pad from the counter, scribbles something on it, and tears off the page. He hands it to me and says, "It is close to the train station. Please don't let him know that I sent you. He will hurt me."

I take the paper and shake my head. "Don't worry, he's not going to be hurting anyone ever again." The look of surprise on Franco's face is a little sad yet amusing.

I walk away from Franco and head back to the bridge to cross it and make my way to Cannaregio to find Nino. I am thinking so many things in my head – should I kill him? Should I beat the crap out of him? One way or another this is going to end today.

*

I find the building where Nino is staying, and I slip into a spot on the other side of the narrow street to watch the place. As I stand there, I can hear a train arriving in the station behind me. This building looks rundown, but the front door appears to be new. An old broken door is inside the gate next to the steps. It seems like there was some kind of problem here.

About waiting for hours, it gets dark and cold. I have to take a leak, and I do not know how the cops on those TV shows can be on a stakeout and sit in their cars and drink coffee and not have to go to the bathroom. I move behind a column but still have a view of the front door. I quickly take a leak and decide to stay behind the column. I slip on my gloves that help against the cold and will protect my hands in a fight.

About another hour goes by and, just as a train leaves the station, the door opens and Nino comes out wearing a leather jacket. His beady eyes dart around to make sure there is no one there, and then he turns and locks the door. He starts walking in my direction, and I jump out from behind the column. "Nino!" I scream.

He turns around and starts running. I figured that this scenario could happen, and that is why I am wearing sneakers. I run after him toward a canal near an old hotel. Nino pushes people out of his way as he runs, and he goes into a dead end alley. When he turns around, I am standing there staring at him.

"You murdered Elena!" I scream as I point at him.

"No, it was not like that," Nino says.

"You learned she was pregnant and you got angry at her," I say as I start to move toward him.

"No, no, I didn't know she was pregnant," he says. "You have to believe me." As I close in on him, he takes out a switchbade and clicks it open.

Nino attempts to swipe my arm with the blade, but I block his arm as if he was throwing a punch and hit him in the side of his head, sending him into a wall. I lock his arm and force him to drop the blade, and then I punch him in the stomach, causing him to fall down to his knees. He scoots around on his knees and grabs my legs and pulls on them, causing me to fall on the ground.

He reaches for his switchblade but, from a kneeling position, I punch him in the side of the head, and he drops down to the ground. I get up with the switchblade in my hand, close it, and put it in my pocket. I am certain it is key evidence and what he used to kill Elena.

I lift him up by the collar, but he shoves me aside and starts running. I quickly catch my breath and run after him along this quiet canal. I see a bridge up ahead that he is trying to reach. A private water taxi is zipping under the bridge as I catch up to him. I grab him by the shoulder and pop him in his face under his left eye. He reels backwards as I hit him again with a left hook, causing him to almost flip over the railing into the canal.

Grabbing his legs, I bring him back over the railing. He makes an attempt to punch me, and I flatten him with a right hook to his temple. Nino is spread out on the bridge at my feet. I take out my phone and dial 112 as I keep an eye on him to make certain that he does not move.

*

I go into the taverna, and it is late, but there are a good number of customers still there. The music is low, with soothing jazz dripping out of the speakers. I go up to the bar and Gina makes me a gin and tonic.

"Where's the boss?" I ask.

"She's in the back," Gina says, "I'll tell her that you're here."

I turn around and lean my elbows on the bar and look around the place. In a shadowed corner in the back of the room, I see Mireille sitting at a table with a young man whose face I cannot see. They are talking and having drinks, and Mireille has that glowing smile on her face. She glances over at the bar and sees me. I raise my glass like I am making a toast, take a sip, and then turn around and look at Paula standing there wiping her hands on a towel.

"Who are you toasting to?" Paula asks as she walks up to me.

"An old friend at the back table," I say.

"How are you doing?" she asks.

I sip my drink and say, "I found Nino tonight."

"And?"

"I'm not a killer," I say. "He is in custody."

Paula goes behind the bar. "I'm going to make you one of my signature martinis on the house to celebrate that accomplishment."

"Sounds good to me," I say, watching her make her magic with vodka, a hint of vermouth, olives, and a generous amount of ice in the shaker.

Paula places the drink before me, and I lean down and look at it closely. "What are you doing?" she laughs.

I look up at her. "I'm appreciating a work of art."

"Well, thank you," Paula says.

I take out my phone and take a picture of the drink. "I'll be sending that to the cocktail hall of fame."

"Oh, you," Paula says with a slap on my hand, "there is no such place like that."

"It may not be a physical place, but it is online – Difford's Cocktail Hall of Fame," I say. This is a site that I like to visit to read about various cocktails, and Paula's martini should definitely be featured there. "They have hundreds of cocktails on there, and I think yours should be too."

"Well, that's very nice of you to say," Paula says.

I lift the drink and raise it. "To the artist who crafted this cocktail."

"Oh, I do like it when I get some recognition." She leans both hands on the bar and asks, "So why didn't you kill him?"

I think about it a bit and answer honestly. "I wasn't thinking of anything before I found him, and then when I saw the switchblade he threatened me with, I figured I had the evidence, and I wanted him to not get off quickly. Death would have been an easy out for him, and then I wanted him to suffer in jail."

"So, you're not a barbarian after all," Paula says.

"I know, Pete said that," I say and sip my drink.

"Well, I'm sure he'll be proud of you. I know I am."

"Thanks, Paula," I say as I lean on the bar and smile. "You know, I am kind of proud of myself too."

Paula goes through the "in" door to the kitchen, and I look up at the bar mirror and see Mireille standing behind me. I turn to her and smile, "How are you?"

Mireille forces a little grin and says, "I'm doing okay."

"Who is the lucky guy?" I ask.

"Someone from work," she whispers.

I look over at him and see that he is on his phone. "Don't worry, I'm not going to cause any trouble."

"Oh, we are not romantic," Mireille says. "We just are celebrating the booking of a big client today."

"Congratulations," I say.

"How are you doing?" she asks.

Looking at her, I think she is more beautiful than ever. "I'm...I'm doing okay. I had to take care of some things, but I'm in good place now." My heart is breaking as I look at her. How could I have lost such a lovely person?

"I'm happy to hear that," Mireille says.

I touch her arm gently and say, "I'm sorry how that situation happened. I never wanted to hurt you."

She nods her head. "I believe that, Bobby. You know, in an odd way, that was good for me. I had never been hurt by someone like that before. It taught me to be stronger and also to be more cautious."

"Well, again, I'm sorry," I say. "I wish you well."

"I feel the same way," Mireille says. She leans forward and kisses my cheek. "Be good to yourself, Bobby. *Au revoir.*"

"Goodbye," I whisper. Something about that *au revoir* seems like it means forever.

When I turn back to the bar, I see Paula throwing a clean bar towel over her shoulder. She stares at me and asks, "Is that the one?"

"Yes, it is she," I say and sip my martini.

"You still love her don't you?" she asks.

Thoughts race through my head and I say, "I loved what I thought we could be, but I was just being delusional."

"How so?" Paula asks.

"A girl like that with a guy like me?"

Paula puts her hand on my arm. "Here we go again – Mr. Self Deprecating. You have a lot to offer someone, Bobby."

I wink at her. "Thank you, Paula."

"Just try to remember that," she says.

"I will," I say, "but I have not had much luck in love."

"You have to give yourself a chance," Paula says.

"Yeah, but I'm not good at doing that," I say.

"Well, I'll keep reminding you if I have to," Paula says as someone calls her name at the other end of the bar.

I glance at the back of the room, but Mireille and her gentleman are gone. I lean on the bar and stare at the olives in my drink. There are three of them – I think one for Beth, one for Mireille, and one for Paula. I have made a mess of things more than once. I eat one olive after another, savoring their soaked in vodka goodness.

There are no more olives and perhaps no more chances for love. I think I have taken three swings, and I missed the ball three times – and with Paula by default. She does not even know that I love her. Whatever the case, three strikes mean that I am out, and I guess I deserve to be. I came to Venice to be far away from everyone and anything I have ever known. This in itself was an attempt to be alone elsewhere. When I first got here it felt blissful, but as the weeks passed by I started meeting people, and then I met Elena in a bar with Nino hovering close by. I wish that I never got involved with her, and then she probably would still be alive.

I close my eyes and listen to that sweet jazz music and think that it is not bad being alone – not that bad at all. I do have friends here, and perhaps I can focus more on my writing now. I look up at myself in the mirror behind the bar, and I raise the glass to my image and whisper, "Here's to not having to dig two graves!"

CHAPTER TWENTY-NINE – Ashes to Ashes

After I retrieve Elena's – and our baby's – ashes from the funeral parlor, I walk out into a rainy, damp, and chilly day. I put up my raincoat collar, open my umbrella, and cover the box to make sure that it does not get wet. Within the box the ashes are inside a beautiful honeycomb shaped urn that I bought online from a place in Modena.

I walk briskly to St. Mary's Basilica, where Carla is waiting for me. She is wearing a black dress under her wet raincoat. We go inside quietly, take off our coats, and sit in chairs as a few tourists have ignored the rain and are walking around the church and taking pictures. The magnicent altar with its painting of Christ ascending to his heavenly father glows even on this dreary day.

"Thank you for coming," I whisper to Carla. I open the slightly damp box and take out the urn.

"Oh, that is lovely," Carla says quietly.

"I thought we could say goodbye to her in this place," I say. "I don't know how religious she was, but I felt like I had to do something."

"Well, when we were growing up, we did go to Mass together," Carla says. She blinks her eyes several times. "I guess later on we lost our way."

"I am not judging her or you," I say.

A lone tear runs on each cheek from Carla's somber brown eyes. "I...I don't know how I could have saved her, but I know that Nino would have killed me if I didn't bring her to him. He also threatened to kill her if she didn't check out of the hospital and go to him."

"Again, I'm not judging you," I say. "Nino did everything he could to ruin both of your lives."

"Bobby, I have to tell you something," Carla says.

"Yes?"

"You know that day when Elena put the ring on the table when you were with that woman in the restaurant?"

"How can I ever forget it?" I ask.

"It really hurt her to do it," Carla says. "Nino threatened her with more violence, so she had no choice. He even scripted what she was to say. Any variation from what he wanted would have resulted in severe punishment."

I nod my head. "I figured as much."

"Please forgive her," she says.

I look down at the urn and say, "I already have."

"Thank you," Carla says, touching my arm.

"I guess we should just quietly pray for a few moments," I say.

"Yes, okay," Carla says.

We both bow our heads. I pray without speaking. "Dear God, I hope that you have forgiven Elena. I know she is with you and so is our baby. The baby never had a chance to live, so I imagine you'll have Elena be with her and comfort her. I don't know why I think the baby was a girl, but I guess because I wanted a girl when Beth was pregnant. Please allow them both to rest in peace now. They deserve happiness in paradise with you."

When I look up, I notice Carla still has her eyes closed and her hands together in prayer. More tears are coming down her cheeks and, although I used to be mad at her for bringing Elena into that terrible life, I feel sorry for her now. Carla is a victim too, forced into prostitution by an evil man. Nino is in jail and will eventually go to prison where I hope he rots for the rest of his life.

Carla finishes praying, and we both sit there and stare at the altar in silence. I close my eyes and breathe in the damp air of the church when I suddenly feel a cool breeze brush by me. I want to believe that is Elena's way of letting me know she is okay on the other side.

I look at Carla and whisper, "I want you to have the urn.

"Really?" she asks.

"Yes, of course," I say as I hand the urn to her. "Maybe if you go home one day you could bring it to Elena's family."

Carla holds the urn with both hands and stares at it. "The only family she has left is her uncle and his children. From what Elena told me, he was a mean man who made her poor mother work so hard in his factory that she got sick and died."

"Well, then you keep it," I say.

"Yes, I will keep it. Every time I look at it, it will remind me of how lucky I am to be alive after all that Nino did to me."

"That's a good idea," I say with a smile.

"You know, I'm dating someone now," Carla says.

"Oh, I'm happy for you," I say.

Carla looks up at the altar and whispers, "One day, if we are together for a long time, I will have to tell him about what I used to do. Right?"

"That's up to you," I say.

"He might hate me when he learns about it," Carla says.

"Carla," I say as I touch her arm, "if he loves you, none of that will matter to him. If it does, then he is not worthy of you."

"Not worthy of me?"

"Yes, exactly," I say. "The past is *your past*; you have to decide if you want to share it with him or not."

"Thank you, Bobby," Carla says. "You are much kinder to me than I deserve."

"Hey, if you didn't tell me about Franco, I would've never found Nino," I say. "So you deserve to move forward now with a fresh start."

"Thank you, Bobby," Carla says. She looks at her watch. "Oh, I have to get back to work."

I put the urn back in the box and hand it to Carla. We get up and walk out of the church. The rain has stopped, and the sun is shining, making everything dripping with moisture glitter like liquid gems. I close my umbrella and look at Carla. "Good luck to you, Carla. I wish you all the best."

She puts out her hand, and I shake it. "I wish you all the best too. Try to find a way to be happy."

I look out at the canal and the people crossing over it on the bridge, and say, "I'm working on it."

*

Later that day, after taking a nap and having something to eat, I sit down at my laptop and open the file Probie sent from his client who wants me to write a book about Venice. I start reading the criteria he expects to be followed and even the specific characters he wants in the book.

I look at my watch, and it is almost five o'clock, meaning it is eleven o'clock back in New York. I lean back in my chair and call Probie, who answers saying, "Long time no hear, Bobby."

"How are you doing, Probie?"

"Good. Very good. That deal in Milan went through, so I'm set for life. Are you calling about the Venice book?"

I look at the laptop screen. "Yeah, I am."

"Have you gotten started yet?"

"Probes, there is no way I can do this," I say.

"What are you talking about?" he says in a louder voice.

"I can't do it; I can't write like that," I say.

"Hey, he's willing to pay you top dollar. Are you crazy?"

"Probes, when I write a book about my time here, it's going to be the story that *I want* to write," I say.

"Oh, well, if you feel that way," Probie says, "I'll let the guy know."

"Everything else okay with you?" I ask.

"Yeah, except the Jets are breaking my heart," he says.

I follow sports on the *USA Today* app on my phone, so I know they are not doing well again this season. "Hey, come on, Probes, the Jets and Mets are always breaking our hearts. You should be used to it by now."

"Yeah, I guess," he moans.

"Take care, my friend," I say.

"Hey, Bob, are you ever coming home?"

I glance out my window at San Marco's bell tower in the distance. "You know, this place is my home now."

*

Serge and I meet for dinner in small trattoria with a view of the illuminated Rialto Bridge in the distance. We have a table by the window, and we can watch the passersby in their coats and hats. It is warm and cozy inside, assisted by a roaring fireplace, and there is a soothing soundtrack of classical music mingled with low conversation.

We have both ordered chicken Milano with a creamy pasta and sun dried tomatoes. Serge ordered a homemade house red wine, and we are on our second bottle. "This wine is outstanding," I say.

"It is a strong wine, good for the colder weather," Serge says. "It goes well with the chicken and this pasta."

"And this is an excellent place," I say glancing at the decor which is meant to look like an old country kitchen. "I must have passed it hundreds of times."

"That is the way of things," Serge says as he slips a piece of chicken into his mouth and chews. "We miss so much in life because we are focused on things that don't matter and miss the things that do."

"Well, now that I know about it," I say with a smile.

Serge sits back and sips his wine. "So, how are you, Bobby?"

"I'm doing...well," I say.

"Pietro has told me about how you took care of that criminal," Serge says with a raised eyebrow. "Very nasty business."

"Yes," I say, "but I had to do something to get justice for Elena. The police weren't able to find him."

"Pietro says the young lady was carrying your baby," Serge says as he spears a tomato with his fork.

"Yes, she was," I say and sip my wine. "Sadly, the baby died too."

Serge shakes his head. "I'm very sorry, Bobby."

"Thank you, Serge," I say. Oddly enough, I have come to accept what happened; I am still upset and cry sometimes, but I am not looking to bring other people down with my tale of woe. I cut into the chicken and chew a piece; it is crispy and delightful. "Man, this chicken is awesome!"

"It is quite something," Serge says.

"I'm aways looking for new places," I say.

Serge leans forward and whispers, "Are you ever coming back to the writing group? We miss you."

I sip some wine, purse my lips, and then say, "I...I am just not productive right now. I don't see any benefit of coming emptyhanded."

"Rolando sat there emptyhanded for weeks," Serge says, "and now he is the most prolific contributor after Pietro."

I put my knife and fork down, sit back, and sip some wine. "It's just that I need some time. Anna's death was very difficult, but losing Elena and our baby has been even worse for me."

Serge lifts his hand and moves it back and forth several times. "I'm not trying to pressure you, Bobby."

"I understand," I say.

"I'm just conveying the feelings of the whole group including myself," Serge says. "We are there every Friday at the appointed time. You're welcome whenever you want to come back to us."

"Thank you, Serge," I say softly. "I will remember that."

"I heard that you have seen Mireille," Serge says as he gently puts some pasta into his mouth.

"Really? How have you heard that?" I ask.

He finishes chewing. "A little birdy told me."

I think quickly and ask, "Do you mean Pete?"

Serge shrugs his shoulders. "He was in that establishment near Campo Erberia that you like to frequent, and the barkeeper told him that Mireille and you talked."

"Boy," I say, "it is hard to have a private life around here."

"It's only because we care," Serge says. He gathers a few sundried tomatoes on his fork. "My word, these things are delicious."

"Yes, we ran into each other," I say, trying to downplay the encounter. "She is doing fine and seeing a young man."

"Oh, I see," Serge says.

"So, don't get any ideas, Serge," I say, "besides she will never go back to the group."

"Oh, well," Serge says and sips his wine, "I thought it was worth giving it a go."

"Look, I'm okay," I say, even though I am far from okay.

"Well, perhaps you would like to meet one of Arabella's friends," Serge says with a smirk. "Remember the nurses and the Barbies at our Halloween party?"

I nod my head. "Yes, I remember them. They are lovely young ladies, but I am just good with being alone right now." I want to say that they are too young for me, but I do not want to imply that Arabella is too young for him.

Serge skews his eyebrows and says, "Fair enough, but take it from me – it is better not being alone."

"Oh, so how are things going with Arabella?" I ask with a slight grin.

"They are...going," Serge says.

"Any plans moving forward with her?" I ask.

"The Seychelles are in the forecast," Serge says.

"The Seychelles? Wow," I say.

"She came across some old photos of my family and me when we were there about 35 years ago," Serge says. "I was so young that I don't recall much about it except that the sand was very white, and the sea was very blue."

"Well, that sounds like a great vacation," I say.

"We will go after the new year," Serge says, then eats another piece of chicken. "My sisters and their families will be coming in for the holidays this year."

"Oh, I'm happy for you, Serge," I say.

Serge finishes chewing and points a fork in my direction. "You are more than welcome to come to Christmas dinner."

I think about it and say, "Okay, I would love to be there."

Serge leans forward again and whispers, "Remember, try not to be alone so much. It is not good for you."

I look out the window at the illuminated bridge and say, "Yeah, I know."

*

After saying goodnight to Serge, he heads off to his palace on the Grand Canal, and I start walking home through the narrow streets toward my building. I have been thinking a great deal about my life after what happened to Elena. I am not sure that I am on the right path yet, but I think that I am going in the right direction.

I come to a small bridge over a canal, and as a gondola glides beneath it, a young couple standing on the bridge leans against the railing and starts to kiss deeply. I stop walking and turn away because I do not want to intrude upon their sacred moment. In that instance there should be a kind of purity that goes undisturbed.

A few moments later, the girl is giggling as they go down the steps on the other side and off into the night. Perhaps I am over accentuating the importance of that encounter on the bridge, but I think not. It is at the heart of what is all good in life. Elena never had a chance for romance, and it is a shame because she deserved it.

The last time Mireille and I kissed was sacred like that. There was an essence of purity in the moment – it is the tingling phase of desire that is above and beyond lust. It is when the soul is more important than the body because it transcends physical need for emotional satisfaction.

I continue walking and thinking about how Mireille and I had reached a pinnacle in our relationship at that time. When we were eating in that restaurant and talking about love, the possibility of intimacy was emerging. And then Elena came along, slapped my ring on the table, and ruined everything.

When I reach my building, I turn the key in the outer door, enter, hit the light switch, and shut the door. Up the 62 steps I go, into my flat, and I look around at the bare walls. I have lived here for seven months, and I still have not decorated to make the space personal. Perhaps that is intentional, but perhaps not.

I change into shorts and a Mets T-shirt, grab a beer from the fridge, and sit by the window staring at the illuminated bell tower. Since I have lived in this flat, I have come to appreciate the view more and more. I feel like I have a connection to that elegant bell tower. There is something personal between us, as if its presence makes me feel like I belong in this city because of it. Like a lighthouse, it is a

beacon of hope to ships and souls lost in the darkness. I find

this symbol provides some sort of dubious comfort to help

me get though another long, lonely night.

CHAPTER THIRTY – Friends Without Benefits

I take my morning walk on a foggy, chilly December day that includes a trip over the Rialto Bridge. I make my way through Piazza San Marco where there a few shoppers and seemingly no tourists. Because of the overcast skies, many of the Christmas lights remain illuminated in stores and restaurants, and they twinkle resiliently through the mist hovering above the square. A large Christmas tree is in the center of the square, decorated with many small white lights and large illuminated balls that make for a stunning effect on this dark winter's day.

Once I reach the waters of San Marco's Basin, I see the gondolas bobbing in the cold lagoon waters. The gondoliers are valiantly bundled up against the chill, and their gondolas are festooned with lights and Christmas decorations. It seems that they – who are at not just the heart but the very soul of Venice – have copious amounts of Christmas spirit.

I look out over the water, and remember last Christmas season when one act of stupidity changed my life forever.

Beth was in our bedroom zipping up her laptop case. She looked up at me and said, "I'll be back by Christmas Eve morning." We always celebrated Christmas Eve with my mother and brother and his family.

I was still annoyed with her for going away – not so much with the trip but with her rising up the ranks in the company while I kept stagnating in the same position that I had when Beth first came to work there. "Okay, that's great. It will make Mom happy."

She put on her coat, put the strap of the laptop bag on her shoulder, and leaned over to pick up her suitcase, but I bent down to pick it up. "What are you doing?" she asked.

I decided that I would drive her to the airport. "I'm going to take you to JFK."

"You don't have to do that," Beth said. "I can call an Uber."

"Remember, I used to live near there," I said. "I know all the shortcuts to get there quickly that even Siri doesn't know."

Beth stared at my face and said, "No, it's okay. I know you aren't happy about me taking this trip, so let me call an Uber."

"It's not that I...I envy your success," I said – but that was exactly what was the matter.

"Look, Bobby, we can talk about this when I get back," she said taking out her phone. Within less than a minute, she had a ride to the airport.

"Be careful," I said and gave her a halfway hug. "It's cold in London at this time of year."

"You take care of yourself, and go to the office

Christmas party and have fun. Okay?" she said.

I really did not want to go without her, but I nodded

my head and said, "Yeah, okay."

Now, I regret going to that party every time I think

about it. I wish I just stayed home and watched *Die Hard* – a

tradition I practiced every Christmas season because it is a

Christmas movie despite Bruce Willis saying that it was not!

I was vulnerable back then, and vulnerability and drinking

are not a good mix. Add into the mix a young co-worker who

– despite knowing I was married – flirted with me and got me

to take her home, making certain everyone at the party knew

about it. *I was such an idiot!*

As I turn to walk away from the waterfront, I hear

someone yelling, "Bobby, Bobby." I look around to see who

it is, and Isabella is standing there in a jogging outift. Her

beautiful face is glowing in the cold, misty air, and her long

blonde hair is up in a bun.

"Hi, Isabella," I say. "How are you?"

She takes a deep breath and exhales as she has just stopped running. "I'm doing well. How are you doing?"

I glance out over the water and say, "It gets a little better each day."

She puts a hand on my arm and says, "You have been through a terrible ordeal. It's going to take time."

"Yeah," I say – and truthfully I am not sure how I am really doing but say, "Catching Nino was a big help."

"Yes, I saw it on the news," she says. "When I heard about all his past crimes, I felt even more impressed that you went after him."

I shake my head. "It wasn't meant to do anything but find justice."

"But you didn't use street justice as you seemed to hint about doing," Isabella says.

"No, when the time came, I was able to subdue him and find the murder weapon, so I felt good that I got to punch him a few times. That was enough. The weapon must have traces of Elena's blood on it, so they will have a strong case."

"I'm glad to hear that," Isabella says. "I wanted justice for Elena too."

"I know you did," I say.

"You know, Bobby, I would have texted or called you to check in on you," Isabella says, "but I didn't want to violate your space or anything. I know mourning is difficult and personal from my work at the hospital."

"Yeah, it is," I say. "Carla – the girl with the red hair – and I recently took Elena and my baby's ashes to church and prayed over them."

"Oh, that is wonderful," Isabella says. "That was a way to provide some closure."

"This fellow Tinno, who has a shop in the Rialto Market, told me that I could spread her ashes at San Michele, but I got a beautiful urn and put the ashes in it instead."

"That sounds lovely, Bobby," Isabella says with smile.

"I let Carla keep it because she and Elena knew each other since they were little kids," I say. "She was the closest thing Elena had to family."

"Well, I think that is a grand gesture," Isabella says.

"Thanks, Isabella," I say. "And thank you for all your efforts with Elena. I know you really cared about her."

"I did," Isabella says. "We got to talk and get to know one another. I just wish I could have saved her."

I look out over the water again and say, "Yeah, I wish I could have saved her too."

"What are you doing for Christmas?" she asks.

I think about Serge's invitation. "Oh, I am invited to a friend's house for Christmas dinner. What about you?"

"Oh, I'm going home to see my family in Ortisei," she says.

"Where is that, Isabella?"

"It is a town in the Dolomites," Isabella says.

I have always wanted to visit the Dolomites because I have heard much talk about the area from Serge and Pietro. "Oh, wow, that must be lovely."

"Yes, the whole town becomes a Christmas village," Isabella says. "We have relatives who join us for dinners and walks through the magical town and market. It is really quite lovely there."

"It sounds wonderful," I say, and then I think about Serge going skiing up there. "A friend of mine has a place up there and likes to go skiing."

"Oh, yes," Isabella says with a wide smile, "my brothers and I will go skiing during the week."

"Well, if I don't see you, Isabella, Merry Christmas to you and your family," I say.

"Thanks, Bobby," she says, "Merry Christmas to you." Isabella smiles, turns around, and starts jogging away.

I look out over the basin again and watch the waters swell up and rock the empty gondolas tied up there. I wonder how I can have any kind of Christmas this year, but I will try not to be alone and make the best of it.

*

A few days later I force myself to go to the last writers' meeting before the holidays. Serge has had his staff decorate the foyer and outside of the house in grand style, and the ballroom where we hold our meetings has a twelve-foot tall Christmas tree that is shimmering with lights and gold ornaments.

Once the business of the meeting is over, the group begins to gravitate over to the buffet where the Three Germans are always first on line. Rolando and Pietro are standing behind them waiting for the men to load up their plates.

Serge is wearing a festive red Santa cap to match his red tie, and Arabella is wearing a red and green dress that is lovely. Serge sits in his chair as Arabella scoots over to the piano. I take a clean but hot white plate and stand behind Pietro just as Arabella starts playing "Jingle Bells." He turns to me and says, "Now she is butchering another song."

"Well, at least she is branching out," I say.

"I think she is getting better," Rolando chimes in with a smile.

"Please," Pietro says, "let us just end the agony now!"

Heinrich must have heard us talking, and he turns to us and says, "I think Miss Arabella plays a nice piano."

"Yeah," Pietro snarls, "but *nice* is not the word for it."

We bring the food over to our table, and then Pietro goes up to the bar to get our drinks. Rolando eats some pasta and looks at me. "Why no story tonight, Bobby?"

I shake my head. "I...I still can't write more than a few sentences at a time."

"Well, that is a start," he says with a smile.

"No, they are practicaly incoherent," I say. "It is like I forgot how to write. I know I can, but it is not working for me."

"They call it 'writer's block' or something," Rolando says as he chews a meatball.

"Yeah, more like blockhead," I say.

Pietro hands me a martini, Rolando a beer, and he has what looks like a gin and tonic. He lifts his glass and says, "Cheers, gentlemen."

Rolando repeats the word but I cannot say it. "Sorry guys, I'm not in a festive spirit," I say.

Pietro leans toward me and says, "Your even being here is testimony to your resiliency, considering what you have been through this year."

"Thanks, Pete," I say.

As Arabella finishes her continued loop of "Jingle Bells," Whitman turns on the sound system and Nat King Cole's "The Christmas Song" flows across the glittering room. Serge comes up from behind us and puts his hands on the backs of Rolando and Pietro's chairs. "Well, my friends, we had some fine readings tonight."

"Yes we did," Pietro says.

"Your Christmas poem was melancholy but still in keeping with the season's joyous aspects," Serge says to Pietro.

"Why thank you, Serge. It sums up how I feel after the events in my life this year," Pietro says.

Serge turns to Rolando. "And your story about the little boy and Babbo Natale was quite moving."

"Thank you, Serge," Rolando says. "It is really a tale that comes from my childhood when I went to see him at the Christmas market."

"When I was a boy, I preferred waiting for La Befana," Serge says. "Christmas Eve and Day were more religious for my family."

"La Befana?" I ask.

"A very old woman who leaves presents on the Eve of the Epiphany," Pietro says. "She never brought me anything – that witch!

Serge chuckles and says, "Well, your story was lovely, Rolando." He turns and looks at me with his usual deadpan expression. "And I was hoping for something from you, Bobby."

I shake my head. "As I was telling Rolando, I am still not getting anywhere with my writing."

Pietro sips his drink and says, "Your muse has gone into hiding."

"Yeah, it's like she is on another planet," I say.

"Well, don't give up hope, Bobby," Serge says. "We've all gone though those dry spells as writers." Someone calls to Serge from across the room, and he says, "Excuse me."

Pietro chews his food and looks up at the ceiling as if he is thinking. "You know, I just realized that I have come to every meeting this year with something to read."

Rolando sips his beer and says, "That is quite commendable."

"Thank you, Rolando," Pietro says. "My binder runneth over."

I eat some pasta and think that he missed that one meeting because of Brian breaking up with him, but I will not stoop to his level. This is a tough night for me because this was the date of last year's office Christmas party back in New York – the night that changed my life forever.

*

After leaving Serge's home, we decide to go to the taverna. The place is decorated festively, and music is playing with a Christmas song slipped into the mix here and there. The place is usually filled with a mix of locals, expats, and tourists in the warmer months. Recently, it is just the locals and and a few expats.

Pietro gets the corner table that he likes for he assumes he has privacy there. I go to the bar to order the drinks from Gina. I ask her, "Where's Paula?"

"Oh, she had to go the doctor today," Gina says.

"Is everything okay?" I ask.

"Yes, as far as I know," Gina says.

I take the drinks over to the table – gin and tonic for Pietro, beer for Rolando, and a Smirnoff Red on the rocks for me – and I sit down and say, "Paula is not here tonight."

Pietro sips his drink. "Hmm. That's a first."

"I hope everything is okay," Rolando says.

"Gina told me that she had to go to the doctor today," I say. "She is not aware if it is anything serious."

"Well, she has always been there for us," Pietro says, "so we can be there for her if it is anything serious."

Rolando leans forward and asks, "Did you think Serge seemed a little different tonight?"

"In what way?" I ask.

"He seemed more – serious. Like something was on his mind," Rolando says.

Pietro sits back and sighs. "That's our Serge – he always has the weight of the world on his shoulders."

"How so?" I ask.

Pietro raises an eyebrow and says, "Sergio Matteo Rossi is the keeper of the flame – his family's legacy. He has six centuries worth of heft of legacy to keep balanced. And his sisters and brother don't always make it easy for him."

Rolando looks at Pietro, sips his beer, and asks, "How long have you known Serge?"

"Oh, since our college days," Pietro says. "He was a handsome young man for whom the girls were very attracted. Let's just say he was never not accompanied by at least one of them."

I think about Arabella and say, "It seems he still is not lacking for company."

Pietro snickers, "Always younger, always prettier than the last one."

"Poor contessa," Rolando says.

Pietro laughs. "Not at all. I've seen her out on the town with another older gent who has lots of money. Her family is struggling, and they're trying to marry her off well to help the family."

"Wow," I say, not having known this before. "Serge seems to have been wise to the situation."

Pietro nods his head. "Not much gets past him. That's why I don't understand this thing with Arabella."

I think about it and say, "I think Serge loved Anna."

"We all did," Pietro says.

"Of course," I say, "but I think he just found Arabella to be this young girl who was in trouble with finances, and he wanted to help her."

Pietro slaps his hand on the table. "That's what I mean – just like the contessa!"

I sip my drink and shake my head. "No, not at all. The contessa came from old money that dried up; Arabella never had anything to begin with. She is more worthy of his attention because she was poor."

"Well," Pietro says, "perhaps Serge is trying to make up for the way he treated his first wife."

"The mother of his child," I say

"Serge has a kid?" Rolando asks.

Pietro looks at him and says, "A son, who would be around thirteen now. I know that he regrets not having much of a relationship with the boy."

I start thinking about that and ask, "Does Serge recognize him as his heir?"

Pietro finishes his drink and says, "Well, I think young Sergio Matteo Rossi VI definitely is his heir."

"Wow," Rolando says as he looks up at the ceiling, "that kid is going to inherit this palace."

Pietro gets up and says, "I'll get the drinks."

I think about Serge's son and how that could be an interesting story, but I would not want to insult him, so I will forget about that for now.

*

The next day my phone rings as I wake up groggily to the sound, and I discover it is under my bed and, as I try to reach it, I fall down on the floor.

When I finally answer it, I hear Paula's voice. "Hi, Bobby."

"Hey, Paula, we missed you last night at the taverna," I say.

"I had things to take care of yesterday," she says, her voice sounding sad.

"Oh, is everything okay?" I ask.

"Can you meet me today?" she asks

I run my fingers through my hair and am worried about her. "Yeah, sure, where do you want to meet?"

"There's a place on the other side of the Rialto right over the bridge," she says.

"I know exactly where that is," I say.

"Is noon okay?" she asks.

I look at my watch, and that gives me about an hour. "Yeah, sure, noon will be fine."

*

I bundle up on this very chilly gray day; the mist is hanging over the streets like waves of dreariness. I wonder about Paula and what is going on – she is usally so upbeat and positive! Her voice on the phone was chillingly somber. I am not sure if I can handle any more bad news about someone I care about.

When I get to the restaurant, Paula is sitting outside on the wall that runs along the steps up to the Rialto Bridge, wearing a coat and crooked New York Yankees baseball cap – which can be seen worn by people all around the city who probably have no clue about the team. I point to my Mets cap on my head and say, "You really could pick a better team."

"Yeah, I suppose," she says with a low dull voice.

"Are you okay?" I ask.

"Can we just go back to your flat?" she asks. "It's really cold, and I don't want to just sit inside."

"Yeah, sure," I say.

We walk back across the bridge in silence. I think about it, and I have never seen Paula outside of the taverna or in the daylight. Her face is even prettier in the outdoor light, and yet she walks with a sort of cloud over her head that is concerning.

After we enter my building, Paula has no issues with the 62 steps up to my flat. When we reach the top of the stairs, I say, "Those steps nearly killed Pete."

She smiles for the first time and says, "Not surprising."

We go inside to the warmth of my rooms. I ask, "Would you like some coffee?"

She shakes her head. "Tea, if you have it. No milk, please."

I look in my drawer and do have some tea, so I put the kettle on the stove and start the coffee for me. I look in the fridge and say, "I have a couple of old croissants. I can microwave them if you like."

Paula stares at my bare walls and says, "The tea is fine."

Once her tea and my coffee are made, I sit down on a chair across from her and watch as she sips her tea with a sullen expression. "What is going on, Paula? I've never seen you like this before."

"You know," she pauses and looks up at the ceiling as if she is gathering her thoughts, "I'm better at helping others than I am myself."

I sip my coffee. "Hmm. That's an interesting observation."

"I am upset because things with Viv and me are not going well," Paula whispers.

"Oh, I'm sorry to hear that," I say and sip my coffee. "I always thought the two of you were the most stable couple." I do not want to get hopeful, but could this be my opening to have a chance with her?

"We usually are," she says, "but things are always okay until they aren't."

"So, what's happening?" I ask.

"Well, Viv wants to have a baby," Paula says. "She wanted to be the mother but went to the doctor, and it turns out she...she is not capable of having a baby."

"Oh, I'm sorry," I say.

"So, when I wasn't at the bar, I was at the doctor," Paula says.

"Oh, yeah, I was a little worried because Gina didn't tell me much," I say.

"Because she was under direct orders," Paula says with a glimmer of a smile.

"Okay, so what happened?"

Paula puts down her cup and grasps her knees with her hands. "My eggs are viable; I can have a baby."

"Well, that's good news, right?"

"The thing is, I am 34, so I have to get pregnant soon," she says.

"Yeah, I guess," I say. "My wife was 34 too when she got pregnant." I realize I should not have said that since Beth lost the baby.

"Bobby, I am ovulating now," Paula says. "Viv and I both agreed that we want you to be the sperm donor."

"What?" I ask incredulously.

"If you would agree," she says.

I put down my cup and say, "I would be honored, of course."

Paula bites her lower lip and says, "The thing is, we don't have time for you to go to the doctor's office and do this because I am ovulating *right now*!"

"What?" I think I know what she is saying, but I am not certain.

"We are asking...I mean, I'm asking for you to do it the old fashioned way for expediencey," she says.

"Really?" Now, I have always found Paula extremely sexy and attractive, but I never thought this would happen.

Paula says, "You know, I used to live my life as a bisexual before I met Viv. It's not like I haven't been with a guy before."

"So, Viv is okay with this?" I ask.

"Yes, she is," Paula says and smiles. "This is simply business."

"And you both approve of me?"

Paula bends her head a little sideways and says, "You're the nicest man I've ever known, except for my father."

"Well, I'm honored," I say.

"So, you will do it for us?" she asks.

I run my hands through my hair and smile. "I don't know if I appreciate being used this way." We both look at each other and burst out laughing.

Paula stands up and looks lovely in her jeans and tight T-shirt. "Come on, in the beginning before I told you about how I was living with Viv, you kind of fancied me."

I stand up and say, "Yeah, sure I did. You're beautiful, funny, sexy, and you make the best martini this side of Manhattan."

"Okay, then," she smiles. "Let's make a baby."

*

After Paula leaves my flat, I go into the bathroom to take a shower because I am all sweaty from our session. As usual, I take off my wedding ring and place it on the sink. I get into the shower and rub the shampoo into my hair, I think about my conversation with Paula after we had sex.

I was not sure if it was good for Paula or not. I felt like she was robotic as she went through the motions. I understood that this was not an attraction thing for her but rather it was sex with a purpose – to get Paula pregnant. When we finished, I fell down on the bed and looked up at the ceiling, catching my breath.

After a few moments of silence, Paula whispered, "I hope this doesn't affect our friendship."

I leaned my elbow on the bed and put my head on my upturned hand. "Why should it affect our friendship?"

"I don't know," Paula said, "sometimes sex changes things between people."

"Well, did it feel okay for you?" I asked.

She glanced at me and grinned. "Yeah, it was okay."

I wanted to think it was great for her. "No bells or whistles?"

Paula closed her eyes. "It was what it was, Bobby."

Okay, I think, but it was great for me, but I was not going to say that. "Well, you said this was about making a baby," I said. "I think what we did was done in the spirit of friendship." I was lying. I have always wanted her and am just realizing it now.

Paula sits up, and I can briefly see her seahorse tattoo, but she glances at me and covers her breasts with the sheet. "I want it to be that way."

"You said that Viv approved, right?" I asked.

"She is...okay with it," Paula said.

"Look," I started feeling nervous at that point, "I'm just a sperm donor here. As long as everyone is okay, it's good for me." I am saying this, but I do not believe it. I have always liked Paula – sort of lusted for her in the beginning – and now I feel she is not just a friend. I feel something more for her.

Paula got up and started getting dressed. "Let's hope that this works, so we don't have to do it again."

"Hey," I said, "was it that bad?" How can I tell her the sex we had was not just good but amazing because I have feelings for her?

Paula hooked her bra and then pulled the sweater over her head. "No, it's just that I'm not used to having sex just to have sex like you are."

"Ouch," I say as I put on my underwear. "You have to remember that I did that with Elena because I was lonely."

"I know," Paula said as she put on her jeans. "I'm not judging you at all."

I walked her to the door and said, "Good luck. I hope this works."

She rubbed my arm and said, "Viv and I appreciate your help."

I watched her go down the stairs, turned around, and locked my door.

After the shower, I stand there dripping wet with a towel around me staring at my wedding ring on the sink. Usually, I put it right back on, but today I open the drawer next to the sink and drop it in there. I think that ring has caused enough pain, and it is time for me to stop wearing it.

After I dry off and get dressed, I sit down in front of my laptop and have the urge to write something about Paula and me. It is definitely an odd feeling now – a resounding sense of weird vibes overwhelm me. Am I guity for having enjoyed sex with Paula and realizing that I care about her more than just as a friend? Am I wrong for being upset that she did not enjoy it? Were we just like animals in the wild having sex to procreate? In some ways, we are worse than that because we know what we are doing.

I finally decide not to write anything about Paula – if I read it during our writers' meetings, Serge, Pietro, and Rolando would know that I was writing about her. I can only imagine how much Pietro would enjoy knowing that. I am not going to give him the satisfaction, but what else can I write about?

After finding no inspiration, I get up and grab a beer and stand at the window looking at San Marco's magnificent bell tower slighty obscured on this misty day. I think about the idea of Paula having my baby. I should have asked more questions – will the baby even know who I am? Or will Paula and Viv eventually tell the child I was an anonymous sperm donor? I secretly wish this situtation will make Paula want me and breakup with Viv, but I know that is never going to happen. In the grand scheme of things, the kid is probably not going to know anything about me, and maybe she will be better off that way.

CHAPTER THIRTY-ONE – Dust to Dust

It is a week after Paula and I were together and a week before Christmas. I walk along the dark streets brightened with Christmas lights, illuminated stars, and the happy faces of people rushing from shop to shop and enjoying this festive season. A few resilient diners here and there are bundled up and sitting at outside tables of the restaurants I pass. Other restaurants have their tables and chairs stacked up outside, and those places are more crowded inside where there is warmth.

After eating leftovers at home, I am making my way to the taverna. Yes, in some ways I have avoided going there this past week. I did not want to text Paula to see how she was doing – I was hoping that she would text me. Despite how I feel about Paula, I do want to see Viv and her have happy lives with a healthy baby – even if it is my kid.

When I go inside the taverna, I say, "*Come stai, Lorenzo?*" The music is playing and people are talking loudly almost over one another.

"Very good," he says as he motions toward the crowded room. "We are very busy tonight!"

"Take care, my friend," I say as I navigate my way through the packed sitting area toward the bar. I see Paula and Gina talking near the service bar, and Gina motions in my direction, causing Paula to smile at me.

She walks over to where I am standing at the bar and asks, "Hello, stranger! Where have you been?"

I am not sure how to respond, but I say, "I've been trying to write something, so I've been staying in and working."

"I thought you were avoiding me," Paula says with a smirk.

"Never!" I say with a smile.

"How about a martini?" she asks.

"Sounds good," I say. I go over to the corner and hang up my coat. When I return to my spot the martini is glistening on the bar in all its glory. "Another masterpiece!"

Paula leans on the bar and stares at me. "*Are we okay?*"

"Yeah, of course, *we are*," I say. "How's Viv?"

"She's excited about the possibility of a baby," Paula says. "Obviously, it's way too early to be anything but patient."

I sip my drink and wink at her. "Another glorious success."

"Are you really, okay?" Paula asks, flipping a bar towel over her arm.

"Yeah, I'm fine," I say, but that is a lie. "But I was wondering about something."

"What is it?"

"Didn't you feel anything for me when we had…"

"Bobby," she says as her eyebrows arch, "what are you trying to say?"

"Oh, nothing," I lie again because I want her to have felt something more for me than just being a sperm donor. "But what are you going to tell the child about me?"

Paula's eyes widen and she takes a deep breath. "What do you want us to tell the child about you?"

I sip my drink and say the truth. "I don't want anything. I just was wondering if I will get to know the child."

"Yeah, sure, you can be *Uncle Bobby* who comes over for dinner on Sunday occasionally. How does that sound?"

By the position of her eyebrows, I understand that she is a little annoyed with me. "Look, I am not asking for anything. I'm just wondering."

Paula's face softens and she smiles. "We will see what happens, Bobby. Will you even still be living here five years from now?"

"Trying to get rid of me?" I chuckle.

"No, not at all," she says, looking at me sideways as she walks toward the other end of the bar.

As I sip my drink, the song "In a Dream" by Rockell starts playing, and it cuts me to my heart.

I was at the middle school dance, and the DJ started playing "In a Dream," and I was wearing my Sunday clothes I wore for church. I heard the words "In a dream, my love/you will find my heart" just as I gazed over at Bonnie, all blonde and beautiful in a polka dot dress as she danced with her friends.

Probie slapped my arm. "Go over and ask her to dance!"

She looked up at me, smiled, and then went back to dancing. I mumbled, "I can't; I just can't!"

I wanted to go up to her and dance with her, but I was frozen. Instead, I walked over to the snack table and took a cold Sunny D with a shaky hand. I could not do it. I was just too scared to tell her how I felt in fear of being rejected.

All these years later, and I have learned nothing. After all this time, how can I tell Paula that I love her. I know, I thought I loved Mireille, but it was perhaps more like an infatuation. She was way out of my league anyway. And poor Elena, I cared about her and had sex with her, but I was trying more to protect her. I do not think it was love, but I did care about her.

How can I tell Paula now that was all *Sturm und Drang*, my going through the turmoil of post-divorce and living in a strange new place. All this time I have been in love with Paula and would not let myself realize it until now. Just like the kid at the middle school dance, I have no way to tell Paula how I feel.

Pietro comes up to the bar, and his nose is twitching those whiskers. "There is not one available table."

"Oh, so now you have to stand up here with the peasants," I say.

He quickly hangs up his coat and then grabs his arms and shivers. "There is a chill in the air tonight."

Gina comes over to us and asks Pietro, "What can I get you?"

Pietro looks up at the ceiling, taps his fingers on the bar, and says, "I'll take a glass of Vecchia Romagna." He glances at me and my drink. "How can you drink that cold swill on a night like this?"

"It is my perfect drink no matter the weather," I say.

When Pietro gets his drink, he spies people leaving a table and scrambles over to it to stake a claim. It is very strange how much sitting at a table means to him rather than standing at the bar. I walk over to the table and join him. He looks at me and says, "Now, isn't this more civilized?"

"Whatever makes you happy, Pete," I say.

"I heard that Serge invited you for Christmas dinner," Pietro says as he sniffs his drink and then takes a sip.

"Did a little birdie tell you this?" I ask with a smile.

"No, Whitman did," Pietro says as he sips his drink. "He has always been my confidant in all matters Serge."

"How lucky you are," I say and sip my martini.

"I've also heard that Serge is going to make a big announcement at the dinner," Pietro says, "ahead of his trip to the Seychelles with Arabella."

"Wow. You are on the inside now, Pete," I say with a smile. It is always a game with him, so I play along.

"It is believed that he will tell us that he and Arabella will be married early next year," Pietro says, his whiskers vibrating with excitement.

I am rather surprised that Serge would do this since everything he has said to me has indicated that he would never marry again. "Well, that is a shocker."

"I also heard that his son will be coming in for Christmas," Pietro says, cupping the brandy snifter in his hand and swirling the dark liquid. "He hasn't seen the kid in years."

"Well, it sounds like it will be interesting," I say. "And thank the Lord for Whitman's inability to keep quiet."

"Yes, that Whitman likes to talk," Pietro says.

I sit there thinking that a year ago my life was so different. Now I have all these new friends, I am living in another city in another country, and I am spending Christmas in a palace on the Grand Canal. Fate has certainly brought me to a place I never thought I would be.

Somehow, I feel at home here. I know that it should not make sense, but after Beth left me, I found myself feeling like other – meaning I did not belong there anymore. I felt as if my whole life had changed so drastically – losing my job, my wife, and my friends that I had known for years before Beth arrived on the scene – and felt that I was out of place.

I remembered being in Venice many years before with two friends from college. We had such a good time, and I recalled happily riding around the canals and feeling a freedom that invigorated my sense of wanting to be independent and out on my own. I loved my parents, but this was a whole new world to explore. I knew I would come back one day, but not in a way like this – a lonely person in search of love and sanctuary.

*

The next morning as I am making coffee, my phone rings. I check the screen and it is Carla. I answer it saying, "Pronto."

"Bobby, it's Carla," she says sounding all flustered.

"What is wrong?" I ask.

"Bobby, I'm having very bad dreams," she says.

"What kind of bad dreams?"

Carla starts to cry. "Ones where I see Nino killing Elena – over and over again. They seem too real."

"Oh, I'm sorry to hear that," I say.

"The thing is I think I know what's causing the dreams," Carla says.

"Yeah, what?"

"I think it's Elena's ashes," Carla says. "I see shadows in my room at night, like she is moving around and over my bed."

I take a deep breath and exhale. I think that she believes this is happening because of the ashes, so there will be no reasoning with her. "Why would Elena be doing this to you?"

"Maybe because I am the one who brought her here," she says. "She's haunting me because she is angry with me."

"So, what do you want me to do?" I ask.

"I…I want you to take the ashes," Carla says and starts crying again. "I can't have them here anymore."

I suppose there is no other way to resolve this, so I say, "Okay, I'll come and take the ashes."

"I have to leave for work now," Carla says. "Please come to the store to get them, okay Bobby?"

I say, "Yeah, I'll see you soon."

I get dressed quickly, take a few sips of my coffee, take my backpack, throw on my coat, and put on my Mets cap and sunglasses, and then I am out the door. As I am walking toward the Rialto Bridge to cross over to get to the Prada Store, I wonder about people's superstitions. Surely, in her rational mind, Carla must know that those ashes are not causing these dreams. She is really dealing with her guilty conscience, but Carla wants to believe this is something supernatural. Maybe thinking that way eases her suffering, but it seems to me that it only enhances it.

When I arrive at the store, I realize how beautiful it is shining in the sunlight with its awnings flapping in the wind. As I head for the entrance, Carla pops outside with a small but distinctive Prada shopping bag. She is wearing a red sweater, black skirt, and looks tired from lack of sleep. "I'm sorry to have bothered you," she says.

I take the bag and put it inside my backpack. "It's not a problem," I say. "But you look like really tired."

Carla nods her head and says, "Yes, I know I do."

I touch her arm and say, "Take care of yourself, Carla. Get a good night's sleep tonight."

"Yes, I will," she says, "*grazie*, Bobby."

"*Ciao*, Carla," I say and start walking away. I wonder if Carla will sleep well tonight, or will the guilt continue to haunt her.

*

Back at my flat, I put the urn with Elena's ashes on the mantel of my closed-up fireplace. I heat my coffee, and then I sit down at my laptop to research scattering the ashes

on San Michele where I have heard it can be done. As I read

about it, there are forms to be filled out and a fee of 16 euros,

but it seems to take about six months to get approval.

I get up and look at the urn again, and I figure I will

keep it. The ashes are all that are left of Elena and our baby

that never had a chance to live. Sadly, they will be a reminder

of two lives taken way before their time. I do not understand

any of this, but I will try to make sense of it as I live my life.

Maybe I can look at the urn each day and be reminded to

enjoy the gift of life that I have sometimes taken for granted.

Each day as I wake up and take my first steps, I will pass that

urn and remember to live life to the fullest for them.

CHAPTER THIRTY-TWO – Something Wicked Comes This Way

It is a few days before Christmas, and as I buy my apple from Tinno in the Rialto Market, the warmth of the sun is comforting. He points up to the sky and says, "God is good to us today. I don't need my scarf or my gloves."

I bite into the apple and chew as I say, "We must enjoy life's little blessings."

"Are you religious, Bobby?" Tinno asks.

I think about my time in Catholic school. For a while after that experience of mixed emotions, I did not reject God but rather his emissaries who made my life miserable. However, over the years since I have grown to appreciate God's subtle way of being with me, even when I faltered with Beth. Perhaps God inspired me to come to Venice to start anew. "Uh, yeah, I say my prayers and count my blessings," I say.

Tinno smiles, exposing some bad teeth. "Good for you, Bobby."

"Have a nice day, Tinno," I say as I start walking toward the steps to go over the bridge for the rest of my daily walk. My phone rings, and I see that it is Adamu calling.

"Hey, what's up?" Adamu asks.

"I'm just taking my daily walk," I say. "How's it going?"

"I'm coming there tomorrow for my annual Christmas visit with my father," Adamu says.

"Hey, that's great," I say. "We have to get together."

"Well, you are invited to celebrate with us on Christmas if you have nothing else to do," Adamu says.

"Uh," I think about Serge's invitation and say, "I am invited to dinner on Christmas Day."

"How about Christmas Eve?"

"Yeah, I'm free," I say.

"We will have the traditional fish feast," Adamu says.

I remember my father's mother making that dinner each year. "Oh, so you guys do the seven fishes too?"

"Of course, so get ready for some good old baccalá," Adamu chuckles.

"What about some fried sardines?" I asking, remembering my favorite dish that Nonna served on that night.

"Yes, they're on the menu. We will have the works, man," Adamu says. "And lots of vino."

"Then I'm definitely in," I say.

"Okay, I'm gonna finish packing and head over to JFK. See you soon, Bobby," he says enthusiastically.

After I hang up, I start walking up the steps of the bridge to get to the other side, but I stop at the top, lean on the wall, and savor the view of the Grand Canal. There are no clouds in the sky, and the sun glitters on the water. The gondolas with Christmas decorations on them float along the smooth surface of the canal, and even a few of the gondoliers are wearing Santa hats. There is a cool holiday vibe in Venice that is much more subdued than in my frenetic hometown during the holidays.

I walk through the square where shoppers are walking on both sides of the large Christmas tree in its center. Making my way to the water, I look out at San Marco's Basin and love the view – I never tire of standing in this spot.

I turn around and start walking, heading for Giardini dell Marinaressa, a public park that has some very interesting and unique sculptures. It is also a nice place to sit on a bench and soak in the view without having too many people around.

I am happy to have heard from my old friend, and I am glad he is coming back to town. I would never have believed that I would have invitations for Christmas Eve and

Christmas Day on my first holiday season in Venice. At this point, I am not even thinking about New Year's Eve.

Once I am in the park, I sit on a bench and take a deep breath. I can see San Marco's bell tower from here in the distance. Directly in front of me is a very red sculpture of a man doing a handstand – with extremely large, exaggerated feet. There are people standing next to it to get their picture taken. I think I will skip that. There are many other sculptures, and my favorite is a large white elephant.

My phone rings, and I see it is Carla's number. I pick up and she is breathing heavily. "Hey, Carla," I say, "what's up?"

"Nino is out of jail," she says catching her breath. "He came to the store and caused a scene."

"How is he out of jail?" I ask. "And how does he know where you work?"

"He said he saw me give you the bag with the ashes in it the other day," she says. "I'm afraid, Bobby."

"Why didn't you call the police?" I ask.

"The store manager did," Carla says, "but Nino ran away."

My head is spinning with a million thoughts. How the hell did Nino not get convicted? Why is he not in jail? My first thought is about Carla's safety. "Okay, Carla, you have to stay in the store in case he is still around. I'll come and get you."

"I can take my lunch in about 30 minutes," she says.

"Okay, tell them you are feeling sick and going home for the day," I say.

"Yes, Bobby," she says. "I'll see you soon."

I get up and start running and going over bridges to get back to San Marco Square. I cannot believe that Nino is free. I thought that I did the right thing and called the police. How can this be happening?

My phone is ringing, and it is Isabella. "Pronto!" I say.

"Did you see it on the news?" Isabella asks.

"See what?"

"Nino is out of jail," she screams.

"Oh, yeah, I just heard," I say.

"They say that the case was dismissed," she says.

I stop walking and lean on the bridge wall. "I said I was willing to testify. I gave them the switchblade he used."

"They say there were no traces of blood on the blade, Bobby," Isabella says, "so he got out. They may believe he is guilty, but he got out on what they said were technicalities."

"Okay, well I am glad your legal system is as messed up as mine. Elena's friend Carla was already threatened by him today at the store where she works," I say. "I'm going to the store to get her out of there safely."

"Bobby," Isabella says, "please call the police."

"The police?" I ask. "Did you see the long list of all his arrests? He knows how to play the system."

I start walking again and Isabella says, "Be careful, Bobby."

"I will be," I say. I hang up the phone and put it away. My gloves are in my coat pockets, so I put them on. I am not sure if Nino will be waiting around outside the store, but it is a possibility.

When I reach the store, the police are already there. An officer is talking to a well-dressed young man who seems to be the manager. The store is roped off, so I cannot get inside, but I see people standing around outside, so I ask a young woman, "What happened?"

"A crazy man was here and caused trouble," she says.

Another woman says, "I work here. The man came into the store before and then he came back again and took one of our girls with him."

"He took a girl?" I ask. "Which girl? Carla?"

"Yes, it was Carla," she says.

I look all around the area and more people are gathering to see what is happening. As I walk toward the water to get away from the crowd and gather my thoughts, my phone rings – it is Carla's number.

"Hello," I say.

"Hello, *hero*," Nino says snidely.

"Where is Carla?" A thousand thoughts run through my mind – most of them scary and ugly.

"She is with me, and I'm treating her very *nice*," Nino says. I can hear Carla crying in the background.

"Okay, what do you want?"

"Come here to get her," he says. "No police – or she will end up like Elena."

"Okay," I say, "no police."

"Come to the place where we last met," he says. "The front door will be open."

"Okay," I say, "I'm coming."

I start running along the narrow streets, over bridges, and I am thinking about how I am going to get out of this alive. He is in his home territory, and he could have any kind of weapon in that flat.

As I come down the narrow lane toward his dilapidated building, I hear a train coming into the station. I see the door ajar, and I walk into the hallway and notice garbage on the floor and peeling paint on the ceiling and walls. I try to catch my breath after running the whole way, and then I start up the old stone staircase slowly. The short first floor landing has a flight of wooden steps going up to the next floor to my left, and there is only one flat on the first floor with the door left open.

I cautiously go up to the door and, just as I am about to go into the flat, Nino comes rushing toward me swinging a hammer. He misses me as I move away from him, and the hammer crashes into the wall leaving a big hole. I hit him with a right hook in the side of his head, sending him against that wall.

Nino bounces back, yanks the hammer out of the wall, and swings at me again, this time hitting my left arm that I put up to protect my head. I crumple to my knees in pain but know the next time he hits me with that thing I will be dead, so I punch him hard in the gut, and as he goes down, and I hit him again in the side of the head. I push myself to stand up as he struggles to get up to try to hit me again. My left hand hangs uselessly at my side, but I pivot away from his hammer and slug him with a right cross that sends him staggering backwards. As he attempts to take another swing at me, I punch him under his left eye, and Nino loses his balance and tumbles down the steps. I hear him squeal like a pig when he hits the bottom floor.

I slowly amble over to the stairs holding my throbbing left arm, and I look down and see Nino lying there with his eyes wide open, staring lifelessly at the peeling paint on the ceiling above him with the hammer on the floor next to his right hand. I then think about Carla, and I shuffle into the flat and find her battered and bruised on the sofa, but she is breathing thankfully. She is covering her face with her hands, and as I touch her arm, she screams. I say, "Carla it's me – Bobby!"

She takes her hands away from her face and stares at me as if in a trance. "Bobby?"

"Yes, you're going to be okay," I say.

"Nino…Nino…"

"He's dead," I whisper. "He's never going to bother you again."

*

I sit on a table in the ER as Isabella wraps my arm with a bandage to keep the splint in place. "You are lucky," she says. "He could have killed you."

I nod my head. "Yeah, I know that."

"How are you feeling?" Isabella asks.

"Well, the arm really hurts," I say.

"No," she says as she stops wrapping my arm. "I mean how are you feeling about killing a man?"

I have not thought about it up until this moment because everything happened so fast with the police coming and getting Carla and me into the ambulance boat quickly. "I…I didn't want to kill him. I just wanted to save Carla and stop him from killing me."

"But he is dead," Isabella says as she continues to wrap my arm. "You must have some feelings about that."

"Yeah, I know," I say, "I am going to have to deal with that." I do not know how I really feel about killing Nino. All I know is that I was not deliberately trying to kill him. I think I would feel much worse if that was the case.

"You are also lucky that this was a simple break," Isabella says. "You could have had damage to nearby blood vessels or nerves, then it would have been much worse."

"How is Carla doing?" I ask.

"Also lucky," Isabella says, "he didn't beat her severely like Elena."

I think about it. "He only wanted to hurt Carla; I was the one that he wanted to kill today."

"Yes, I know that." Isabella finishes wrapping my arm and gently maneuvers it into a sling. "Now, take it easy for a while. You must restrict movement of the arm as much as possible for it to heal properly."

"How long do I have to wear this?" I ask, annoyed with having my arm being compromised like this.

"You will wait a week until the swelling goes down," Isabella says. "Then you will come back, and they will probably give you a cast."

"A cast? Damn, I've never broken a bone before." I look down at my useless arm in the sling and then up at her. "How long am I going to have to wear the cast?"

"About two to four weeks perhaps," Isabella says. "We will have to check it again to be sure."

"That's going to seem like forever to me," I say as I hop off the table and remember that Isabella said that she was going home for the holidays. "Aren't you supposed to be in the Dolomites?"

"Yes, actually, I am leaving tonight," Isabella says.

"Well, Merry Christmas, Isabella," I say. "Enjoy your holiday."

As I start walking toward the door, Isabella says, "Bobby."

I turn around and say, "Yeah?"

"I was worried about you," she says. "I'm glad you're okay."

I am not sure how to take this, but I say, "Thanks."

"You should take a water taxi home," she says. "No exertion for a while."

I nod my head and say, "Yes, doctor."

*

That evening, I sit in my flat watching the local news on TV with my arm in the sling, and the story about Nino comes on screen. I sip my beer as they describe his "long history of criminal behavior" and that "he died after falling down a staircase while attacking a person who came to the defense of an innocent young woman that he had beaten in his flat." Well, they have most of the story right. I am glad I avoided the press and got right into the ambulance boat with Carla as we were being chased by them.

My phone rings, and it is Carla. "Hey, how are you doing?"

"Thank you for saving me," she says.

"Hey, Nino took you because of me, so I had to," I say. "How was Nino able to take you out of the store like that?"

"After I called you the first time, Nino came back into the store about a half hour later. I was at the front of the store arranging a shelf, and he must have seen me through the window. He just came in and grabbed me, punched the security man, and dragged me outside."

"Oh, crap," I say. "I tried to get there as fast as I could."

"I understand," she says.

"How about the guy you're seeing? Does he know anything about this?" I ask.

"The guy is done with me," she says.

"Oh, I'm sorry," I say.

"Well, I had to tell him about Nino," she says. "He wanted to know why this lowly criminal had anything to do with me."

"And what happened?"

"He asked me for the truth, so I told him," Carla says whimpering. "And now he is done with me."

"Well, then he wasn't worthy of you," I say.

"Bobby, I think I'm done too," Carla says sounding like she is on the verge of crying hysterically.

I sit up and my left arm hurts as I move too quickly. "What are you talking about?"

"I can't take it here anymore," she says. "I come from a good family, and they want me to come home."

"Oh, well, I guess it's not like Elena's situation was then," I say.

"No, I love my parents and they love me; I just came to Venice for a little fun and adventure. I think I must go home because I haven't had any fun or adventure at all."

"How did you end up with Nino?" I ask.

"When I got off the train at Santa Lucia," she whispers. "He was waiting on the platform and talking to other girls who kept walking. Then he saw me and said that he would give me a job and a place to stay."

"Oh, that sucks," I say. "What a bastard!"

"I was 18 and had planned to stay in a hotel I found online," she says. "I was innocent as Elena was. He ruined us both!"

"Yes, you both didn't deserve to have this happen to you. Too bad someone didn't kill him a long time ago."

"He was always afraid, always owing people money," she says. "I just got sucked into a life that wasn't like being alive. Now I want to put it all behind me. I want to go home and be with my family again."

I think about it and say, "Well, you have to do what is best for you, Carla."

"I was going to go home for Christmas," she says, "but now I'm just going to stay there."

"I wish you well, Carla," I say.

"Thank you for everything, Bobby," she says. "I'll never forget how you took care of me when you didn't need to do it."

"Okay, well, good luck to you, and may God be with you," I say.

"*Grazie mille*," she says softly and ends the call.

I lean my head back and sip the beer. I am happy that Carla is not another tragic ending like poor Elena. She will go home and hopefully start over; sadly, Elena did not have that option.

As for Nino, something wicked has been destroyed. I do not know why he turned out that way, but no one will cry for him being gone. There is no tragedy for him because he only caused pain and suffering. I did not go there wanting to kill him. I only wanted to save Carla, but I do not feel sorry about him being dead. From the first time I saw him with his greedy face and beady eyes, I wanted to beat the crap out of him.

Now he is dead by my hand, and I feel no remorse because he made Elena and Carla's lives miserable and eventually murdered Elena. I hope that he will suffer eternal justice somewhere in the seventh circle of hell where he belongs.

CHAPTER THIRTY-THREE – Christmas in Venice

I sit with my left arm in the sling in Serge's ballroom at a long table filled with many guests. The biggest obstacle to my being here was getting dressed – normally a simple task that I take for granted. In fact, everything I once did easily is a challenge. Getting my shirt on and then my jacket over my thickly taped broken arm was difficult. Tying my tie was impossible, so I went with an open collar. I do not like that look – it feels unfinished! But in my condition, I am certain no one is going to question it.

Serge is at the head of the table with his son Sergio to his right and Arabella on his left. Serge's brother Giacomo sits next to Sergio. The brother looks like a younger version of Serge, while the son has hints of Serge's appearance in his facial features.

At my end of the table, I am sitting with Pietro, who already

has had too much wine.

Pietro glances at me and asks, "How is the arm?"

I answer truthfully. "It hurts, but I can handle it."

"You had to be a hero," Pietro says and sips his wine.

"Unfortunately, all of you Americans have this inclination."

I think about how Nino sarcastically called me

"Hero" when we spoke on the phone. "I'm no hero; I just did

what I had to do, Pete."

He sits back and nods his head, "Ah, the reluctant

American hero, even more annoying."

This is a lovely dinner in a festively decorated,

opulent room; however, last night's dinner with Amadu and

his family was more my style. The Christmas Eve dinner –

La Vigilia – was called the Feast of the Seven Fishes by my

Italian Nonna, for which she cooked amazing dishes.

Amadu's father and the rest of the family welcomed me into

their home and treated me as if I was family.

In Adamu's father's cozy flat with an illuminated Christmas tree in the living room, I sat at a table with his father Arturo, his stepmother Maria, and their son Arturo, whom they call Arti. Arturo was a short but handsome man, and I realized where Adamu got some of his facial features. Maria was a lovely middle aged Italian woman with dark shoulder length hair streaked with gray, and Arti was 19-year-old college student who looked more like his mother than his father.

We had just finished linguine with lobster and a dish of mixed seafood. I sat back, sipped my wine, and said, "This is the best food I've had since coming to Venice."

"Oh, Adamu," Maria said, "I like your friend."

"You are an excellent cook, signora," I said.

Arturo drank some wine and said, "My friends tell me that I am the luckiest man, and I have no choice but to agree with them."

Arti said, "Mama's kitchen always smells like heaven."

Maria got up and started taking our plates. "I will let you relax awhile until I serve you the _secondo_."

As she went into the kitchen, I looked at Adamu and asked, "What is the secondo?"

Adamu poured more wine into my glass, and then his brother's and father's glasses. "That is the best of all – the salted cod fish with potatoes!"

"The _baccalà!_" Arti said with a big smile.

I held my stomach with my right hand and said, "I don't think I'll have room."

Arturo laughed and said, "We eat until our stomachs break!" We all laughed along with him, but I was feeling very full yet did not want to insult my hosts.

"What happened to your arm," Arti asked me.

I looked at Adamu who raised his eyebrows. I turned to Arti and said, "I fell down the stairs."

"Oh," Arti said. "Does it hurt?"

"Yeah," I said, "it hurts a lot!"

After we ate the amazing cod fish, I got up with Adamu, and we walked into the living room area with our glasses of wine. It felt good to stand up and let all that food have a chance to digest.

"Thanks for not saying what really happened," Adamu said.

"Hey, I'm not looking to brag about it," I said.

"Well, you did what you had to do," Adamu said with a hand on my right shoulder. "I met that guy. He had it coming."

"The thing is that I really didn't want to kill him," I said. "The first time I fought with him, I called the police. It should have never come to me having to confront him again, but he was let go on a technicality."

"Like back home," Adamu said, "sometimes things happen in the justice system that are not always right."

"Yeah, I know that," I said. "Now, I have to live with the fact that I killed someone." I still had not come to terms with the enormity of this situation – I had killed another human being – but I kept trying to tell myself that it was self-defense; he was a bad guy and had murdered Elena. Somehow, that still did not seem to justify what happened.

"You were defending yourself," Adamu said. "It was a dire situation – kill or be killed! And what do you think he would have done to Carla if he had killed you?"

I stared at him and felt a shiver go up my battered left arm. "I don't want to even think about that."

"Well, despite your situation, you seem to have enjoyed the food," Adamu says with a smile.

I sipped my wine and nodded my head. "Maria is an amazing cook."

"What are you going to do tomorrow?"

"Oh, the head of our writers' group is having a party."

Adamu pointed at me and said, "That rich guy with the palace on the Grand Canal?"

"Yeah, that's right," I said.

Arti stuck his head into the room and said, "Come back to the table."

Adamu looked at me. "Maria's baked her Christmas cookies."

We sat at the table again, and there was a tray of cookies in the center of the table with red and green icing on them. "Would you like some espresso, Bobby?" Maria asked me.

"Yes, please," I said.

Arturo, still drinking wine, leaned forward, and asked, "So, Bobby, why are you still not married?"

I glanced at Adamu and then looked at the man with a smile on his face. "Truthfully, I am divorced, so I was married."

Arti touched his father's arm. "Just like you, Papa."

"Yes," Arturo said shaking his head and looking at Adamu. "That is not something I ever wanted, Adamu. But I was wrong to take you and your mother to New York. I was unable to be a success there, and our marriage suffered. That was why it was best for me to go home and let you and your sister have a life without your parents fighting all the time."

Adamu nodded his head. "I've always known why you did what you did. It was because you loved us and even Mama."

Arturo smiled and sat back. "I was unsure what would happen to me, but then I met someone who would change my life." He looked at Maria and rubbed her arm. "Bobby, don't let a divorce stop you from trying to find love again."

"Hey, you're not married either, Adamu," Arti said.

"Yes, and I've never been married," Adamu said.

"My son," Arturo said, "you should find a nice Italian woman and settle down."

"I'm working on it, Pop," Adamu said.

"And you should find a nice Italian woman too, Bobby," Arturo said.

I sipped my espresso stoically and said, "I will see what I can do about that, signor."

Pietro, annoyed with the seating arrangements, says, "We might as well be sitting in another room."

I look at all the guests sitting between Serge and us and ask, "Do you know who all these other people are?"

"Well, there are Serge's two sisters and their assorted varieties of spoiled rotten kids. Jack – Giacomo's nickname – is not married yet, but Serge is looking to get him a bride. The rest of the people are other wealthy Venetians whom Serge has known his whole life who have nowhere else to go today. *Boo-hoo.*"

We have just finished a course featuring meat with a green sauce that is delicious. "What was that, Pete?"

"*Bollito con salsa verde*," Pietro says. "Serge never fails to underwhelm."

"I thought it was wonderful," I say.

Pietro stares at me with drunken eyes. "Unlike you, I was here for last Christmas Day. So far, all the courses have been the same. There's no originality in his chef's kitchen."

Arabella has turned off the music and is sitting at the piano. She starts playing her usual mangled version of "Jingle Bells" as Serge stands off to the side with a wide smile on his face. All the guests are quiet and are accepting her rocky rendition of the song without a peep.

When she is done, Arabella stands up and shines in her bright red dress. Serge gives her a chaste kiss on the cheek as everyone applauds except Pietro, who taps two fingers on the palm of his left hand. He glances at me and says, "At least you have an excuse for not applauding with your impediment."

The Christmas music is back on, and some people are on the dance floor moving to Brenda Lee's version of "Jingle Bell Rock." Pietro and I get up as he says, "Let's stretch the old legs."

Serge's son Sergio walks up to me and asks, "Bobby, how did you hurt your arm?"

I glance at Pietro and think that Sergio is just a kid. "Oh, I fell down the stairs."

"He's a clumsy oaf," Pietro chuckles and then walks away.

"Oh, I was thinking it might have been broken while you were doing something exciting and adventurous," Sergio says.

"Unfortunately, I am a writer and most of my adventure happens on my laptop," I say.

Serge walks over to us and says, "I see you two have met."

"Yes, father, he is a writer like you," Sergio says.

Serge looks at me and says, "Oh, Bobby is a fine writer."

"Thank you, Serge," I say. "You really know how to throw a party."

"It's Christmas," Serge says, "it is time to embrace joy because of our Lord's birth. It's the season of miracles!"

This is not the first time I have heard Serge mention something religious. "Well, I appreciate being here."

Arabella comes up to us with two glasses of red wine and hands one to Serge. "Are you having fun, Bobby?" she asks.

"Yes, of course," I say. "I always have a good time here."

Whitman rings a bell signaling the next course is being served. We all find our seats as roast baby lamb with golden potatoes and peas is served. Pietro looks at me and frowns. "Ugh! Same as last year!"

I taste a piece of the lamb, and it is succulent. "Oh, man, this is delicious, Pete. How can you not enjoy this?"

He eats a piece of the meat and says, "It will suffice."

"I spoke with Sergio," I say. "Seems like a nice kid."

"Yeah, he can afford to be nice," Pietro says as he chews his food with malice.

"What the hell does that mean?" I ask.

Pietro takes another piece of meat, shoves it into his mouth, and chews it quickly. I do not understand Pietro sometimes. I am not sure why he is angry with Serge's son.

After dinner is over and we are waiting for dessert, there is more dancing and wine and everyone is having a ball in the ballroom. Sergio is dancing with Arabella, and Pietro sits at the table moping and sipping his wine.

I walk over to Serge and say, "Everyone is having a great time, including me."

"Oh splendid, Bobby," Serge says.

"Sergio is having fun," I say.

"I wanted him to come here and experience this festive night," Serge says. "I want him to know what he is missing."

I remember what Pietro said about Sergio coming to live here. "He does seem to like it here."

Serge glances at me. "I want him to understand the possibilities available to him here that are not possible where he lives with his mother."

"What do you think he will do?" I ask.

Serge stares at his son as he dances joyfully. "I am hoping the end of the year is the best time for him to make the break."

"What about your ex?" I ask.

"Why do you think he is here?" Serge says in his deadpan fashion.

I am surprised. "She wants him here?"

"She knows it will be financially beneficial for her," Serge says. "She has a young man who caught her eye, and she would like to live free to travel with her toy boy."

"Wow," I say, thinking that Serge probably meant to say "boy toy," but who am I to say anything? "That's surprising."

Serge shakes his head and says in his deadpan fashion, "Not to me – I have always had her number." He stares at me and asks, "I do hope you will be here for our New Year's Eve ball. If you're up to it, that is."

I am happy that he has invited me. I would hate to be alone on New Year's Eve. "Oh, yes, of course, I wouldn't want to miss that."

Whitman comes into the room, and Serge looks at me and says, "Excuse me." He walks away from me and heads over to talk with Whitman about something, which turns out to be about serving dessert.

The dessert consists of a generous piece of panettone and all sorts of cookies. As I sip a lovely cappuccino, Pietro flops into the chair with brandy in a snifter. He looks at the cake and cookies on his plate and shakes his head. "From beginning to the end this has been the same exact meal as last year."

I bite into a cookie and say, "I wouldn't mind having this meal once a year. I thought it was amazing."

"Well, you're an American, so I guess I shouldn't be surprised," Pietro says as he takes a drink.

"You were right about Sergio, Pete."

He looks at me over his brandy snifter, "I usually am, Robert."

"Well, you might be interested to know that Serge told me that he is trying get Sergio to move in here in the new year."

"I told you," Pietro says as he takes a victorious sip of brandy. "Whitman can always be counted on."

The music suddenly stops, and Serge is standing in the front of the room holding a microphone. "Ladies and gentlemen, my beloved family, and dear honored guests. Thank you for coming this evening. I appreciate your presence here. It has made the night wonderful and joyous for Arabella and me. I ask you all to take a moment to bow your heads and think about those we love who have been lost in this past year."

Everyone in the room is quiet. I think about Anna and Elena, and in my mind, I ask God to care for them on the other side. After a few more seconds, I can hear Serge banging the microphone as he turns on the stereo, and John Lennon's song "So This Is Christmas" fills the room, and the people start singing along. He hands the microphone to Arabella, and to my surprise she sings like a choir of heavenly angels.

Pietro looks at me and asks, "Am I very drunk or does Arabella have a good voice?"

"You're very drunk, Pete," I say with a chuckle.

Pete shakes his head. "I was waiting for Serge to make his big announcement. I guess Whitman was wrong."

I chuckle. "Well, even Whitman can be wrong once and a while."

Pietro stares at me with bleary eyes. "I'm too drunk to care at this point."

*

I go home in a water taxi, and the driver helps me get out of the boat because of my left arm. I get inside the building, hit the light switch, and climb up the 62 steps to my flat. Once inside, I turn on a switch, and a light goes on as well as the small Christmas tree that I have on a table by the front window.

Falling onto the couch with a beer in hand, I stare at the tree and listen to Christmas songs on my phone. A year ago, Beth left me and my mother died during the second week of January. I did not think about her before when Serge asked us for a moment of silence because I still cannot believe that she is gone. Life without Beth has been difficult, but life without my Mom is just unbearable. My only solace is that she is in heaven with my father. I hope that they are watching over me.

It is Christmas, but it really does not feel like it to me. I went to Adamu's place for Christmas Eve and Serge's home today, so at least I was not alone. But, at the end of this day, I am alone. I thought I was getting used to it – not just being alone but being lonely – but it still bothers me. I close my eyes and listen to good old Bing Crosby singing "White Christmas," but there is no solace in his voice as I used to feel when I heard that song.

Sady, I am all alone on Christmas night, and all I can think about is that it is going to be a hell of a long week until I get to New Year's Eve.

CHAPTER THIRTY-FOUR – Carnevale

When the two-weeks of Carnevale began, I enjoyed the first day when large parties kicked off the celebration, and the streets were flooded with masked and costumed characters of all sizes and shapes marching in parades across the bridges and converging in Piazza San Marco. However, there seemed to be a bit of a lull on weekdays, and while there were some people wearing costumes and masks here and there in the streets, the atmosphere was rather sedate until the weekend came again.

Today is the Saturday before Shrove Tuesday – the day before Ash Wednesday – and as I walk through the streets on a cool March evening toward the taverna, I am wearing a simple black mask that covers my eyes and nose only. Hey, I want to keep my mouth free for drinking.

Drunken revelers fill the streets. A group of young girls, all wearing cat masks with sparkling feathers, comes up to me laughing, and one of them throws confetti over me. Another yells, "*Buongiorno, signora maschera!*" They all laugh and walk away.

The stores are decorated with glittering lights, and gondolas are filled with masked and costumed passengers gliding up and down the canals. Two weeks of partying are coming to an end soon, and I wonder what it is going to be like on Tuesday at Serge's house. I still have time to get a costume, but I think I might just wear this mask because I am not sure what costume to wear.

Once I am inside the taverna, I realize that most of the customers are in costumes and masks. I wave to Lorenzo – who is unmasked – and make my way to the bar. I see Gina carrying a tray filled with drinks and wearing a sparkling green mask with matching feathers. Some of the waiters are wearing simple masks like mine.

I lean my right elbow on the bar and lift my left arm out away from my side. It feels so good to not have that cast on my arm anymore. I still have some discomfort, but Isabella has told me that I healed much faster than she expected. I am going to physical therapy three times a week, and it seems to be helping me.

"Hello, mystery man," I hear Paula saying behind me.

I turn around and am surprised by her bare face. "What? No mask?"

Paula touches her small baby bump with one hand and wipes down the bar with a towel. "I don't like masks and don't want it to affect my breathing with the baby." She points at my head. "I like the confetti; nice touch!"

I look in the bar mirror and brush the glittering specks out of my hair while asking, "How are you feeling?"

"Fine," she says exhaling loudly. "I went to the doctor today and everything is good so far."

"That's good to hear."

She hands me a copy of her ultrasound as she asks, "What are you drinking?"

"I love this image of the baby," I say. "I guess I'll have one of your famous martinis to celebrate."

As Paula makes the drink, she says, "That image is the baby at 10 weeks, and everything looks normal. It is amazing to be carrying a child. I can't even believe it sometimes."

I put the ultrasound image down on the bar as she places my martini in front of me. "I can't believe how clear that image is."

Paula picks up the photo and stares at it. "It's a miracle, Bobby. I want to thank you for helping us."

"So, how has Viv been handling it?" I ask and then sip my drink. I want to tell her that I love her, but I'm too scared because she is in love with Viv, so it is useless to try.

"She's loving the experience. She has already ordered so many clothes and toys. I don't know where we are going to put it all."

I like seeing the wide smile on her beautiful face. I do not think I have ever seen Paula look happier. "You'll figure it all out." I do not know if she would be that happy with me.

"So, your mask is appropriately cool," Paula says. "Are you enjoying the Carnevale experience?"

I think about it and say, "Yeah, there have been entertaining moments, but some lulls too. I think tonight the streets are the most crowded I've seen these past two weeks."

"Wait until Tuesday," Paula says, "that's the biggest night of all. I hope you can come by; it should be rocking in here."

I turn around and look at the crowded room filled with noisy people and loud music. "Seems pretty wild tonight."

Paula flips the bar towel over her shoulder. "Tuesday will be like Halloween and New Year's Eve combined."

"Oh, wow," I say and sip my martini. "I'm going to a party on the Grand Canal."

Paula smiles. "Oh, our friend Serge I suppose."

"Yes," I smile and say, "I'm not sure what to expect."

Paula leans against the bar. "Expect the unexpected. Carnevale is about going beyond boundaries. The masks and costumes make everyone someone else. You can see how far people will go on that night."

I sip my drink and squint as I think. "I didn't realize it was like that."

"Yeah, it is something that defies reality. It is all about mystery – who is wearing that mask?" She taps on the bar and says, "I have go take a piddle – it's the one thing I hate about being preggers. I'm always in the loo."

I watch her walking away. I am happy for her and Viv, but I do think about the baby she is carrying. It is my child, but I am not sure if I will ever know him or her. I went into this with an understanding that I would have nothing to do with or say about the baby. Whether I like it or not, I have to live with it. There will be no happy ending for Paula and me and our baby, so I have to stop having these crazy thoughts.

When I turn to look around the room, I see a woman in a luxurious purple gown wearing a glittering purple mask with purple feathers on top of it. She has long brown hair down to her waist, snowy white arms, and exquisite lips that look like the delicate petals of a purple orchid. She walks over to me with a drink in her pale white hand, and she sips it through a straw.

"Well, hello," I say. "Nice costume." I look at the drink and ask, "That's a Bellini, right?" She silently nods her head. I remember that Mireille liked drinking those, and I say, "I used to know someone who liked to drink Bellinis."

The woman takes the straw out of her mouth, leans toward me, and places a wet kiss on my cheek with her soft floral lips. There is something so intriguing about the moment that makes me think about what Paula had just said about "expect the unexpected" during Carnevale.

I watch the woman as she places the straw back in her purple mouth, turns around, and walks away from me as if she is gliding on air and disappears into the crowd.

When I turn to take a sip of my drink, Paula is standing there chuckling. "I saw what just happened with *La Donna Viola*. Now you get an idea what Carnevale is all about."

I shake my head and sip my drink. "That may have been one of the weirdest but exciting moments of my life."

"Wait until Tuesday," Paula snickers. "Then let's talk."

"Okay, well, I'll *expect the unexpected*," I say. I am a little nervous and do not know what is going to happen.

"All I can say," Paula says, "is that if I was going to a party on the Grand Canal, I would get myself a proper costume."

I nod my head. "Okay, I guess I'll look into it." Now, one thing I have always hated – those days before Halloween when I had to get a costume – will probably be even worse

here in Venice for Carnevale. Maybe I should just stay home,

but I do not want to insult Serge. I will have to figure out

something by Tuesday.

*

The next morning I call Pietro and ask, "Do I need a

costume for Serge's party?"

"If you're asking me that question, then I am sorry for

you," Pietro says. "It's like the biggest night of the year, and

you're going to come in cargo pants I suppose."

If I was back in New York, I would go to Party City

for a costume, but I have no idea where to go, so I ask,

"Where will I go for an appropriate costume?"

"You have to go to the atelier – you have to see Boffo

– he makes the finest masks and has the best costumes."

"But what is an appropriate costume?" I ask.

"Oh, dear," Pietro says with a sigh, "look for

something that is Baroque or Renaissance, with an

appropriate mask. They make the masks at Boffo's place. You can even make your own if you want to."

Armed with the address, I go out into the bright morning wearing a light jacket because the weather is good, and there is not a cloud in the sky. I cross over the Rialto and make my way to the shop, passing the Acqua Alta Bookstore that I once visited, and it is crowded with customers once again. I turn into a narrow lane and find the atelier – hundreds of masks and costumes are in the windows.

Once inside the crowded shop, I see tables filled with masks and shelves loaded with dummy heads with creepy faces sporting an assortment of wigs. There is a wide selection of all kinds of masks lining the walls, and the music in the store is increduously like from an American pop radio station in some greasy spoon diner back home. In the corner there is a large statue of the plague doctor with bird like curved beak holding a long stick used to probe sick patients.

An older gentleman approaches me, and he is wearing a wig that makes him look like Louis XIV. "May I help you?" he asks with no accent.

"Are you Boffo?" I ask. "My friend Pietro sent me here."

"Yes, I am Boffo. Hmm. Pietro – the little guy from Florence, yes?" he asks with a wry smile.

"Yes, that's the guy. I'm going to a party, and I'm looking for a costume and mask," I say.

"What do you want to project?" he asks.

"What do you mean?"

"Well, Carnevale has many aspects to it, but above all there is a slightly dangerous tone to it. It is kind of like your Halloween on drugs. There is a mixture of fear and luxury, if you know what I mean," he says with a slightly sinister grin.

I do not know what to say."Uh, yeah, I guess so."

"Where is your party being held?" he asks with a raised eyebrow.

"Oh, in a palace on the Grand Canal," I say, and then I regret saying it because he will think he can charge me more because I must have money.

He turns to the statue of the plague doctor and says, "I think this one is appropriate – it is always nice to remind the wealthy that Death can come to anyone – you know, like in Edgar Allan Poe's story."

"Yes, I know the story," I say, remembering "The Masque of the Red Death" scaring the crap out of my when I read it in high school. I start feeling like this whole thing is nothing like me. Even at home I never went all out for Halloween. I would buy a big plastic knife and a goalie mask and be Jason or whatever else that was simple. "You know," I say, "I have to think about this."

"Please come back," he says, "so I can make you something that you are not. That is the whole point of Carnevale. Everyone can be different and yet the same."

"Yeah, okay, thanks," I say as I run out of the place.

I go back over the Rialto and walk through the market. Tinno is there sipping orange juice from a little bottle. "*Buongiorno*, Bobby," he says in a raspy voice.

I buy an apple and rub it against my jacket. "What do you think about Carnevale, Tinno?" I ask.

"Ah, *the farewell to meat*," Tinno says with a grin.

"What are you saying?" I ask.

"That is what it means – *carne vale* – farewell to eating meat. It starts the fasting of Lent," he says.

"Up until this moment, I had no idea that was what the word meant," I say.

"People forget that this time is all about faith," Tinno says, "and instead it has become this decadent celebration."

I nod my head. "Yeah, I guess you're right."

I say goodbye and, as I start to leave, Tinno says, "Don't forget to get your ashes on Wednesday, Bobby."

As I make my way back toward my flat, I think about my Catholic school days and how we got the ashes in church.

The priest would dig his thumb covered with ashes into my forehead saying, "Remember that you are dust, and to dust you shall return." Oddly enough, those words have more signifcance to me now more than ever.

*

I was in my bed and sleeping restlessly. I felt cold and hot at the same time. When I sat up, the room was filled with vibrating colors. There was a violin playing somewhere – an eerie kind of music from another century that was dripping with sadness.

Getting out of bed, I stumbled over something and rushed to the front door to get out of the flat. As I opened the door, The Grim Reaper was standing there with his scythe in his skeletal hands. He moved toward me and I backed up, frightened by his appearance.

Again, I stumbled over something, but this time it caused me to fall on the floor. The Grim Reaper stood over me and looked like he was a hologram. I struggled to stand up, and as I did the ghoul pointed down to the floor. I saw a body lying face down, and when I bent down to turn it over, I saw Elena's face.

I was shocked and recoiled from her battered appearance. The Grim Reaper kept pointing at me accusingly as if I was responsible for her death. He started walking toward me still pointing a bony finger at my face, and I backed up into a wall and shut my eyes, as he put his icy fingers on my neck.

I wake up and am covered with sweat. My heart is beating wildly and my hands are shaking. I throw the blanket off my body, get up, and rush into the bathroom to splash water on my face. I look up into the mirror, and my eyes are distorted by guilt. I have felt responsible for not doing enough to help Elena, but I also did not know where she was until she slapped my wedding ring on the table when I was dining with Mireille, and then disappeared into the ether again with Nino.

When I saw her with Nino, I should have done

something, but I was more concerned about

explaining everything to Mireille. I turn away from

the mirror and go into the other room, take the urn

with Elena's ashes from the mantel, and fall onto my

couch. I close my eyes and whisper, "I'm sorry,

Elena." Nothing I can say or do will ever ease my

guilt and suffering.

*

As I walk into the foyer of Serge's palace, I am

wearing my wedding tuxedo and my black mask. Whitman is

dressed in a white volto mask with a black hooded cape. I

say, "Good evening, Whitman."

"Welcome to the party, sir," Whitman says as he

points his white gloved hand to the entrance of the ballroom.

The double doorway has an enormous glittering mask above

it, and shimmering curtains hang down from both sides of it.

Inside the room, strings of glittering masks hang from every chandelier. Black silhouettes of gondolas with a gondolier and passengers hang from garlands strung along the walls. In the corner near the DJ booth is large black pergola covered with black and white balloons with a huge glittering mask on top, and people are taking pictures under it.

As I walk around the ballroom in my half mask, I see a wide array of characters. There are vampires, a person with stars and planets on the costume, a black mask, and glowing crescent moon as a hat. There a horned goats, couples in Baroque and Renaissance clothing and wigs, and many people wearing white bauta masks and multi-colored robes. I also notice that the waiters are all wearing volto masks like Whitman with short black capes.

The music is pounding – at this moment it is Donna Summer's "Hot Stuff" – and I move over to the bar and order a Smirnoff Red on the rocks. As I lean on the bar, someone dressed as who I think is Mozart, due to the wig, mask, and costume, leans on the bar and says, "How come you're wearing a tuxedo and didn't get a costume?"

I know the voice. I ask, "Rolando?"

He takes off the mask and laughs. "I should have remained quiet."

"Nice costume," I say. "I went to the atelier but I couldn't decide, and then I found my wedding tuxedo in my closet. Considering how my marriage turned out, I suppose it qualifies as a costume."

Rolando laughs, orders a beer, and says, "So, this is your first Carnevale, yes?"

"Yes, my first in Venice," I say. "I went to Mardi Gras in New Orleans once years ago. It was wild but in a different way." Saying that reminds me of a simpler time in my life.

"Carnevale was originally designed as an equalizer," Rolando says and then sips his beer.

"Really," I ask. "How so?"

"In Venice since we are living on small islands, we all live close together – the rich and the poor! Serge is here in a palace on the canal, and we are living on simple streets in San Polo. When everyone is out in the streets in costume and masks, they are all the same. The rich rub elbows with the poor, and we all join the parades and parties. It is a distinctly unifying moment for all citizens whether rich or poor."

"That's very interesting," I say, impressed by Rolando's take on the holiday.

Rolando says, "What is also possible is for a person to become someone else – even if it is for only two weeks during Carnevale or even one night at a party. You can become what you are not."

I point at him and say, "Like Mozart!" Rolando smiles and then we turn and notice a short person standing in front of us wearing a colorful horned hat and robe and a white bauta mask. "Hey, buddy," I say. "What are you supposed to be?"

Rolando taps my arm. "He is wearing the corno ducale – he is the Doge of Venice. It is a famous costume."

"Well, it looks great," I say, elevating my voice as the music seems to get louder.

The duke takes off his mask, and we are both surprised to see Pietro under it. "Man, that thing is sweaty," he says twitching his whiskers.

"What are you drinking?" Rolando asks.

"I'll take a glass of Soave," Pietro says. He looks me up and down. "Seriously, you couldn't have tried harder?"

"This is me as my dark side," I say with a smile.

Pietro takes his glass of wine and asks, "Did you guys see Serge and Arabella?"

Rolando and I both say "No" at the same time. I look at him and say, "Jinx – you owe me a soda."

"What?" Rolando asks.

"Oh, I'm just kidding," I say.

Rolando points in the direction of the DJ booth. "Look over there! I think I see them."

I turn around and see a man in a tall wizard's hat and matching robe with stars and moons on it holding a long wand. A young woman stands next to him in a long golden gown, a gold mask, and wears a wig of long black curly hair with a glistening crown on top of it.

"I'm assuming he is Merlin and she is Guinevere," I say.

"Good call," Rolando says.

Pietro points to the buffet table and says, "Oh, *frittelle*!"

So, the Duke of Venice rushes over to the table and fills a plate with round pastries. Rolando says, "That is a traditional treat for Carnevale. You can't get them any other time of the year."

I go over to the buffet and put a few of the pastries on my plate. I try one and it has a uniquely sweet taste, with raisins and nuts mixed in it. I sip my drink and ask, "Should we go over and talk to our host?"

Pietro shakes his head. "I would let him be. He always gets very much into his character, kind of like a method actor. He won't talk to anyone as Serge tonight."

"Why does he do that?" I ask.

"He believes that it is not just a costume but that he becomes *incarnate* – he is that actual person tonight," Pietro says and then shoves more pastries into his mouth.

Rolando laughs and says, "To be a medieval wizard for a night isn't so bad."

"Or the Duke of Venice?" I say to Pietro.

As the night goes on, the drinks keep flowing and people are dancing. The music keeps pounding, and Serge and Arabella are in the center of the dance floor doing some kind of old fashioned dance with courtsies and bowing.

When I go down the hallway to the bathroom, there are two people in Renaissance clothing and wigs in a dark corner having sex. Oddly enough, they are wearing their masks during the act. The guy on top glances at me with a sinister devil's mask, then gets back to business quickly.

When I leave the bathroom, I notice that the amorous duo are gone. I get another drink and go over to a table where Rolando and Pietro are sitting with their drinks. "This is a long night," I say.

"It will end at midnight," Pietro says. "That is the start of the fast – and Serge is very serious about that religious mumbo jumbo."

Rolando looks at his watch. "That means we have 30 minutes to go."

"Yet another disappointing event," Pietro sighs. "Except, of course, for Serge's chef's excellent *frittelle*."

For some unknown reason, I get an urge to look across the dance foor, and I realize that *La Donna Viola* is standing amidst the dancers and the confetti being thrown and the frenzy of the room. She is staring right at me. Looking back at Rolando and Pietro briefly, I am impelled to stand up and gravitate towards her. As I approach her, she turns and starts walking away toward the exit.

I follow her through the swaying curtains out into the foyer, where there are people sitting on the red velvet chairs drinking and laughing. She goes out the back door, down the steps, and glides around the side of the building and reaches the wall overlooking the Grand Canal. The street and canal are illuminated behind her, as people in costumes and masks go by in gondolas.

As I come down the steps, a raucos parade of costumed celebrants marches in between us, blocking my view of her. The person leading the procession has a snare drum hanging in front of his bare chest and is banging it incessantly. Once the parade is gone, so is *La Donna Viola* with it.

I run after the group as it continues moving away from me along the canal, but I find the elusive woman wearing purple standing on top of a bridge over a smaller canal. I slowly walk up to her, and she stares at me silently with her unmoving purple mask and lips, the purple feathers on the top of the mask fluttering in a breeze coming over the canal.

I need to know who she is and ask, "Who are you?"

She turns her head and looks out over the canal. When she speaks, her voice is lower than a whisper. "I am now what I am not," she says.

I think I understand what she is saying, but I want to be sure. "What does that mean?"

"I am an illusion," she says. "Tomorrow I will be gone. In some ways I am like a ghost."

"But it's just a costume," I say.

She turns and stares at me with a deadpan masked face. "Is it?" she asks.

I take off my black mask and hold it up to her. "It's all part of a game, right? It is not the real me."

She turns away from me. "So, your saying that your unmasked self is more real – that we all don't wear a mask even when people can see our faces?"

I stuff the mask into my jacket pocket and say, "I hope that I show people who I really am – like now!"

"If you want to see what you claim is really me, take off my mask," she says softly.

As much as I want to see her face, the allure of not knowing who she is feels exciting. I reach out to touch her mask, and I feel its cold plasticity and the edge of it rough against my fingertips. I ask, "Do I know you?"

"You know this incarnation of me," she says. "Is the fantasy better than knowing what's underneath the mask?"

I am afraid to see her face now, and she takes my hand in her warm one and lowers it. "I...I don't know." Standing there with her holding my hand, I feel frozen.

"Yes you do," she says with a chuckle. She releases my hand, and I watch her as she goes down the other side of the bridge, where another parade is marching on by. She blends into its dancing and cheering members and disappears into the night.

I turn and look at a gondolier pushing his empty gondola toward the bridge. He looks up at me and says, "We are both alone, my friend. *Buona notte!*"

I watch as he goes under the bridge I am standing on. I think about the gravity of the words he has just said, and I realize that is my reality. I turn around, go down the steps, and begin walking towards home.

Who is *La Donna Viola*? She wore a beautfiul gown but the mask was disconserting. I want to think she is beautiful beneath the mask, but my hesitation to take it off makes me wonder about myself. I guess I was not brave enough to see her real face or, perhaps, that is her real face and what was underneath it is a facade. I guess I am happier not knowing who she really is rather than finding out who she is not.

CHAPTER THIRTY-FIVE – The Dream Is Over

On the one-year anniversary of my first day of living in my Venice flat, it is a lovely early May morning, and I am wearing my Mets cap, sunglasses, polo shirt, cargo shorts, and sneakers again. It is warm but not hot, and I know how hot it can get from being here last summer.

Walking through the bustling market by the Rialto, I am not surprised anymore about the crowds of people coming here – I understand this city's intoxicating allure. A slight breeze brings with it the smell of fish from the stalls, and the noisy seagulls are swooping into place to await their scraps.

I find Tinno sitting on his chair reading a postcard. I say, "*Buongiorno*, Tinno."

He looks up at me with tears on his sun-darkened face. "Hello, Bobby."

"What's wrong?"

I see the words LAS VEGAS on the front of the postcard. "It is from my son. His wife lost their baby."

"Oh, I'm sorry to hear that," I say.

He shakes the postcard, and its glossy side reflects the sunlight. "I was going to visit him when they had the baby."

"Well," I am trying to think of something to say, "why not visit him anyway."

Tinno takes the postcard and slides it under his cashbox. "It is not the right time; I want to celebrate with him and not mourn."

I pay for an apple and say, "My wife lost our baby over a year ago."

Tinno wipes his face and stands up. "I'm sorry for you."

"Yeah, well, life is not easy at times." I think of the truth of those words.

Tinno looks up at the sky and says, "We know what we want, but sometimes God has other plans."

I think about my life and nod. "Ain't that the truth!"

I leave Tinno and walk over the bridge, heading for what will be my last appointment with Isabella. I think of Isabella sometimes as beautiful but aloof. She must know she is attractive, and yet there is something about her, a sort of invisible veil that prevents me from getting to know her better, or even to have the courage to ask her out.

*

Standing next to the examination table, Isabella holds my file and studies the latest X-ray of my arm. She looks up at me. "You are remarkable. You have healed completely."

"Well, I did whatever you told me to do," I say.

"Are you still going to PT?" she asks.

"Yes, twice a week now."

She closes my file and puts it on the table. "You have strong bones, Bobby," she says with a smile.

I laugh and say, "I guess I'm happy my mother made me drink my milk every day when I was a kid."

"Let's go into my office," she says.

I follow her down the hallway into her office, and she sits behind her desk as I sit in a chair. "I want to thank you for everything," I say.

"How are you doing, Bobby?"

I squeeze my left forearm and say, "I feel really good now."

She puts her hand on her chest and asks, "But how are you doing here?"

I want to answer honestly. "Look, I have good days and bad days. Sometimes I have bad dreams about Elena. I am dealing with it the best I can."

"Just as the physical therapy helped your arm, there are those who can help with your emotional health," Isabella says. She picks up a card from her desk, leans forward, and hands it to me. "This is a doctor whom I have worked with for years. You may want to call him when you need someone to listen."

I look at the card and then back at her. "Okay, I'll think about it."

"Bobby, I care about you," she says.

"Oh yeah?" I ask, and she nods her head. "How about we go out to dinner one night and *you* do the listening?" I cannot believe I am brave enough to finally ask her out.

Isabella's lovely face gets a little contorted as she says, "Bobby, I don't fraternize with my patients like that. It wouldn't be professional."

Gut punch! I nod my head and say, "I…I understand." I get up, put the card in my pocket, and start to leave.

"I'm sorry, Bobby," Isabella says.

I nod my head again. "Yeah, so am I."

As I leave the hospital I walk up on a bridge and watch a vaporetto rumble toward me and then go under the bridge. Why would I even think someone so beautiful as Isabella would want to go out with me? Besides, she knows I was seeing a prostitute and even got her pregnant, and then after her pimp murdered her, I ended up killing him. That is not such a great resume for a prospective suitor. I am certain that a woman of her quality would not think romantically of me – she is out of my league and then some.

I start heading home because I want to work on my manuscript for tonight's writer's meeting. I think I finally have something that can become the novel I want to write here in Venice. I wonder about including Isabella in the story or not. Elena is in it, as is Pietro, Serge, and Paula. That will be the most difficult part of writing this book – deciding who is in it and who is left on the cutting room floor.

*

As I sit in my chair at the meeting, I nervously look over my first two short chapters of the novel. Pietro comes into the room carrying his battered binder with papers sticking out of it. The Three Germans are sitting there with plates of food on their laps smiling like kids on Christmas. Rolando nervously looks at the papers on his lap, and the rest of the members are all staring stoically forward looking at Serge who is standing behind the podium.

Serge looks up from his notes and says, "Good afternoon, everyone. I just want to remind you that Arabella and I are going away for two weeks, so we will not be having our meetings because I am having some work done on this house while we are away, and I don't want to impose on Bobby to take over for me. Our next meeting will be three weeks from today."

The Three Germans look at one another and nod their heads. Pietro glances at me and whispers, "He just cancels the meetings like that. He doesn't care if some of us look forward to this meeting every week."

"A few of us could meet informally," I whisper.

Pietro rolls his eyes. "It's just not the same."

Serge looks down at his papers and says, "By order of rotation, our first reader will be Bobby. Have you brought something to share with us today?"

I nod my head, stand up, and say, "Yes." I walk up to the podium, Serge takes a seat, and I look out at everyone. "Good afternoon. What I am reading today is the first two short chapters of the novel I am starting."

"That's wonderful," Serge says.

I look down and say, "The title of the book will be *Life and Death in Venice*." I take a deep breath, swallow, and begin reading.

After everyone has read, Serge returns to the podium. "Well, we had some very interesting readings this week. Now, please help yourselves to the buffet and drinks at the bar. Please don't forget to email your peer reviews to the readers who shared their work tonight."

The Three Germans rush to the table faster than racehorses. I get up, fold my papers, and put them in my big cargo shorts pocket. Pietro gathers his papers, shoves them into the binder, and snaps it shut. Rolando is putting his papers into his inside jacket pocket as he walks over to me.

"Really, just a beautiful story," he says. "Will I appear in future chapters?"

I nod my head. "Yes, but you can already see I used different names for Elena and Paula, so names will be changed to protect the innocent."

"You mean *the guilty*," Pietro chuckles.

I stare at him and say, "Very funny, Pete."

"Well, I'm very happy for you," Rolando says.

"Thanks, guys," I say. The overall positive reaction to my story is very encouraging. At least I know I am on the right track.

We all get food from the buffet. I grab a bottle of water, but Pietro and Rolando get drinks at the bar. When they sit down Pietro asks, "Robert, you're not drinking? Is someone on the wagon?"

I shake my head. "No, Pete. I'm going over to the taverna after this, so I'm waiting to drink there."

"How is the little mother to be?" Pietro asks and shoves a forkful of spaghetti into his mouth.

I smile and say, "Paula's in her second trimester and everything is good."

"That's good news," Rolando says and then sips his beer.

"Yeah, but she keeps working and plans to work as long as she can," I say. I will not tell them, but I am concerned about her being on her feet during those long nights behind the bar once she moves into her third trimester, but I am not a husband or even boyfriend and have no say in the matter.

"I'm just wondering," Pietro says as he twirls spaghetti with his fork, "what will Paula do if something happens to her partner?"

I put down my knife and fork. "What are you talking about?'

He chews his pasta quickly then says, "If her partner fell into a canal and died, what would Paula do?"

Pietro can be such a little creep sometimes. I sip my water and bite my lower lip. "We've never had that kind of discussion."

I eat one of the little pizzas that Serge's chef makes that are perfectly delectable. I chew vigorously as Rolando leans forward and says, "Maybe that is something reasonable you can discuss with Paula."

I think about it and say, "Maybe you guys are right." I remain quiet as we sit there eating, wondering if I have any rights at all in this matter. I mean, what if something did happen to both Paula and Viv?

As everyone is leaving, I see young Sergio in the foyer who comes running over to me. "Hi, Bobby!" he says and shakes my hand.

"How are you doing, Sergio? How is school?"

"Everything is going well. I love it here in Venice," Sergio says with a big smile.

Arabella walks through the front doorway coming in from Serge's luxurious boat – the one he uses to go out to his even more luxurious yacht – in a green dress with matching pumps. Whitman is following her carrying shopping bags. She looks at us and says, "Hi, guys!" and continues walking down the hallway toward the grand staircase.

Serge exits the ballroom and walks over to us. He looks at his son and says, "Did you finish that project that is due on Monday?"

Sergio shakes his head. "I'm about halfway there, father."

Serge puts both his hands into his pants pockets. "I want to see that project finished by tomorrow morning. Everything must be done tomorrow because I am leaving on Sunday, and I will be occupied the whole day and unable to go over it with you."

"Okay, father," Sergio says. He glances at me and says, "Goodbye, Bobby."

After Sergio leaves, I look at Serge and say, "It seems bringing him here has been successful."

Serge takes the unlit pipe from his jacket pocket and puts it into his mouth. "It has not been without difficulties. His old school never challenged him, but the private academy I'm sending him to does, meaning he needs my help."

"Still, now he has every advantage," I say.

"That was why I wanted him here," Serge says. "By the way, that story you read today was marvelous."

"Thanks, Serge," I say. "I appreciate hearing that."

"But calling the leader of the writers' group *George* is a bit disappointing," Serge says.

"Oh, I'm sorry," I say, stopping myself from laughing.

"Perhaps you can think about changing it to a nice Italian name like, hmm, Rocco," Serge says.

I nod my head and say, "Okay, I'll think about that."

*

The taverna is busy on this Friday night as I walk in and say, "Hey, Lorenzo" to the affable bouncer who stands near the door. The tables are crowded with people talking loudly because the music's volume is turned up high. I push my way through the crowd to the bar and see Gina making the drinks. I wonder if Paula is on a break or off tonight.

Finally, Gina comes over to me and asks, "What can I get you, Bobby?"

"Smirnoff Red on the rocks," I say. I purposely do not ask for a martini because I know that she will not make it right. She quickly makes my drink and puts it on the bar in front of me. "Where's the boss tonight?"

Gina smiles and says, "She's in the kitchen. I'll tell her that you're here."

"Thanks, Gina," I say.

I look around the room, and there are so many people sitting together at the tables, sharing drinks, and laughing. Nothing is worse than being in a bar alone.

"Hello, stranger," I hear coming from behind me. I turn around and see Paula – her baby bump looks much bigger under her apron. "Where have you been lately?"

I am not sure what to say. "Oh, I've been doing things and working on my book." Since realizing that I am in love with Paula, I have been avoiding this place. I feel like I am back in middle school avoiding Bonnie because I liked her and had no way of expressing myself properly. "Hey, Paula, how are you feeling?"

She holds her stomach with both hands. "I've got a big baby in there; that's how I'm feeling."

"How many weeks are you now?" I ask.

She leans on the bar and squints. "You have trouble remembering things, Bobby?"

I think about when we were together and say, 'It's about 19 weeks now, right?"

"There you go; you can do your maths!" she says standing up, and then putting her hand on her back. "This baby is killing my back."

"You shouldn't be on your feet so much," I say.

"It's hard to be sitting down when you're tending bar," Paula says.

I see a stool in the corner next to the coat rack. I go get it and put it over the bar and onto the elevated netting on the floor behind it. "Please take a break once in a while."

Paula stares at me. "You're acting like my mother."

"Your mother? Not the seahorse one, right?"

"Don't be silly. If I was a seahorse, you'd be carrying the baby," she chuckles.

"Well, that's scary," I say.

Paula sighs. "My very human mother is begging me to come home and have the baby. She wants me to give birth in the U.K."

"Well, I would think she would also want to be part of the baby's life," I say.

"I'm going on six years living here now," Paula says. "We barely talked anymore, but when she found out I was preggers, now she calls me every day."

I think about Beth and her mother. "When my wife was pregnant, her mother called her every day too. I think something kicks in – the maternal instinct or something."

Paula sees Gina at the bar taking care of the waiters' drink orders, so she looks at the stool and reluctantly sits down. "Oh, that is good. Thanks, Bobby." She looks up at me and says, "Viv doesn't want to go back to the U.K. ever, so I have to deal with that too."

I think about it and say, "I thought I detected a British accent when I met her."

"She tries to talk like an American," Paula says. "Don't ask me why." She stares at me and asks, "Whatever happened with *La Donna Viola*? Last night Pete and Rolando were in here and told me that she was at the Carnevale party and that you followed her outside."

Now I realize that Pietro and Rolando are coming here without me, and I would have preferred that Paula did not know about that encounter. "Oh, yeah, I did follow her out of the party. We walked together, held hands, and stood on a bridge."

"That's all?" she asks like she cares what I did or did not do like an old girlfriend or something.

"Yeah, that's it," I say. "She dared me to take off her mask, but I got spooked and didn't do it, and she walked away."

"Seems a shame," Paula says. "That night I saw her here with you, I thought there was something going on there, and she was a stunning young woman."

"As usual, I dropped the ball," I say and sip my drink.

"There you go again," Paula says, "always putting yourself down."

I want to change the subject, and I think about what Pietro had said to me about Viv and ask, "Can I ask you a question?"

"Yeah, of course," she says.

"Paula, I don't mean to be morbid, but have you and Viv ever thought about who would take care of the baby if something happened to both of you?"

Paula's eyes widen, and she stares at me sullenly. "What would make you think a thing like that?"

"Pete," I say, "he asked me that question."

"I'm not at all surprised about that," she says. "And no, Viv and I have never discussed that."

"Well, I'm asking because…"

Paula jumps off her stool and puts her face close to mine. "You're not going to have anything to do with the baby. Remember?"

"I do," I say, backing up a little and sipping my drink.

"Your name is not going to be on any papers or on the birth certificate," Paula says. "I thought you knew and understood that."

I nod my head and say, "I know that, but you should have a plan in place. It doesn't have to involve me, but you should have someone in mind who you can trust just in case."

She glances at the end of the bar. "Gina! *I trust Gina!*"

I sip my drink. "Good, then you have a plan."

Paula looks at me as if the rage is boiling inside of her. "Bobby, sometimes you make me so angry."

"I'm sorry," I say. "I'm sure you know I care about you and the baby."

Paula sighs and wipes her hands on the apron. "Yes, I do know that you care, but I don't like things to get complicated. I'm trying to say that you're not going to be involved in the baby's life. I want you to understand and *never forget that*!" Paula walks away from me, and I know it is over now.

I finish my drink and slam the glass on the bar. As Paula looks back at me, I say, "Yeah, I'll never ever forget that!"

As if on cue, Crowded House's song "Don't Dream It's Over" starts playing in the room, and I wonder if Paula has done it deliberately, but I decide the universe itself is letting me know the finality of things between Paula and me. I realize that I am finished here. I turn around and make my way through the crowded tables. I ignore Lorenzo as he is saying something to me, and I exit the taverna. I guess I am done with Paula, and she is done with me. Either way, I will have to find a new taverna to call home.

*

It has been two months since I last saw Paula or my other friends – I have become adjusted to being alone. I wake to another lovely day, but it is hotter than yesterday, so I go out to take my walk earlier and stand on a bridge over a canal. Everyone is racing everywhere, and the tourists are back in droves now. It is the middle of July, and Venice is overly crowded again.

In a gondola below me, a young couple is kissing as the gondolier grins and pushes them forward until they disappear under the bridge. Maybe I am not okay being alone here. I think about Mireille, and I know that she has a kind heart. I want to take a chance – perhaps a crazy one – and go to the hotel and ask her to go out to lunch today. I have not seen her in a long time, so maybe she has forgiven me.

I go along the busy streets, over canals, and reach the lovely old hotel where she works. When I go inside, I am amazed at the old classic wood paneled walls, the ancient glowing lamps, and the hush provided by the thick red and green carpet in the lobby. Guests are coming in and out of the adjoining dining area, and I walk up to the desk and see an older man with a badge that says "Maurice" on it.

"Good morning, sir," Maurice says in a friendly tone.

"Hello, good morning, Maurice. I am sorry to bother you, but I am looking for Mireille Martel," I say.

"My Mireille?" he asks. "She is my niece."

"Yes, I would like to speak with her," I say.

"Oh, that will be quite impossible," Maurice says. "She has moved back home to Paris."

"Really?" I ask. "Do you know if there was a reason?"

"Yes, her father died, and she went to home to console her mother," Maurice says.

Another gut punch! I am trying to process this information, and I nod my head, turn around, and walk out of the hotel. I make my way to the Grand Canal and lean against a railing and look out at the gondolas and vaporetti on the glistening water, the people crossing over bridges, and the city seems so vibrant with life and purpose. How come everyone has someplace to go and something to do and someone to love? How come I have nothing and no one?

Mireille, sweet Mireille. I blew it with her just like I blew it with Beth. I am my own worst enemy, always getting in my own way. I am turning 39 this year, and still have no clue as to how to do things the right way. I am just very bad at the thing they call love. If they gave me a grade for it, I would receive a well-deserved F on the report card of life.

I start walking and make my way toward the Rialto. I go into the bustling market, find my way to Tinno, who is selling a bag of oranges to a young couple who are holding hands. Everyone is in love except me.

After they leave, I buy an apple and say, "Tinno, what's the secret to love?"

"Secret? To love?" the old man asks.

"Yeah, how do you know what to do? What is the secret to it?"

Tinno leans toward me and whispers, "Always give more and take less. Always listen more and talk less. And in a fight, always lose, because that way you win in the end. Those are my secrets to love."

"And how do you deal with being alone? Especially here in Venice?"

Tinno turns his hands up to the sky, and the sunlight shines on them. "You are never alone, Bobby. God is always with you. Pray and find strength there."

"Thanks, Tinno," I say, sliding the apple into my cargo shorts pocket. As I walk away, I think about praying, but in my experience when I have prayed things only got worse.

I make my way over the Rialto, through all the tourists milling around in the Piazza San Marco, and keep walking until I reach the water. I think about how Mireille refused to live with her father for so long, but now she has

gone back to comfort her mother who must be hurting after

he died because she loved the man so much. Now, I guess I

will never see Mireille again.

I watch the tied-up gondolas bouncing with

the wake of the vaporetti passing behind them.

Although the gondolas are famous, those vaporetti are

representative of life here in Venice; everything

seems to be tied to those who have ridden in them.

There is consistency in that, and stability too. There

could not be anything more ingenious; Venetians are

linked together by that common experience. It is kind

of like how the subway connects everyone in New

York City for better or worse.

I have made so many mistakes, and now I

stand here staring at the water in one of the most

glorious cities in the world, but I am all alone. I have

no one to blame but myself, and I have nowhere to

go. Going back home will not solve anything and would probably make things much worse. Mireille is in Paris, and I could go there, but I would only be rejected just as Isabella and Paula have rejected me. I cannot even go back to the writers' group anymore because Rolando and Pietro go to Paula's place now, and I do not want them telling me anything about her or her pregnancy and eventually the baby, so that door is permanently closed.

Everyone is trying to tell me something – the people I know, this city, this country, the whole world is trying to tell me something, but I cannot hear it. I am not sure if I even want to hear anyone. They are all chattering in my head like a bunch of incoherent monkeys, and I am like a different species that cannot understand them. I must cut them all off – why do I need them in my life anymore?

Even poor old Tinno tried to tell me about love, and I did hear what he had to say because I like him. Perhaps Tinno will be the one person I allow to remain in my life, but he is the one who warned me about dying alone in Venice. That is something I am trying to put off indefinitely.

I should take Tinno's advice, but maybe tomorrow. Praying seems almost like a foreign thing to me right now, and I am not certain, but I think my prayers are not being heard. If all my time spent in Catholic school taught me anything, there are no saints or sinners among us. We are what we are – human beings in all our frailty – trying to navigate a world that is a spiritual maze where hopes and dreams go to get lost.

I am about to turn my head when I see the image of the Grim Reaper standing in one of the tied-up gondolas bouncing in the basin water, his face lost in shadows cast by his hood and his scythe glistening in the sunlight. When I shut my eyes and open them again, the ghastly ghoul is gone, but his appearance has shaken me. I turn around and start going back to my flat, where I will eat alone, sleep alone, and one day die alone, but I am determined that Death is not going to get me today. *No, not on this day!*

As I walk away from the water, I feel an urge to start running. I am plowing through the crowds of people who move aside for me in St. Mark's Square. I feel panic and come to a stop because my heart is beating madly, and I am out of breath. I bend over, hold my knees, and try to calm myself down.

I glance at the café to my left, and I figure I will sit down, get a drink, and try to get myself thinking straight. I walk up to the waiter, and he tells me to sit anywhere. I choose a table in the middle of the seating area, sit under the shade of the umbrella, and order a big bottle of still water.

How have I come to this moment? I have always sensed that Death was present here, leering at me from windows, rooftops, and bridges over canals. I could handle that because he and his minions are keeping tabs on all of us, waiting for when it is time to collect us, but today I saw him for a moment standing in that gondola. Maybe he is just reminding me that he is there.

A young woman walks toward the waiter, and he tells her to sit anywhere as he brings me my drink. She has long brown hair that hangs down to her waist, pale white skin, and she wears purple lipstick. She sits at the table next to mine and orders a cappuccino. I sip my water and glance at her – those lips look like *La Donna Viola's* fragile ones that resembled the petals of an orchid. Her face without the mask is lovely and has an ethereal glow.

I try to focus on my drink, and I am rather thirsty after my mad dash away from the water. I glance at her and see that she is looking at her phone; her fingernail polish is purple and matches the color of her lipstick. She is wearing a light blue skirt and a frilly white blouse. Her white low-heeled shoes are polished and shine brightly.

The waiter brings her coffee, and as he leaves, I turn to glance at her again. Her profile! I am not imagining anything – *I believe she is <u>La Donna Viola</u>*!

Am I going to be so stupid now like my frightened adolescent self who could not manage to ask Bonnie to dance? I may never see her again, so I turn to her and ask, "How are you today?"

She looks at me for the first time and smiles. "I am fine? And you?"

"I'm fine, and it's a beautiful day," I say.

She looks up at the sky and says, "Yes, it is."

It is around noon so I ask, "Are you on your lunch hour?"

"Oh, no," she says and smiles. "I'm waiting for my cousin. She is here on holiday from Boston. We are going to visit the Doge's Palace today."

"Oh, splendid," I say and think, what the hell! When did I ever use "splendid" in a sentence? I am starting to sound like Serge.

She sips her coffee and says, "You're an American, yes?"

"Yes, I'm from New York, but I live here now," I say.

She sips her coffee again and looks at me. "I think I have seen you somewhere before."

Yes! This is my opportunity to say something. "Yes, you look familiar as well."

She turns and stares at me. "Oh, yes, *I do know you.*"

"You met me during Carnevale," I say. "You were wearing that lovely purple gown and a purple mask."

She leans forward and studies my face. "*It is you.*" She smiles and takes a deep breath. "We stood on the bridge and you almost took off my mask."

"Yes, that is true," I say, "but I was afraid to do it."

"But the moment was such magic like we were in a dream," she says. "I'm glad you didn't take off my mask. Now, that you see me, how do you feel?"

"Well, is this the *real* you now?" I ask.

She smiles and says, "It's the everyday me."

I put out my hand and say, "I am Bobby."

She takes my hand in hers – it is as warm as it was that night on the bridge. "I am Sofia," she giggles. "Nice to meet you *again*."

I release her hand and am still not sure of myself. "I guess this is just a strange coincidence us meeting again."

Sofia turns and sips her coffee. "Oh, no, my mother always says that there are no coincidences."

I would like to believe this is true. "So, we were meant to meet again?"

Sofia sits back in the chair and sighs. "I remember seeing you in the taverna. I was there with my friends and a little drunk, and when I saw you, I wanted to kiss you. They dared me to do it, and so I did."

Now I understand what happened in the taverna. "Oh, wow, I just felt that was a strange moment."

"Yes, it was for me too," Sofia laughs. "I don't do that kind of thing usually."

"But what about the party at the palace?"

"Well, I hope this doesn't bother you, but my parents are friends with Signor Rossi," Sofia says.

"They told me that I could bring my friends, but I didn't expect to see you again."

Hmm. Her parents are Serge's friends? "It certainly doesn't bother me," I say, "but I'm surprised."

"Of course, you wouldn't know," Sofia says. "I came late to the party that night with my girlfriends, and as we were dancing, I saw you – even with the mask, I knew it was you because of that hair."

I self-consciously run my fingers through my thick head of hair. "Well, I guess it's good for something."

"No, it is wonderful hair," she smiles.

"So, why did you run away from me?"

"I wasn't sure about what to do," Sofia says and then sips her coffee. "It was the whole aura of the Carnevale – you know the mystery and the fear and the delight of it all."

"But when we met on the bridge…"

Sofia closes her eyes. "That was magical. I am glad you didn't take off my mask. It would have changed everything."

"But now the masks are off," I say.

"Yes, but it is different now that we are not in the dream anymore," she says. Her phone timer beeps, and she turns it off. "Oh, I have to go meet my cousin now." She stands up and is preparing to leave.

I cannot let her slip away from me again, but she seems to be in a hurry, and I falter as usual. I blurt out, "Maybe we will run into each other again."

She smiles and says, "I would like that." She takes one last sip of coffee. "I must run, Bobby. *Ciao*."

"Enjoy your tour," I say. I watch her as she rushes across the square into the evanescence of time and space. I keep staring at the cobblestones as if I could trace purple glitter, marking the path of her magical steps until she vanishes into the crowd of people.

I pay for my drink and start walking back to my flat.
The steps seem unfamiliar to me, as if I have forgotten how
to get home. I feel elation and fear as I process meeting Sofia
– is she any less beautiful than *La Donna Viola*? Should I
wish that we had not met so that the fantasy of meeting her
and holding her hand on that bridge is not tarnished?

I make my way home, go up the 62 steps, and enter
my flat. I turn on the AC, grab a beer, and go sit by the
window and enjoy my view of San Marco's bell tower. I
think about how Sofia said we were not in the dream
anymore. What does that mean? And who was dreaming?
"We are not" suggests we were both in the dream together, or
does it mean we were having the same dream?

My phones buzzes, so I take it out of my pocket,
foolishly hoping it was a text from Sofia; I imagine she has
sent a picture of herself. Alas, how could she, when I did not
have the courage to ask her for her phone number. I close my

eyes and visualize her face. Man, she is beautiful. I want to suppress my negative thoughts – but I cannot; *she is out of my league!*

Yes, the dream is over. In that dream we had a magical moment on the bridge, but all dreams are intangible and never last. I did meet her in the café and that is real and something I can hold onto. Also, I did find out her parents are Serge's friends, but it would seem rather desperate act if I had to contact him to connect with Sofia, so maybe it is just not meant to be.

*

The next morning, I feel a bit depressed about botching my opportunity with Sofia. Last evening I imagined talking to Sofia for hours on the phone, just like I used to do with Bonnie when I had no worries back in high school. I was in my room with my Mets, Jets, Van Halen, Metallica, and *Star Wars* posters on my walls and no dream seemed too big. At this point I am not even sure what I imagined Sofia and I talked about, but now I have learned the hard way that dreams are always eventually over.

I take my usual walk to the Rialto, and I go up to Tinno and say, "*Buongiorno*, my friend."

Tinno stares at me and frowns. "You seem no better today. You still have a cloud over your head."

"I feel a bit out of it," I say, wishing that I was having dinner with Sofia tonight.

"You seem like you lost a girl," Tinno says.

I buy my apple and say, "Yeah, more or less."

I cross the bridge and make my way to the square that is bustling with tourists and citizens all busily going into different directions. I reach the water and watch the gondoliers, pushing loads of passengers bathed in sunshine.

Sofia seems very different than Mireille, Paula, and Beth. Each of them had issues that complicated our interactions. Sofia seems so stable, so positive, and I do not believe I have ever known a woman like that. I wish that I will run into her again, but I am leaving that to fate because to try to do anything else would feel wrong to me.

I am going to miss the writers' group, the taverna, and what will happen to Paula and my baby, but I have let go of them all. My life is moving in a new direction, and I am starting over again, and I am resigned to that now.

An elderly couple gets into a gondola, and the gondolier starts pushing them away from the dock. They are smiling and holding hands – just like the ones in Mireille's story – and I think I see the Grim Reaper on the bridge behind them. I shut my eyes, open them again, and the specter is gone.

Even he cannot ruin this day. I will not allow it. I turn away and start walking back through the square. I will go home, do some writing, and prepare dinner for myself.

As I am almost out of the main area of the square, I see a very pregnant Paula carrying a shopping bag. She stops walking when she sees me. "Hello stranger," Paula says.

"How are you doing?" I ask, feeling awkward.

She touches her stomach with her free hand and says, "I'm doing as well as I can. Where have you been?"

I stare at her lovely face and still feel something for her, but it is different now. "I'm writing my book, keeping busy with going to the gym, and just getting on with my life."

"You never answered my texts." She puts down her bag, smiles, and says, "I'm glad to know that you're okay."

"I changed my number," I say.

"Are you ever coming back to the taverna? Everyone has been asking about you. I don't know what to tell them."

I look up at the sky and sigh. "You can say that I'm dead – the old Bobby anyway."

Paula gently puts her hand on my cheek. "I liked the old Bobby. In other circumstances, maybe we could have been good for each other."

I touch the back of her hand. "How odd for you to say that now." I pull away from her hand on my face. "Goodbye, Paula!" I turn and quickly walk away from her, fighting against an urge to go back and say more. I know I cannot play that game anymore. I must forget about her, the baby, and the friends I made. I must go a different way now.

I continue to walk home, confident that I know this place in an intimate way – *Venice is my city!* I stop on a bridge and watch a traffic jam of gondolas laden with tourists in the narrow canal below me. This is exactly what my life will be like now, but I will continue navigating my way around this city and appreciating those waters that incessantly flow in from the lagoon, and I will withstand the highs and lows of the tide.

Afterword

Thank you for reading *Life and Death in Venice*. I hope that you enjoyed the book.

My books – *The Stranger from the Sea*, *Love in the Time of the Coronavirus*, *Unicorn: A Love Story*, and others – are available on Amazon.

Please follow me and learn about new releases of books and read my articles at Victor Lana's blog.

After you have read this book, please leave reviews and ratings on Amazon and Goodreads. Honest reviews and ratings are encouraged and appreciated. This is the most important thing you can do to support me and other writers.

Thank you for your interest in my work.